calm, cool, and adjusted

Other Books by Kristin Billerbeck

Ashley Stockingdale novels

What a Girl Wants
She's Out of Control
With This Ring, I'm Confused

Spa Girl Series

She's All That
A Girl's Best Friend
Calm, Cool, and Adjusted

Split Ends

kristin billerbeck

THOMAS NELSON
Since 1798

NASHVILLE DALLAS MEXICO CITY RIO DE JANEIRO BEIJING

Published in Nashville, Tennessee, by Thomas Nelson. Thomas Nelson is a registered trademark of Thomas Nelson, Inc.

Published in association with Yates & Yates, www.yates2.com.

Thomas Nelson, Inc., titles may be purchased in bulk for educational, business, fund-raising, or sales promotional use. For information, please e-mail SpecialMarkets@ThomasNelson.com.

Library of Congress Cataloging-in-Publication Data

Billerbeck, Kristin.
Calm, cool, & adjusted / Kristin Billerbeck.
p. cm. — (Spa girls collection)
ISBN 978-1-59145-330-7 (tradepaper)
ISBN 978-1-59554-376-9 (repack)
1. Chiropractors—Fiction. 2. Santa Clara Valley (Santa Clara County, Calif.)—Fiction. 3. Chick lit. I. Title. II. Title: Calm, cool, and adjusted.
PS3602.I44C36 2006
813'.6—dc22 2006019854

Printed in the United States of America
08 09 10 11 RRD 9 8 7 6 5 4 3 2 1

Dedication

This book is dedicated to all the men and women in natural health management who helped me fight my way out of multiple sclerosis, especially Doctor Lambertson of Fort Wayne, Indiana, and Carolyn Rüeben of Sacramento, California. And to my writing partner, Colleen Coble, who got me started and prayed me through to its finish.

And most of all to my husband, who has lived "in sickness and in health" with integrity and much love.

Acknowledgments

To have a trustworthy editor is pure gold. Leslie Peterson, thank you for all your time, effort, and encouragement. You are the best in the business, and I am so grateful to have you. I know when I send you something and you tell me it needs work, it does. That in itself is a calling and I'm so glad you heeded it.

To Jeana Ledbetter, my agent, who not only puts up with my whiny phone calls but is there when I have a stupid joke I have to share or a question about a single line of copy. You go above and beyond, and I trust you implicitly to keep me on track. Even if you weren't my agent, I would love you unconditionally.

And finally, to my writing "group," Colleen Coble, Diann Hunt, and Denise Hunter, for seeing me through each day and keeping this job from being lonely and solitary. You are each my daily blessing.

Desperation has a scent. I'm certain there's a science to it—a research grant out there somewhere. I'm waiting for the *National Geographic* special on some poor, unsuspecting Capuchin monkey in the rainforest. Silently, she watches the next tree, full of capuchin bachelors as they mix and mingle, reveling over some juicy fruit morsel. Suddenly, overcome by their sheer numbers and her endless options, she leaps across the branches. A riot ensues. She startles the fray of monkey men, who abandon their tree in a frenzy of flying, frenetic fur. The insistent, excited monkey squeals peal through the rainforest as the jungle stampede unfolds before her unsuspecting eyes. And then, just as quickly as the ruckus began, all is silent, and our capuchin heroine rests alone on the top branch, catching her breath while watching the last of the tails disappear into the green canopy. Her dreams dashed, she sits and analyzes where she went wrong . . .

"The human spirit can endure in sickness,
but a crushed spirit who can bear."
Proverbs 18:14

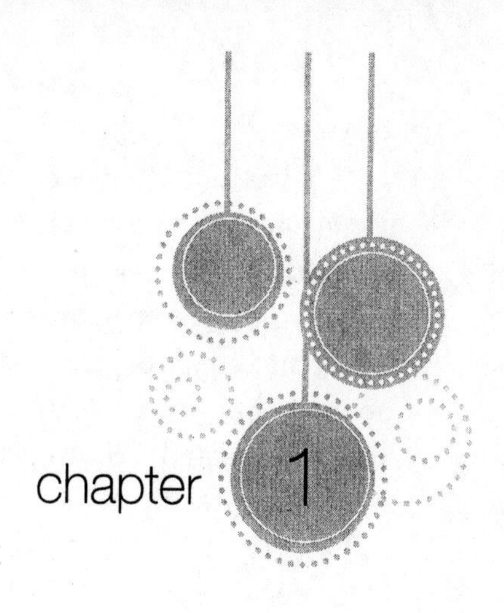

Miles run: 6
Laps swum: 24
Desperation scale: 2

Contrary to popular opinion, I am not desperate. Not yet anyway. I would just prefer to have an escort for my best friend's wedding before my friends find me a mercy date. I suppose I just don't understand why anyone cares that I have a date for the wedding. It's not like I have a reputation for being normal. When I show up to any event, it's expected that I'll dance to the beat of my own drum. It's part of my charm.

Besides, a mercy date is so demeaning. I shudder to think about the reading of the vows next to someone I barely know. There's the uncomfortable shifting, the avoiding of glances while the romantic promises are read. Does anyone facing thirty really need that kind of pressure? I think not. A girl of my age should be allowed to show up at a wedding unencumbered, to pluck from the trough of the buffet without fear or recriminations. I am a modern woman. I'll get my endorphins from chocolate, thank you very much.

Why must we always come down to the men? Men are a dime a dozen. (Well, not the good ones, but my point is still valid.) I'm not doting or cutesy or even able to hold my tongue at the point when most women know better. My goal is health: to make as many people healthy as possible. Most people simply aren't concerned about their health, and when I look into a pair of green eyes surrounded by a yellowish tint, how can I not comment on their liver function? I'm a doctor, after all! Granted, I didn't actually take the Hippocratic oath—I'm a chiropractor. However, I did earn the "Doctor" title and so I like to think that brings me in under an umbrella clause. One of the benefits of doctor status is my free advice. Am I right? What's the first thing people do at parties to a doctor? "Oh, Doc, I have this ache in my shoulder."

Emma, my receptionist, comes in gnawing on a carrot. Emma is the epitome of health and beauty—what the women's magazines put on their covers—and yet she sees none of it. Wastes her life on a useless boyfriend and working here. Not that I'm not grateful, mind you. I just see her accomplishing so much more with her life and healthy habits. Perhaps finding a sexy marathon runner and settling down. But Emma will have none of it. Her ambition is to have conversations all day with my patients, and then fill me in on the gossip. It's a quest for her. To know more about everyone than they know about themselves.

"Hey, Poppy, Dr. Nip/Tuck is here to see you." She bites off another piece of carrot as she finishes her sentence. "He's so fine. You be nice."

I force down a smile because I know exactly why Dr. Jeff Curran is here. I push through the custom curtain to the office foyer, which is a muted red to inspire energy, wealth, and romance. The plastic surgeon from the office next door sort of matches the wall—his face is a deep shade of scarlet, and something tells me he's not getting the peaceful feeling from my waterfall feature in the office.

Dr. Jeff is a bit of a dichotomy. You get the impression he used to be ruggedly handsome and hardily masculine before succumbing to the evils of his trade. Now, his skin is as smooth as a baby's bottom—as if he's microdermabrasioned daily. Truth be told, he scares me a little because this man is wielding a knife to bring others into his plastic fold.

Perhaps I'm too harsh on him. He is quite handsome; it just pains me to admit it. He's attractive in that high school quarterback way. But I imagine the only kind of woman he wants is his own mirror image with implants. At least that's my assessment. As I said, maybe I'm too harsh on him.

"Hi, Dr. Curran. Is there something I can help you with?" I use my sweetest, low-toned voice to inspire calm. His eyes thin in immediate challenge, which makes me sigh. Why are there people on earth who make Christianity so difficult? Those who seem to make you an immediate hypocrite just because they are so grating? I suppose it's the weeds in the field, a product of the fall, but Jeff Curran makes me feel so spiritually weak. He claims Christianity, actually goes to my church, but he and I could not be more opposite if he were a Hindu and I a Muslim. We are, most certainly, unequally yoked in the Christian sense.

"You parked your Subaru in my space again." He tries to keep the anger from his voice, but he doesn't succeed. He says *Subaru* like it's a main course on *Fear Factor*.

I did park my car there. On purpose, actually. It's not technically his space, but he's so attached to it I just can't help but taunt him with my inferior car. I sort of enjoy forcing humanity upon him, making him deal with us little people. Yes, it's childish, but what else do I have going on? When life is boring, you spice it up. Granted, it's the same way I did it in second grade, but what can I say? I'm easily amused.

"Have I defiled the space? How will you ever park your Beamer there again? Did I leave an oil stain?" I ask hopefully.

His jaw clenches. "My reputation is everything in this career, Ms. Clayton." (He refuses to call me Doctor.) "Would you like it if your earthy clients caught you driving a Hummer?" He crosses his arms, waiting for my answer. "I didn't think so."

"Maybe you'd like me to get you a nameplate for the spot so everyone will know what you drive." This makes me laugh a little. As though his personalized "TuckMe" license plate doesn't tell everyone just whose car it is.

"Poppy, you are the most peaceful woman I know. I come in here and there are scented candles burning, soft music playing, a water fountain. So tell me, how is it you're so peaceful . . ." He pauses. " . . . to everyone else? Why must I endure your wrath? What makes me so special?"

That's a good question, and the simple answer is that I don't like him, and I don't like what he does for a living. Feeding off the insecurities of women. Hmm . . . I suppose I believe I must be his voice of reason. Oscar has Felix, SpongeBob has Squidward, and Dr. Jeff has me. It's the natural course of life.

Since I didn't answer him, Jeff continues. "Since we must share office space, would you mind keeping your clients' cars from my side of the parking lot? It's closer for them, anyway. I think the more convenient we make it for our clients, the better—" He swallows abruptly. "—doctors—" He chokes on the word. "The better doctors we'll both be. Certainly we can agree on that much."

I hate to be patronized. For all intents and purposes, I've been an adult since I was thirteen. At thirty, I hardly need someone to dumb it down for me. "I can't exactly go outside and direct traffic. I have a business to run here. Besides, maybe if your clients walk more, they'll need less liposuction," I say.

He stands over me menacingly, and I have to admit, he is prettier than me. He's like a work of art, and I find myself getting lost in his baby blues, which hold no sparkle at the moment. Even angry, they're beautiful. "You're sabotaging my practice, Poppy, and I know you wouldn't do that on purpose." Again with the patronization. "My clients see the beaters your patients drive and worry that I'm a hack surgeon. They need to trust me with the knife, and part of that is creating an environment they trust. Like your Zen spa space here."

"Red is the color of energy. My clients should leave here energized and ready to face the world, not relaxed." Somehow, that seems different to me than judging a surgeon by the cars in the parking lot, but what do I know of his world?

He gazes up at the wall. "Whatever. Listen, when I have my own surgical center in a few years, I won't be here. So let's do our best to coexist, shall we?" He moves a hanging leaf away from his face. "After that, your jungle can reclaim its own and you can go back to smoking incense or whatever it is you do over here."

"Jeff, you park your car in front of *my* office. Granted, I understand you don't want your beloved Lexus scratched, but it makes it look like I'm here for the money. Just like you don't want the beaters in front of your office, I don't want the status symbol in front of mine. It says that I value the wrong things in life."

"Status symbol? I beg your pardon, but I drive a very practical car and the space in front of your office is bigger. No door dings, as you pointed out."

"It really bothers you this is a free country, doesn't it? All these people running around with wrinkles and fat you can't suck out. It's just criminal that God makes you deal with the riffraff, but I'm afraid that's the way it is. I park there because I want my patients to trust me. It's the same difference."

"Uh, no, it's not. I'm not charging them seventy-five bucks a pop for voodoo. My clients actually get what they pay for. I promise and I deliver. With you, it's just the luck of the draw."

I gasp audibly at his true belief in my practice. "I beg your pardon. Chinese medicine has been around longer than your rudimentary surgery skills. Which will, I'm sure, be out of date with the next brilliant procedure that plasters the skin tighter to the bone. I cure the whole body, not just focus on the superficial."

He looks around my office and at the water feature in particular. "I'm doing important work over there. I'm not just creating an ambiance."

Just as he says this, a woman with lips the size of inflated tires comes through the door. "Oh, thorry," she lisps. "Thought thith wath the exit." She quickly retreats, and I have to cover my giggle. I'm not sure where plumping lips the size of life preservers comes in on the importance scale, but that's his problem, not mine.

"Your lips thin when you get older, Ms. Clayton. Someday you too may want injections and just so you know there're no hard feelings, I'll be happy to plump them up the first time for free."

"If you're hoping I'll give free adjustments for oversized implants and their effects on the back, I'm afraid I won't return the favor."

"I don't do implants for cosmetic reasons, and you know that."

I've heard him make a point of that, and as much as the rest of his work disgusts me, I can respect that. But we rarely give each other the benefit of the doubt. It's part of our insane and ludicrous mutual attraction, I suppose.

"Poppy." He lowers his voice to that sexy purr he possesses. "Does it *really* bother you that I park there?"

I pause for a moment to really ponder the question because he sounds as if he's really interested. "No," I admit. *Just your very presence in my building annoys me*, I think with regret for my own control tendencies.

As much as this man drives me crazy, he's a very warm spirit. He's gentle and kind, just incredibly misguided. And Lord forgive me, there's something within me that wants to set him on the path to righteousness on a daily basis. If I wasn't visited weekly by people who had destroyed their health over something cosmetic or unnecessary, I wouldn't have this attitude. I really wouldn't.

"My patients just don't want to get old before their time. I know we disagree on methods, but—"

I interrupt him. "How can you perpetuate the myth that it's about nothing more than being an ornament?"

"I don't perpetuate that myth, as you put it. But it seems selfish that you would stop women from trying to improve themselves. It's a choice, you know, and most women aren't blessed with your looks or that body."

"Is that a professional opinion?" I ask him. I have no idea why I love to see him squirm, but I apparently live for it. I see his eyes fall on my figure and quickly come to my eyes as if he hasn't noticed a thing.

"As I was saying . . ." I see him visibly swallow and for some reason, this gives me a small thrill. "Clients seek my help when they aren't given what nature has been so generous with for you. I would think being beautiful—"

I look down. I'm above this. I know better than to fall for smooth talking, but as I meet his gaze I realize I'm only human.

"And don't play coy as if you don't know it, Poppy. Women know the power beauty yields them, and you're no different. As I was saying, I think you'd have a little more mercy on your fellow woman."

Dang, he knows how to make me feel small. I want people to know the power that healthy living can bring them; I want them to know they hold the gift of God's creation right at their fingertips. But I stumble and become so very human when Jeff calls me beautiful. I am so petty. So vain in my own way. "I won't park in your beloved space, all right? Are we done now?"

"I appreciate that." He flashes those teeth once more and retreats into his world of Botox and silicone. Plastic surgery. Even the name drives me insane. Everything about it says fake, facade, industrial, when we, as doctors, should be teaching the world all things natural: eating habits, renewable resources, exercise. If he wasn't so Neanderthal, he would see that. But I hold out little hope for him as he slinks back to where he came from.

"I don't know why he annoys you so much," Emma says, staring at the closed door our offices share. "He's always nice to you. He tries, Poppy—you have to give him that."

"He's really not that kind, Emma. You're just charmed by him. Like a snake in his basket. He plays a tune, and we all follow blindly." I click my tongue, "And I'm no different."

"Maybe I am charmed, but so what? Does everyone have think like you?"

"Of course not, but it would help if my office staff did. Do you know how many people I see sick from all the environmental triggers in the air? That man deliberately injects people with botulism for vanity's sake. It's his entire worldview I have trouble with. Not him, per se."

"It's not like he's forcing it on people. He's not at a loss for clients. That place is like Grand Central over there, and have you seen they're carrying that really good mineral makeup at the medical spa?"

I look at her with my naked face. "No, I hadn't noticed."

One thing about Emma, what she lacks in ambition she more than makes up for in opinion. "What makes you think you have any right to change him, Poppy?"

"Don't you see, Hollywood is forcing it—people have an unnatural desire to be youthful. It's so important to maintain balance in all areas of your life. If you don't want to age, you should live a healthy lifestyle."

"Remember that Grape Nuts guy did that, and he still died. Besides, it's not all about health; it's about looking good too. No one wants to go through life with 9 percent body fat and the face of a troll, am I right?" Emma asks.

"How can the body work against those poisons he injects, Emma?" I shake my head. "He just wakes up wrong every day. We can't all age like Cher. We shouldn't. It isn't natural."

"Of course it isn't natural. That's why it's called *plastic surgery*. Plastic, not so natural. Surgery, not natural. What does that have to do with you taking his parking space every-day?" Emma asks.

"It just makes me feel better, all right? Sort of my own way of balancing him out. I'm the yin to his yang. I bring balance to his world."

"I don't know. I like him. He's always very complimentary of you." Emma looks at the door, like a retriever waiting for its owner to return. "You don't have to agree with each other to share office space." She shrugs. "What do you say to each other at church when you attend?"

"Nothing. And he's complimentary of everyone, Emma. It's how he makes his money. 'Oh, you're beautiful, dahlink!' Let me flash my fake smile at you as an exclamation point. He's a used car salesman with a knife. No wait, that's too unkind to the car salesman!"

"I just think you could work a little harder to be neigh-borly. Love thy neighbor as thyself, and all that."

"I am being neighborly. I'm showing him that his neighbor is valuable even in an American vehicle."

"No, you're being motherly. Like you always are—you think you're Mother Earth and you can parent the rest of us so much better than we can handle our own lives." Emma grabs up her purse, which is weighted down with foodstuffs. She gnaws constantly, like a chipmunk, usually on some grain, and has such a high metabolism she even makes the scales nervous. "Want something from next door?"

I shake my head. There's a café next door. It's a tiny, Greek place with wonderful delicacies like hummus and grape-leaf sandwiches, but my encounter with Dr. Nip/Tuck has left me without an appetite. "I have a full schedule this afternoon. I want to keep the patients moving through, and I think I'll just run for a while. I need to clear my head."

"You already ran this morning. You're going to look like one of those Hollywood starlets with the stick figure and a big balloon head perched on the shoulders. Is that what you want?"

"I'm just going a mile. I won't be ten minutes. I'll eat something fattening when I get back, all right?"

As Emma shuts the door for the lunch break, I allow my body to fall and mold into my ergonomic chair, made especially for my spine. Who wants to be loved for her beauty anyway? Anyone can be beautiful. If they're not by nature, Jeff seems to be able to boil just such a brew next door.

This morning's situation makes me anxious about the wedding all over again. Why should I bow down to society's whims? I don't believe in plastic surgery; that's easily explained. So why isn't it just as easy that I don't want a date for Morgan's wedding? This is my second best friend to get married within six months. I don't want to go with just anyone. Of course, if I go alone, people take pictures, and I get to remember I was alone during the day. It's just not a history I care to relive either way. Is that so wrong?

The way I see it, I have two choices: first, I can tell Morgan and Lilly, my best friends and Spa Girls, that I already have a date for Morgan's wedding. This would involve lying and I'm a terrible liar. I'd never get away with it. Lilly's got the eagle eye for truth.

My second option is that I can act as though the wedding means nothing to me and lure some unsuspecting male friend into being my escort. The wedding of course involves two full months of festivities. There's the couples' shower, the dinners with out-of-town guests, and, naturally, the rehearsal dinner and wedding. Where am I going to find a date to fill two months of drudgery? Between thoughts of the first shower and the final wave from the "Just Married" limo, my head starts to hurt.

I haven't had a boyfriend that lasted for two months in, well, I don't want to say. A long time. Statistically, my chances of holding onto a boyfriend for two months are not pretty, especially since I have no current prospects. Okay, technically, I have no future prospects at the moment, either, but I'm not about to admit that. I must seek out a different avenue in telling my best friends that I'm right on this one.

It wouldn't be a big deal that I was dateless in San Francisco if I didn't know Lilly and Morgan were looming with someone to fill the vacancy. Friends always think they know best in terms of your dating options, and let's just say I'd let them pick me an entire wardrobe before I let them find me my wedding date.

I look up at the clock and realize my running time is quickly dwindling. "I'm just going to call Morgan and Lilly and tell them I'm coming alone."

The phone rings. And rings. Emma has obviously left for

lunch already—and why wouldn't she? It's 11:30 and it's been at least ten minutes since her last snack.

"Dr. Poppy's office," I answer.

"Poppy, it's Lilly."

My stomach twirls a bit as I think about my next move. "Hey, Lilly, how's everything coming for the couples' shower?" I ask.

"What? Oh, fine, fine. Morgan and George are going to love it. I've got the invitations all set. And hey, did you get the times and gift suggestions prepared for the Round-the-Clock shower? I'm going to need those soon."

"I'll e-mail them to you today. I've got them all finished. You know what I did?"

"Do I want to?" Lilly asks.

"Every two hours is an organ meridian in the Chinese acupuncture clock. I came up with gifts that go with those two hours, to nurture their health. Isn't that terrific?"

Lilly sighs. "Example, please?"

"Okay, you know how everyone needs a pick-me-up at three in the afternoon? That's your bladder meridian, and lack of a healthy meridian there can cause fear and a tensed nervous system. So gift suggestions are aromatherapy candles and bath products."

She sighs again. Louder this time. "You know, Poppy, what's wrong with just saying the afternoon's for tea time? Three to five can be tea time, and you can suggest that someone buy a teapot. It's better than reminding people of the bride's bodily functions, don't you think?"

"Well, that's weird," I shrug. "Who has tea time in America?"

"Right," Lilly says. "Because in America, we're busy having bladder time instead."

"We should be," I say. "Improper bladder function is what causes that afternoon fatigue. God created your organs to work in harmony, Lilly. It's not a joke to ignore them."

"I'll do the time features. Thanks for trying. I don't even want to know when colon time is."

"Lilly, you can't just take everything over."

"Poppy, you can't just make Morgan's shower sound like a New Age gift show. If you show up with healing rocks, you're outta there."

I'm quiet. I can't really answer to that. I don't believe in the healing power of rocks. But hello? I worked hard on those gift suggestions. Sure, I knew they weren't the norm, but neither is Morgan. She's special and I wanted her shower to reflect that. Anyone can do a twenty-four-hour shower. Big deal.

"What I really called about, Poppy—and don't hang up until you hear me out."

I look around my office thinking of my alternatives, and yeah, I can hear her out. "I'm listening. Have you been taking that elixir I sent you home with?"

She ignores my question. "Now, we know you have no trouble meeting men. Heck, we've been beside you long enough to know all hail the redhead. But Morgan and I met this great guy last night and we thought maybe—"

No, I certainly don't have any trouble meeting men. It's the red hair—it's like a guy magnet. I think all those Maureen O'Hara-John Wayne movies conditioned men to believe taming the fiery redhead is some sort of hero ambition. Of course, I'm nothing like Maureen O'Hara, and I usually turn out to be a big disappointment to those with preconceived ideas. Once I've told a man how he needs to improve his kidney function or pump his adrenals, the O'Hara fantasy generally evaporates quickly.

So a blind date is not on my priority list. "Lilly, you know I appreciate you two, but I've decided I'm coming to the wedding alone. The pressure of getting a date is just doing nothing for my peace levels. Every time I think about it, I want to run. I'm sure this guy is wonderful, and you can invite him to the wedding and maybe it will be love at first sight. I'll be overcome by his magnetism, and you can tell me that you told me so. All right?"

"Really, Poppy, you'd like him, and he has a great spine. Very tall. His color is good. He could star in a vitamin ad. Really. You'd love him or I wouldn't have picked him out for you."

"Funny, that's exactly what my dad said about my stepmother—that I'd love her. And we all know where that headed."

"You're not going to even give this a chance, are you?"

"Not even a whisper of a chance." If there's anything more pathetic than not having a date, or wanting one, it's being told the perfect man is out there. Here's the problem with this: your friends, well meaning as they may be, set you up with some form of an ape, and then you question not only yourself, but what your friends must think of you. So I start to pedal quickly. "I'm training for the triathlon in Hawaii and that's my focus. What's it to you if I show up alone?"

She's quiet for a minute—which, may I say, is not like Lilly. "Don't take offense, Poppy, but lately, your natural-health thing is consuming you. The running, the swimming, the eating weird foodstuffs . . . We're starting to get concerned."

"I'll eat what I'm served at the wedding, Lilly."

"Morgan has taken a lot of flack in the city, what with her father being in jail and a lot of the socialites thinking she belongs there too. Her wedding day is a chance to start fresh. To walk down the aisle with George and little Georgie and know that her history is just that: history. We just need to do what we can to make this day great for her."

"What do my health interests have to do with Morgan's wedding?"

"Isn't it true that at my wedding reception you told the mayor his teeth-whitening system had been linked to cancer?"

"Yeah, but it has and—"

"And isn't it also true that you told my Nana's boyfriend that his esophagus spasms could be helped with a proper diet? And you started to write it down?"

"He can't eat like that and not expect some repercussions."

"Nana lives to cook for him, Poppy. You ticked both of them off and I had to explain how you are a natural health food promoter."

"So what does this have to do with Morgan's wedding? You don't want me to talk about health, fine, I'll shut up."

"Morgan's had a rough year. She's been in the newspaper for nothing but scandal for a long time now. This is her day, and no one needs to be diagnosed at the wedding."

I catch my breath and feel a welt in my throat as I realize my friends don't really want me at the wedding. They want the Stanford Poppy—the one who graduated with them and was little more than a bad dresser.

I embarrass my friends. I know I'm different. I'm not prone to care what the world thinks, but I realize, with a sharp pain, that I do care what Morgan and Lilly think. I've always been proud to be different. Until this moment, anyway.

Lilly's already married. I obviously didn't do any real damage at her wedding. She's pregnant, too, so I fail to see how my actions could harm anything in Morgan's celebration. George loves her. His son, Georgie, loves her. If I tell someone they need more whole grains, how is that going to hurt anything?

I let out a deep breath. "Fine. I won't say a thing, even if someone's liver is puffing their face up to the size of a super tomato. I'll say nothing," I vow.

"You can't help yourself," Lilly continues. "You're a natural mother, and you want to mother everyone, and I'm just asking, for this one day, can you put a muzzle on it?"

Can I? I'm sure I probably could, but what about *me* will be at the wedding? If they want my shell, maybe they could call Stepford.

"I put up with your hair obsession. This is *my* weirdness; you have to accept it. That's the cost of being my friend." Lilly thought at one time that all of her life's woes were caused by bushy, frizzy Italian hair. She eventually learned it was merely an excuse.

But Lilly doesn't back down. "Get a date, or I'll find one for you," she says. "You're not going to try and make me feel guilty. He can be as earthy as you like. Just get one or I'll get one for you."

"I don't believe you'll get me one," I say, challenging my best friend.

"Try me. Show up alone, and I'll have someone meet you at the door, and he might have a lace muzzle I've sewn."

This makes me laugh. "Who would you get?"

"Nate, if you're not careful."

Nate's her former toad neighbor who goes through women like Kleenex. "I'll find a date." So much for Eleanor Roosevelt and my suffragettes. In the world of weddings, a girl is in need of a date. Sometimes we are so Victorian.

Lilly offers one last stand. "This is for your own good."

"What if I'm destined to be single for the rest of my life, and you're upsetting the balance of nature and God's plan?"

"I'll take it up with Him. See ya, love." Lilly hangs up the phone, and I'm in no better place than I was before the conversation.

I slide into my running shoes, lace them up, and exit through the back door of my office. Dr. Jeff is getting into his

Lexus—which I called a Beamer just to bug him—and there's an awkward moment where we should probably acknowledge each other's presence, but don't. *A Lexus convertible*, I think to myself. *Little cars for little men.*

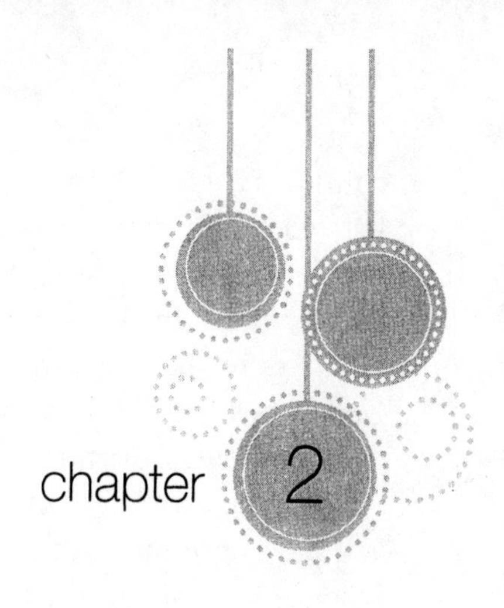

chapter 2

Another mile run.
Desperation scale: 1 (I'm good!)

Running always clears my head. It's my sanity and I thank the Lord that my legs work well enough to carry me into this realm of quiet communion with Him. I can get so bogged down in the day-to-day grind, lost to my anxieties and pressure to make the world a better place. When I run, it feels like I'm leaving my problems behind me, riding the wind to freedom and allowing myself to remember I do not control the universe. I should, but I don't.

As I pass the eucalyptus trees that line the road, inhaling their fresh, cleansing scent, I can hardly believe my friends think I'll embarrass them without a date. Don't they know me by now? I can embarrass them *with* a date too. But I wouldn't do that. My best friends have found their soul mates and that's enough for me. Their joy is enough for me. And I can survive anything for five hours, even a dancing relative with BO. I'll just have to borrow Lilly's Vicks VapoRub. The only thing left to do is decide between curtain number one (mercy date) or curtain number two (finding my own victim).

As I approach the office complex, I start to slow my pace

a little, and for once, I feel a tinge of guilt seeing my car in Jeff's spot. Not because it's his spot; I already explained that. But because I don't really care. Why do I knowingly upset him for pleasure? What kind of sick person does things like that? I don't like what the visual says about me, and I hope God is missing this little portion of my day. Sometimes the definition of Christian feels so narrow.

I pull my car keys from my fanny pack, slide into my car, and move it to the back forty of the parking lot. While there, I notice a small convertible with the top down. There's a blonde talking on her cell phone, loudly.

"Are you going to help me or not? I want a divorce. You want a divorce. Let's just get it over with! If you were this patient in our marriage, we wouldn't have this problem." She snaps her phone shut and eyes me with a smile as though I haven't just overheard her most private and painful conversation. At least, it should be painful. She doesn't look terribly upset.

"I couldn't help overhearing," I say to her as she gets out of the car. Her legs go on forever, and she's wearing spiky heels I can only guess have some sort of name attached to them. I'm sure Lilly or Morgan would know the brand.

"Are you selling something?" she asks me, looking down from her lofty view.

"No, I'm not selling anything. I just wanted to know if there was anything I could do for you. It sounds like you're having a tough day." I point to the complex. "I'm a chiropractor and I also do Chinese medicine. Things that deal with the emotional aspects of health."

She laughs. "Thanks, but my back is just fine. It's my husband who seems to have difficulty with other women's backs, but that's another subject."

"I do all sorts of natural healing. God's first building block was energy, you know. The anger must be eating you alive."

She gives me that look I'm used to by now. "That's sweet. Well, listen, thank you for stopping, but I'm fine. It's nice to know there are still concerned citizens about in the Silicon Valley. Are you licensed to prescribe meds?" she asks me.

I shake my head. "I don't really believe in pharmaceuticals."

"Right." She lifts the corner of her lip. "Well, nice meeting you."

"You're sure you're okay?" I ask.

"I made a mistake. Just trying to remedy it. Do I have lipstick on my teeth?" She flashes me a smile.

I shake my head. She hikes her gargantuan bag over her shoulder and heads for Jeff's office. I guess a divorce is nothing a trip to the plastic surgeon's office can't handle. And he'll be there waiting. The thought ticks me off.

"Good luck," I say to her back. As she walks away I'm almost envious. Not that she's getting a divorce, but that she can handle something so overwhelming with ease. I know it's because she's so out of touch with her own emotions, but that hardly makes me feel better at the moment.

Our office complex has a small gym, and I head to the showers after I've run to wipe as much of the morning's grime off me as possible. Reaching into my gym bag, I drink a soy/ flax seed/strawberry smoothie I brought with me for lunch. It's warm and tastes like sandpaper grit in soy, but I swallow it all down anyway. I need to get those essential oils before starting the afternoon's grind. But as I think about the little Greek café, I wonder if I don't make life harder than it has to be.

I pull on my familiar cotton skirt and slide into my Clarks clogs. A once-over in the mirror tells me my figure is lost in the outfit. I like it this way. I am so glad I got my mom's red hair. I smooth the skirt she used to wear with pride. It's one of my very favorite things, though I suppose it has seen better days. I can't bring myself to throw it away or succumb to the world of fashion. It's Lilly and Morgan's least favorite thing of mine, and they are quite vocal about my wearing it. See why I'm envious of that woman in the convertible? She can throw away a marriage easier than I can a skirt.

When I emerge from the changing room and head to the office, I see my father waiting beside the door and checking his watch. *Uh oh.* I look around for an escape, but it's too late—he's seen me and he opens his arms as he approaches me. I watch his countenance fall as he sees my skirt, but he recovers quickly.

"Hi, Daddy," I say, my face crushed into suit jacket.

"Poppy, how about having dinner with your old dad tonight?"

Is *she* here? I don't say this, but I'm sure my extended silence implies it.

"Just you and me." My dad pulls away. "What do you say? Sharon had an event at the convention center, so I drove her here and I'm free until nine tonight. Just like old times. Are you up for it? Or do you have a hot date that I'm interfering with?"

"No, Daddy, it sounds great." I try to force my enthusiasm, but as I see my dad in his suit, a part of me dies. *All this frippery to drive Sharon to San Jose . . .*

This is not my father. My father was a free-spirited, tie-dye-wearing artist who listened to Credence Clearwater Revival long after it was fashionable and put off any job that interfered with our family. This man who stands before me now looks like an Armani ad, his eyes now dulled by corporate America and proper small talk. This is someone Sharon created, and there's an inability on my part to find my father within the exterior. I've tried, really I have, but all I get is his business advice and our conversations quickly revert to how best to make a buck. The thing is my dad shouldn't give money advice to welfare recipients. I'm afraid the money comes from Sharon, the heart from my father.

"So what will you do until it's time for dinner?" I ask him.

"I thought I'd hang out and watch you work."

His very presence makes me nervous, somehow, and I've already run at lunch, so I can hardly take a jog now. "I don't know if that's such a good idea, Dad. You might make the men uncomfortable. It's been hard as it is to overcome their feelings that I'm not strong enough to be their chiropractor. You don't mind, do you?"

"Sure. Sure, I understand."

It's clear he doesn't.

"Maybe you could sit in my office and read a book, huh? I've got lots of great things in there on health and even some fiction. Lots of Dickens—they make me think of Mom."

He looks down at his expensive shoes. "Poppy, about your mother. I can't help but notice you're still wearing one of her skirts and—"

"Dad, don't say it. I like the skirt. I like the memory of my mom close to me and this reminds me to care for the earth God created. That we don't need something new every five minutes to make us feel better about ourselves. That's what she taught me," I say proudly, circling the skirt with my hands. "Not to be a consumer, but to give something back."

"Poppy, that skirt is nearly twenty years old. Your mother bought it new, you know." He whispers the next part: "You look ridiculous, honey. You're running a business now and your mother would be proud of you regardless of what career path you chose. You don't have to wear that ancient skirt to prove your loyalty."

I feel my jaw twitch. Spoken like someone whose loyalty dissipated quick enough. "I look ridiculous?" I laugh to let him know I'm not offended. "I haven't forgotten who I am, Dad. I'm not dressed like Donald Trump, trying to pretend that I never knew a life of simplicity. My goal isn't to get my wife the biggest diamond in the Junior League."

My hand flies to my mouth as I see him visibly shaken at my comment. My dad's gentility is just not cut out for this type of content, and I feel about an inch tall.

My father's face, now worn from years of pain and of avoiding it, clouds. He starts to nod his head.

"Daddy, I'm sorry." *Why can't I just shut up? Where is my edit button?*

He holds up a palm. "No, you're entitled to your opinion and it's obvious you think I've sold out. That's fair. Poppy, I loved your mother and our family, too, but she wouldn't want you standing still mourning her. Do you think she would want me to spend these nearly two decades alone so I could prove my love to her?"

"This isn't the place for this conversation."

"You don't have anything to prove to her, Poppy. She was proud of you, not what you accomplished. She knew from the day you were born that you were a special heart. You danced everywhere and you delighted everyone who met you. Sometimes your mother would just look at you and cry from the love she felt."

"Stop it," I say as my eyes begin tearing up.

"You don't need to wear gauze for the rest of your life to prove your love, and I didn't need to stay the same person I was twenty years ago."

"Stop." I hold my palm up. "Don't say anything else." There are people entering Jeff's office, and each one of them has stopped to look at us. I want to stick my tongue out and tell them to go get Botoxed and leave me alone, but their stares do get to me. It's official—my run has done nothing for me after the presence of my father and his gloomy tale of devotion. Up that desperation level back to a four.

I unlock the front door to my office, and the bells jingle to announce my arrival. My father holds the door open for me as I pull the key out, and he looks at me and winks.

"What's that smell?" He wrinkles his nose.

"Mint and thyme. It's a stress reliever. A lot of my clients come straight from work, full of angst. I like to provide them with an opportunity for respite from the daily struggles. Even if it's only for a few minutes."

He just nods. A few years ago, he might have asked to try some for his own house, but Sharon has long since squelched his curiosity. "Before you start for the afternoon," he says. "I want to talk to you about Morgan's wedding."

"What?" I stop cold. "My Morgan's wedding?"

Dad nods. "Do you have a date?"

"What?" I ask as though it isn't the question of the month.

"A date," Dad says. "Do you have a date to Morgan's wedding?"

"Why?" I stretch this word out, hoping to imply it's none of his business and maybe we could close down the discussion.

"I just wondered, that's all. Sharon and I—"

"Sharon and you, what? You're invited to the wedding?"

"Of course your best friend would invite us, Poppy. I'm walking Morgan down the aisle. Didn't she mention that?"

I swallow the lump in my throat. "No, she must have forgotten that little tidbit." Morgan's father is in jail for tax evasion, but I still find it interesting she's using my father for a stand-in. Doesn't she remember my father, however sweet he may be, comes with Sharon? Pariah-en-Gucci. So much for loyalty.

"Sharon and I wanted to know if you needed a ride to the

wedding. We could drive up together, maybe have breakfast on the Bay."

"Oh darn," I nibble on my lip, hoping that sounded remotely real and rushing to think up an excuse. Here it comes: my first truth stretch of the day. "I have a date, but that would have been really fun. Darn it."

"Maybe we can double. Sharon is always saying she wants to meet the man in your life."

"My date is really shy, Dad. He's not quite what you'd call a man in my life, at this point." *He's also non-existent, but surely I can find someone shy while I'm on the search. I could put that in an Internet search, after all.*

"So who's the mystery man? Could he be someone serious?" He looks at me smiling, full of hope, and I can't go through with it. I hate having a conscience.

"The truth is Lilly and Morgan are setting me up. I don't know who he is, and I'd rather that the world doesn't know that it's a setup, okay? Maybe you could keep that out of your speech at the wedding. You are speaking, I assume."

He ignores my question. "Poppy, boys have always flocked to you like you were the only stick of candy at school. You need to stop repelling everyone, sweetheart." He pushes my hair over my shoulder in a tender way. "That skirt sends a message, and you know it. Someday, someone is going to make it over the moat, and then what?"

Emma opens the door with a jangle and brightens at the sight of my father, "Mr. Clayton!" She drops her bag at the door and hugs my dad like he's her own. "What are you doing over here?"

We act like my father lives in Outer Mongolia, but he's only over the hill in Santa Cruz. Some people actually drive every day to work from the coast, but not my father. It's a major endeavor to get him over the hill, like he has to come on the wagon train through sleet. Not his climate-controlled Lexus over Highway 17.

"I came to take my beautiful daughter out to dinner."

"She needs it. She's been training, you know. All I ever see her eat is flaxseed shakes and soy mochas."

"Is this true?" My father arches a brow.

"Fourteen percent body fat, Dad." I pull my skirt tightly around my hips. "I'm in the best shape of my life."

"That's debatable," my father sits down and picks up a magazine in one fluid movement and begins thumbing through the pages. "Look, here are nice clothes that are environmentally responsible in this magazine, Poppy. Let's go shopping tonight. Maybe we could find some clothes to show off that great figure of yours. Why be 14 percent body fat when your skirt is 30 percent?" He grins at this. "When you're eighty, you can tell your grandchildren about your body-fat percentage." His eyes twinkle, and he winks at Emma.

I'm shaking my head. I remember shopping with my father in junior high and I think it wounded me for life. *I am not going back there.*

He seems to know what I'm thinking, "Come on, it's not a training bra. We'll start small. Maybe just a skirt that isn't falling apart? We don't have to do an entire wardrobe."

"Don't bother," Emma grins. "I think those clothes are surgically attached to her body. She's allergic to the word *new*. As a matter of fact, she might check with Dr. Jeff next door to see if they could be surgically attached. It would save her the trouble in the morning. You know how some women get their eyebrows drawn on?"

"Do you mind?" I look at Emma with a glance that reminds her who signs her paychecks. "Dad, I know what you're trying to do, but I don't need clothes. It's important to my clients that I retain a life of simplicity. If I come in here dressing to the nines, how will they know they're not in the plastic surgery office next door?"

"The smell?" he asks. "Or the excess of plants, maybe. I feel like I'm in the rainforest. And what is that incessant dripping sound?"

"It's the water feature," I say.

"It's Chinese water torture!"

"She does buy nice workout wear," Emma says. "She gets asked out practically every lunch hour, then she comes back for the sackcloth, and her magical powers disappear. As do the men."

"Emma!"

"We had some cancellations today so I moved everyone around to keep you free for updating charts. You're free for an hour. Why don't you go eat something?"

"I ate already," I say through gritted teeth.

"I bet your father hasn't, and a warm shake doesn't count if that's what you ate, Poppy."

"How did you know what I ate?"

"We'll be at lunch," my father says, taking me by the elbow and leading me out of the office.

This is feeling every bit the Monday it is. I get to endure a lecture on the benefits of dressing for success. I need a spa date with my Spa Girls. Before they're *both* married and weighed down with the plight of motherhood. Lilly's baby will be here in a few months and Morgan becomes an instant mother when she marries George. A blind date is starting to sound like the easiest, most stress-free option. The world is against me, and I feel my energy draining with each step. A hot rock massage might be just what I need to fill 'er up.

I may not be desperate. But I'm close.

chapter 3

Daddy still here.
Desperation scale: 5

Simon Jennings is one of my most regular clients. He's tall—six-feet-four (at least)—with a hulking frame and a horrible spine. To the outside viewer, he would just appear big and athletic, but to the trained eye, he's a bad spine waiting to happen. His spinal subluxations require alignment every week, and he uses that to his advantage—trying each appointment to secure a date for Friday night.

I'm torn with Simon. Sometimes I think he's beyond charming and the next minute I think *annoyed* would be a good term to describe how I feel about him. Not because he isn't handsome and chivalrous, but because I don't understand his purpose in life. He's like Midas, and everything he touches turns to gold, but I never actually see him do anything, and that frightens me. He plays a lot of golf. I imagine he's had to be serious at some point to be able to play all that golf. Somewhere along the line, he made a lot of cash, but there's more to life than cash. Although he does have good insurance coverage; that shows genuine practicality.

Simon is one of those men you just don't take seriously

and yet always wonder if you're missing the true treasure beneath. He comes in with a joke on the tongue, and when he switches to Casanova, I'm just never sure who's speaking. I'm not going to lie—there have been times I've really been tempted by Simon, and our chemistry is inexplicable, but then he talks about his latest golf game and I think about my own father and his lack of a forty-hour week and I'm immediately back in reality.

There's more, of course. Let's just say that when I can't tell if someone is truly asking me out, I'm not generally tempted, but as the wedding date approaches, I'm more open minded every week. Simon would be an easy out. He'd dress up well, put on his best sales smile, be able to talk about golf at the Olympic Club, and generally impress. But at what cost? I'm his doctor, after all.

"Poppy." Simon's large frame maneuvers through the swinging doors, and I light up at the sight of him, but I quickly go into my carefully managed facade. It's probably just me fantasizing about the perfect wedding date.

"Did you miss me last week?" he asks with a wink.

"I'll bet your back missed me more." I smile.

He rolls his head, and I can hear the crack. "You've got that right. So tell me, does absence make the heart grow fonder? Are we on for Friday night?" He wiggles his eyebrows, and on a lesser man, it would just be annoying. But on Simon, there's a certain amount of the cute factor to it. A boyish charm, if you will.

I place a hand on my hip. "You know what they say, Simon: out of sight, out of mind."

"Oh." He grabs his heart. "You know how to wound me, you really do. It's true what they say about redheads. Heartbreakers, every one of you. Tossing us poor men to the lions. You're worse than Nero, you know."

He stops and hands me the toiletries from his recent trips to the Westin Hotels. (I love the smell of their stuff!) "But you're worth the trouble, I suppose."

"Simon, thank you!" I take the collection of shampoos and put them on the desk. "Where'd you go?"

"It's no trouble. I haven't washed my hair for a week, but you don't mind." He winks. "I went to Hawaii. I'm looking for some property there."

"Get on the table," I order, having had enough of his weekly antics. He's all bark.

He lies down on his stomach, and I use my hands to feel down his spine while he moans—whether in pain or ecstasy, I never ask. It's not the kind of thing I want to know. I stop at C5 and C6. "I don't know what you do to yourself on that golf course, but—"

His voice is muffled. "When I'm giving Tiger lessons, he always says great golf costs the master something. The perfect swing requires all of the athlete, and my back pays the price. You ought to be thankful for me; I keep you in business."

"I suppose that's Tiger Woods," I say.

"No, it's Tiger Hernandez. We play once in a while."

While he's giving me his bravado, I adjust his back with a loud crack before he knows what's hit him and he grunts. I don't usually apply such force, but Simon's back seems to require it.

"This guy giving you trouble?" My father comes out of my office, and I cringe. It's like fighting for the training bra with the pink flower all over again. I lower my eyebrows menacingly, hoping to send Daddy a silent message—*I can take care of myself*—but as is expected, he ignores me completely. "That's my daughter you're talking to. You mind yourself. Don't let her size fool you; she could take you down easily enough."

This makes Simon grin. "I have no doubt she could. Did you hear what she just did to my back? And I'm paying for this torture."

"I'm fine, Dad. Just a little harmless banter between a favorite client and myself."

Simon turns over and gives me a smirk. His eyes meet mine in mutual understanding, and for a small instant I forget my father is standing here.

"You're standing up for me. I knew you loved me, Dr. Poppy. What must it be like for you to look at me every week, unable to act on your feelings from a professional obligation? Give into temptation, sweetie. Do it now before it's too late." He reaches out, and I have to physically stand in front of my father.

"He's kidding, Dad." I turn towards Simon. "You'll never understand my pain, Simon. Every week you come in here, and I see . . . I see a spine I just have to crack." I say this while wrestling Daddy back in the office. Daddy finally calms down and backs away, but not without punching his own palm in warning. Just like the gorilla at the zoo. I can almost hear the accompanying "Ooo-ooo." And Simon looks like a linebacker while my father is shaped and dressed like an older model in a catalog (one of those for timeshares in exotic locales). I'm sure Daddy is thinking this man is a slacker of the worst sort, completely unaware Simon could probably buy and sell all of us a few times over. Then play a round of golf before the day is up.

"So this is your father?" Simon stands up and stretches a palm out towards my father, but Daddy just purses his lips, which doesn't stop Simon at all. He steps forward. "I didn't mean any disrespect, Mr. Clayton. Poppy and I go way back. She knows how to shut me down if she wants."

My father grunts a reply, still not completely satisfied.

"She is a little cruel. She has all that beauty in that tiny, stunning package of hers, and she never lets a soul open the gift."

"No one had better try!" My father threatens.

"Trust me," Simon continues. "Everyone tries. But you have nothing to worry about." Simon sets his hand on my shoulder and turns to the door beside my office for his sports massage from Brian the mighty. He wasn't really finished with my session, but I imagine he's done enough since my father isn't leaving. As Simon goes, he looks straight into my father's eyes. "It's a pity too." Then his gaze meets my own. "Because I could give her everything."

At his exit, my father's face is bright red. "That's what you put up with? Paying you to adjust a guy's back does not entitle him to treat you like a piece of meat. Maybe I need to be here every day, Poppy. You always were too trusting. You can't handle men like that. It's not your job to fix everyone, you know?"

I handle men like that every day of the week.

"He's harmless, Dad. I promise. He's been here for three years, and he's one of my best patients. Besides, he needs me. His back is a wreck. We're friends and hopefully when he comes in here, he gets the courage to go out into the world and really ask a woman out. I'm empowering him to change his life—both his spine and his confidence."

"He doesn't seem to need any more confidence. He's already got enough for the three of us. I imagine he's got a few women too. He doesn't seem the type to be lonely."

My father's comment unnerves me. I don't think Simon is like that at all, but I'll admit I follow him with my eyes wondering if my father's sixth sense has picked up on something I've missed all these years. My father is typically nice to everyone. His actions over Simon seem oddly out of character, and it makes me wonder what Daddy is really doing here.

"He's too friendly if you ask me. You running a chiropractic office or a dating service? Flirting is not part of what you offer, I'm assuming."

"Daddy, what's gotten into you? I don't flirt with everyone, I promise. Simon is special."

"I heard that!" Simon calls from the massage therapist's office.

"It seems like my presence might be necessary here."

"Like I said, it's hard enough for me to get the male clientele, Dad. I don't need you scaring them off like seagulls at the beach."

"You're too pretty to be in here by yourself. This is what you avoided med school for?" He shakes his head and looks at his feet. It's not that he's upset I avoided med school. He only wants me to be happy, but I don't think he was ever too keen on the natural route after Sharon came along. If given the choice of a small roaster or Starbucks, my father would choose Starbucks every time. And medical school is the corporate version of health: there's no getting around it. Corporate is comfortable to my dad now. Maybe he got tired of choosing the hard way with my mother, who ground all our grains and grew vegetables. Maybe he just saw how much easier life is on the "outside."

"Brian's right next door, Dad. He does all the massages, and he has a black belt if I ever need him. Jeff, the plastic surgeon, is on the other side of me, and he's here as much as I am. So I'm safe, okay? Besides, I really could take someone out if I had to. My own version of the Vulcan death grip that I learned in chiropractic school."

My dad nods. "Poppy, are you happy with this life?"

"I love my life, Dad. I get to run every day, train for my triathlons. I get to go away when I want with the Spa Girls and relax. I've got everything I could want here."

"Now Poppy, you know I'm not one to pry or interfere."

"Yes, Dad, I do know that." *So enough already.*

"When you decided to drop out of medical school, did I ever question you?"

"I didn't actually drop out, Dad, just didn't go."

"But did I question you?" His voice turns solemn. "And you were accepted to medical school."

"No, Dad, you didn't question me, but it's not like I became a burden to you or anything. My priorities just changed. All the things Mom taught me made sense, and had she stuck with that lifestyle . . . Well, you know."

"There is no easy way to say this, honey, so I'm just going to come right out and say it."

Can those words ever be followed by something good? I know this is not something I want to hear. "I have patients, Dad. They have to get back to work. Could we put off this sermon until later?" I point towards the door, which he slams shut, locking us in the office.

"Sharon and I have been talking."

Which means he's been doing a lot of listening. "And? What did Sharon decide I should do with my life?"

"We think if you're going to continue to live this alternative lifestyle—"

"I'm a chiropractor. I'm not gay, Daddy."

"We think you should move your practice back to Santa Cruz, where you'll be more comfortable." He scans my skirt and looks away. "Poppy, you were always happy there by the beach, and we want to know you'll be happy when we're settling into retirement."

"I like it here, Dad. I don't actually care what people think, or if I'm seen as a weirdo. I'm sort of proud of it. I was pegged early on at Stanford as missing the route to Berkeley." I bite down my smile. "So please don't worry about me."

"The truth is, Poppy, we're downsizing, Sharon and I. We don't spend much time in the house, and we've discussed it. We think it's time you got your inheritance. Your mother left you that house, and we feel we've freeloaded long enough. In other words, we're becoming grown-ups."

"What does that mean exactly?"

"We're retiring from the rat race. We've rented a little place near Phoenix and we're leaving California. Well, actually we've left. But we're moving out slowly. However, the house is empty and while there's a lot of work to be done, the equity on the house should pay for it easily."

"Phoenix? Dad, it's too hot in Phoenix. You're used to the beach, the marine layer, fog, gentle ocean breezes . . . What are you thinking?"

"I'm getting older, Poppy. It's hard for me to manage the lawn and the constant upkeep that living in the salt air requires. The moist air gets into my joints and it's just better for me in Arizona."

"What makes you think I can manage the house?"

He smiles gently. "You can always sell it."

"I can't sell it and you know it."

"Then maybe it's time you find out why. You never came to visit Sharon and me while we lived there. If it really means something to you, find out why."

"I'm not moving back there."

"That's fine, but it's your responsibility now. Your mother and I were to sign this house over to you when you turned thirty, and that's about to happen. It was a decision we made a long time ago, and I've lived out my part of the deal. Now it's your turn."

"It doesn't mean we have to do anything different, Dad. I don't need that house. You and Sharon can stay there." I struggle to find the right words. Anything to keep that house and its legacy far from my grasp.

He pulls out a folded piece of paper from his breast pocket. "It belongs to you. I've done everything legally to make it yours. Actually, I did it a long time ago." He looks down again. "All the necessary legal issues. If you want to get rid of it, it's your business now."

I shove the paper back at him. "Well, I'm not taking it. I have my own business to run. I can't be worrying about retrofitting a house, and I know it's not in the best shape."

"Then you'll have to sign it away legally. Sell it 'as is.' It's still worth quite a bit of money." He shrugs, giving me that innocent twinkle that I imagine gets him out of trouble with Sharon. "There's nothing I can do about it now. Sell it."

"I can't do that, Dad. It was Mom's house."

"It's yours now, Poppy."

"I can't live in that house again." Even the thought of it sends shivers up my spine.

"Sell it, sweetie. It's time to move on. Either that, or move back there and embrace it. One way or another, you've got to face it."

I just shake my head. I can't even avoid her skirts in the closet. I'm just supposed to up and sell her memory, her essence?

"Anyway." Dad claps his hands together. "That's why I came by. I needed to tell you it's officially yours."

Yippee.

"I have the condo. You and Sharon sell it." I try to place the title back in his hands. And all the work the decrepit building needs. I don't mind really being without the house; I just don't want to be the one to dispose of it.

Daddy just shakes his head. "I made a deal with your mother a long time ago. If you don't want the house, like I said, sell it." He pulls his jacket down, smoothing the lapels. "I'll get out of your way until dinner."

"We're not through."

Emma steps into the room, noticing our heated tones. She appears very apologetic. "Your patients are backing up."

"We're not done, Dad." I say again. I step into the examination room and see Dr. Jeff Curran, my beloved plastic surgeon neighbor, sitting on my table. "Oh," I hear myself groan. "What do you want?"

"I just came by to thank you. You moved your car," he says in a low tone.

"Yeah," I draw my hair behind my ear—in an annoyed way, not trying to be cute or anything. "Don't think too much of it. I did it for the good of your business. Your success and my freedom from silicone next door." He gives Silicon Valley a new meaning for me.

"Thank you anyway." He stands up and I'll admit I flinch a bit as he does so. Even though he's exceptionally clean-cut with extraordinarily white teeth, he really is actor handsome. I'm sure he has some sort of ab builder by the mirror at home. Looking at him is like a car accident: he's drop-dead gorgeous, and even though you know better . . . Well, I *am* human.

Emma clears her throat. "The patients are waiting, Poppy."

"Right." I break my gaze from Jeff's. His eyes are blue. Sort of a grayish-green blue like the ocean on a foggy day. Not that I noticed. They're just so natural looking and they don't go with the whole plastic persona. "So thanks for telling me. Thanks." *Yeah, I just said that.*

"You're welcome." Before he has a chance to leave, my father comes out of the office, and their eyes meet in the strangest way. Perhaps it's the doctor coat and my father has stars in his eyes. Somewhere in the annals of history it was decreed that parents should think doctors make good husbands. Quite frankly, I think they make horrible husbands from what I've seen—always working, their minds preoccupied when they're home. And then there's the whole bringing-home-viruses-to-the-children aspect. You're much better off with a professor, I would think. Oh, maybe not. They probably think they're as interesting to you as they are to their students. It's the whole clueless aspect.

An electrician. That's a good husband job.

"Poppy, you all right?"

"Huh? Yeah. Just daydreaming."

Simon steps out of Brian's office, and he looks at Jeff as though he's met the opponent.

"I'll pick you up at six-thirty," Dad says. "You're going to eat a decent meal. Nothing with tofu in it, all right?"

I feel my head bobbing. "Great. Six-thirty. I'll be ready."

My father leans over and kisses me on the cheek. "You may not want to go back to Santa Cruz, but that skirt does."

I flare it out, looking at the bright purples and turquoise, now faded into muddied gray versions of themselves, and I look up just in time to see Jeff's eyes fall on the material. I feel my face flame red. Simon, too, looks at the skirt with new eyes and for once, I wish I'd worn something else. So this is what embarrassment feels like. I definitely need a spa weekend. I'm getting delusional.

chapter 4

My friends diss me.
Desperation scale: 6

When the work day is over, I brace myself for the evening with my father. He's retiring in Arizona. How utterly clichéd and corporate. He couldn't even surprise me by separating from the pack just this once? He couldn't go to Montana or Chicago?

I hear myself sigh. The house is mine now. It's my burden to bear and he knows it. I'm certain he's happy to be rid of the trouble and the pain. It's amazing how our lives can get so intertwined with a material possession. That house represents so much more to me than just a domicile, and I suppose it's the same for him. The difference is he got to be done with it before the hard part started.

I turn up the music, Third Day, and try to erase my thoughts. The lead singer's voice is sheer heaven, and I start to dance around my office putting it back to rights. While I try to keep my office a peaceful environment, after a long day with whiny executives who don't want to wait a second throwing their magazines around, its neat appearance diminishes.

I realign all the bottles of elixirs and enzymes on the

shelves that my patients have haphazardly rearranged. Rearranged, touched, fingered, but not resigned themselves to buy. Why is investing in health such a big deal to these people? They'll spend four hundred dollars on a pair of shoes, but they won't spend twenty dollars for better digestion. It's unfathomable. Unreasonable. Ridiculous.

My cell phone rings and I turn down the stereo. I see, by caller ID, it's the bride: Morgan. My feelings are mixed, as I know she's leery of inviting me, one of her best friends, to the wedding for fear that I'll offer free health advice. I know she'd never actually uninvite me, but even the warnings and threat of a blind date don't exactly evoke warmth. After all I've done for my friends, this is my final thank you before their foray into married life.

"Hey, Morgan," I say without inflection into the phone.

"So you're looking for a spa date? You? Why don't you just take a rosemary bath or swallow one of those green drinks? If you're needing a spa date, we're all sunk. You are, in fact, peace personified."

How I wish that were so. "Not today. The reality is coming upon me. You're leaving me. This is one of the last times I can call and we can still play. Lilly's having the baby soon, and you'll be married with an instant son of your own. I'll have to find new friends." I don't say the last thing nearly as despondently as I feel it. Currently, I'm Eeyore, packing my own rain cloud. Even I don't particularly want to be around me.

"We're not abandoning you, Poppy."

"All friends say that, and then they always end up abandoning. Their lives get busy. Their husbands don't like to see them turn into giggly girls, and the single friends are left to shop for a new pet. Soon, the single friend's grocery list consists of cat food and fiber, and my grocery list already reads that way so I've got nowhere to go but down. Then I start hanging out with the other people who haven't found love, and we get stranger, and our dreams evaporate into nothing."

"You are having a day. Poppy, I'll make the reservations, but in the meantime, you're making me nervous. Can't you take a vitamin or something? Maybe go visit the trees."

The trees are a nearby grove of eucalyptus I often run to on my lunch hour. The scent brings my mother to life and a peace just descends upon me there. When I was a child, we would play hide-and-seek amongst the trees near our home. I always feel her nearby and my problems farther away when I smell eucalyptus or redwoods. But yeah, the trees aren't happening right now.

I try to put on my best front. "I think the spa would help. The office has been so busy, and with training, I haven't had much time to play. My father just had a bit of news too. He's going to Arizona, of all places. See? You are all leaving me."

"You are the only one I know who actually needs to schedule fun, Poppy, but I hear you. Can you go this weekend, then? I'll call Lilly." Morgan still has that nervous lilt to her voice, and I'm sorry I transferred my angst energy. Not a great friend thing to do. And definitely not like me. It's probably the plastic surgeon. He's got me all out of sync. He probably emanated bad silicone vibes when he entered my office, knocking over my energy with his plastic meridians.

"I can go this weekend. I'll just have to cancel all my dates." I giggle, without feeling, but I'm hoping to infuse much needed humor into the moment. I feel relief knowing I'm just going to get away from it all for a time. But as soon as it's confirmed, I start to stress about all I'll need to do while there "relaxing." "I'll have to run while I'm there. I'll swim when I get home to the condo, but I can't stop training or I won't make my goal for the Hawaiian triathlon."

"Poppy, you need to let it go, girl. You are a control freak and it's scaring me."

"See, that's the thing. Control freaks get a bad rap. I mean, even the word *freak*—how rude is that? God is a God of order," I say calmly. "Not chaos. When people operate under chaos, how can they possibly not want to improve upon that? If people could feel the endorphins that I get running . . . If they could know the power of going to the cupboard and finding exactly what they needed immediately . . . If they could feel the energy of a really good diet . . . I'm telling you, there would be no Atkins, no Jenny Craig—just people running and jumping with all their excess energy. I mean, I have the answer, and I'm just supposed to keep it bottled inside? When you eat badly, your body's rhythm changes. Your organs cry out for balance. I just can't understand why people don't embrace these truths. I'm not talking out of ignorant opinion. I've studied this in depth and—"

"Poppy."

"Yeah?"

"It took you a minute and a half to tell me that story. I timed you."

"Why?"

"Because a minute and a half of conversation, without stopping for the other person's comments, is why we're getting you a wedding date."

I think I'm offended. "I was just saying that control freaks get a bad rap after you called me one."

"There's a reason for that. Prove to us you're not. Let the skirts go. You know, it was sort of cute back in college. Now it's scaring us."

What is it with the skirts today? I look down at my current version. "Well, next time you need your shoes placed in an orderly fashion in a new closet, we'll see who you go to. It won't be Lilly. You love my order. What if I just became haphazard and commercialized?"

"Poppy, you know we love you, but you're getting to be like a telemarketer. It used to be just the weird skirts and the digestion of inhumane health drinks. But now . . ." She pauses dramatically. "Now, it's just getting odder by the minute. Lilly told me you organized my twenty-four-hour shower according to the acupuncture clock?"

"That was a surprise!"

Morgan continues, "Do you like it when you tell a story and your audience starts backing up?"

"I just assume they're not open to the idea of their health yet. I just tell them the truth," I cry.

"It's just not really dinner conversation, Poppy. That's all we're saying. There's a time and place. In your office, people pay for your advice; they want to hear it."

I feel an ache in my stomach. "So what are you saying? You don't want me at your wedding?"

Morgan couldn't be rude if she tried, but right now she's on the hairy edge of offensive, and I realize this obviously means a lot to her.

"I couldn't get married without you, Poppy. You're one of my very best friends in the world. You've been there for me when no one else was—do you really think I could get married without you there? No, I'm saying that Lilly and I think you have gone a little over the deep end lately. We want *our* Poppy back, not the one so obsessed with health that she's not living. You know, Lilly grew up eating pasta and sausage and she looks every bit as healthy as you."

"Looks are deceiving. If you could look at her arteries, you'd see the difference. Sure, she's thin—God made her that way. But still, she needs to take care of her temple. See, in the beginning, God created light. Light is energy and energy heals. It was God's first building block, the power He instills in His children if they only respect the creation . . . creation of . . ." I peter out about here. *Man, I do sound like a weirdo.*

Morgan sighs loud and long. "Don't you see? People don't want to eat bark for lunch. They don't want gritty drinks the color of that stuff that grows on a frog pond. People want to enjoy life. To eat, drink, and be merry. They want to dine in outdoor cafés and sip fine wine with fancy cheeses."

"Outdoor cafés!" I'm horrified. "You know, birds just walk all over the tables, and how often do you think they get cleaned? I'm not even talking about a good bleach clean, just regular spray cleaned."

"I don't care and neither does anyone else. Poppy, what's happened to you? When did you stop enjoying life?"

"I enjoy life," I say meekly. But I have to admit, fun to me has become staying on top of my to-do list and counting my body-fat ratio. "I'm looking forward to the wedding. I'll enjoy that. Why don't you tell me about my date?" I encourage Morgan to do the talking.

"He's a runner, Poppy. Max met him on the San Francisco Beach 5k."

"You got me a date off the street?"

"The beach, and no, not exactly. Max brought him to dinner, and Lilly and I interviewed him for the prospective job."

I'm not even going to comment on the word *job*. "Is he a Christian?"

"Of course he is. And he likes to dress comfortably and he's into his health. He even has a good body-fat ratio. He told us what it was, but I don't remember."

"What do you mean he's into his health?" Granted, I'm afraid to ask. That could mean a plethora of things, and considering what Lilly and Morgan currently think of my health topics, it could mean I'm in for a world of hurt.

"He feels perfectly at ease discussing his small intestine at the dinner table. He's you in pants, actually. We were delighted to find him."

"You know I can hold my tongue at the wedding. Why are you setting me up? I am capable of finding myself a date."

"We know that. It's just we think you'd really like this guy and there might be some magic here."

The only magic I'm thinking of is how to make this guy disappear. "You know, if I want magic, I'll go to Disneyland, Morgan. You either want me at the wedding, or you don't. If you could tell Mr. Health, 'Thank you for the mercy date but I'm busy that day,' I'd be most appreciative."

"Poppy! You wouldn't dare miss my wedding."

I slam shut the phone, which, granted, isn't a big deal on a cell phone, but it makes me feel better. I know when Morgan has had a chance to cool off she'll realize forcing me into a date with a guy from the beach isn't her best moment as a friend. I take off a sandal and throw it across the office. At that very moment, Jeff Curran comes in the door, his eyebrows raised.

"Well, I didn't know you had it in you. So this beatnik peace thing—is that just an act?"

"What do you want?" I ask rudely. Sort of my standard tone with Jeff, and I catch myself for my continuous rudeness. Even if he does represent in human form all that's wrong with the world.

"I'm knocking off early, and I wanted to know if you wanted to have dinner with me, but now I'm worried I'd get in the way of flying shellfish."

"I don't eat shellfish. They're bottom feeders. Not that this is relevant. My dad is taking me out tonight. Didn't you overhear that?" (I'm sure he did. Could he be looking for an invite?)

"So tomorrow night, maybe?" he asks, ignoring my question.

I know he heard my plans. "Jeff, I don't mean any offense asking this, but what's up?"

"I've been wanting to do this since I opened my practice, but today's the first day you actually spoke nicely to me. I thought we might be neighborly when I moved my practice in. I see you at church. You see me at church. Maybe we could get beyond ignoring each other. You know, be big enough Christians to overcome our little differences."

This makes me laugh. "It's a little late for that, wouldn't you say?" I've sort of grown accustomed to ignoring him with style. And vice versa.

My cell phone starts to ring. It's Morgan again.

"Aren't you going to get that?" he asks.

"No." I see him eye me as though I treat everyone with this anger. "It's my best friend. I'll call her back."

It keeps ringing, even though I try to shut it down so I stuff the phone into my oversized skirt pocket.

"Let me guess: you've actually got another guy you're torturing on the phone, but you want to finish with me first? So how about that dinner?" He crosses his arms in his elegant suit. He's a young version of my now-corporate father. Granted, he probably makes money, though.

"You know, I really don't believe in plastic surgery." I tell him. I mean, let's nip this in the bud immediately. "It's all about vanity and pride and the Bible is pretty clear on that, so how is it you justify what you do?" I cross my arms, and yes, I'm probably taking my anger toward Morgan out on him. But he is here, after all.

"That doesn't make any sense. Plastic surgery does a lot of good in the world. In fact, I'll bet my profession is more respected than your New Age garble. Listen to the music you have playing. What is that supposed to be about?"

I purse my lips at him. "It creates an air of peace. What did you do today over in your office? Besides inflate women's mouths to the size of those wax lips we wore as kids?"

"I don't have to justify what I do to you, Poppy. I'm proud of it." He crosses his arms, and I watch as his blue eyes flash at me. "Today, I didn't have surgery. Mostly, I did consultations for a few patients to get all the extra skin removed after their gastric bypass surgery. It's painful, you know, all that skin. Burning, chafing, irritation. The skin loses all elasticity when it shrinks so quickly."

"I didn't know." I didn't want to, either, but that's another story.

"So it's a deal breaker that we don't respect what the other does; is that what you're telling me?"

"Well, isn't it?" I ask him, still unsure why he's even here. I thought my musical cars in the parking lot was enough to scare him off but good.

"It's not a deal breaker for me. I know you help people over here, and I figure somewhere deep inside you know I help people too. No one becomes a doctor for the money, am I right?"

Well, except for plastic surgeons. I look at his handsome face, and he grins that electric charm that I'm sure works on every woman alive but me. The fact remains he's being decent, and perhaps one dinner with him can convince him that what I do has value. Maybe dining with someone so absolutely different from me will help me see what my friends want from me, because I sure can't figure it out.

"Are you expecting me to dress in something other than what I wear?" I ask him with my eyes thinned. If he's looking for fashionista clothing, I might as well let him know to lower the expectations immediately. If my skirt doesn't go to the restaurant, neither do I.

He smiles slightly. "I never even noticed what you wear. You'll wear what you like, I would think. I didn't know there was a dress code for two friends having dinner."

"That can't possibly be true. That you haven't noticed what I wear."

"Because you dress that way for a reason? Do you want to tell me what it is?"

"See, you did notice."

"I noticed you spare no expense on running gear. But then, Poppy in spandex? Well, I'd have to be blind to not notice that. In case it hasn't come across your radar, I am male."

"That's sexist!" I accuse.

"See, it's really not. Sexist would be if I thought you were incapable due to your fine, good looks. But I don't. However, like a day in Yosemite, I can't help but admire the beauty. If I didn't, God didn't piece me together right, you know? Didn't your daddy teach you about the birds and the bees?"

"What about looking on a woman in lust?" I force a hand to my hip.

"No, no, you're not going to catch me in that. I never made the jump to lust. I was talking beauty. My job is to assist in *beauty*, so what kind of doctor would I be if I hadn't noticed? Do you want a plastic surgeon who doesn't get what the world thinks is beautiful? Think about that now."

"I don't want a plastic surgeon at all, actually."

My father comes into the office with a jingle of the bells. "Business must be good," he says to Jeff. "You never have to work."

"On the contrary, your daughter makes me work like a coal miner to try and wrangle a simple dinner out of her. Just a little business to discuss." He cocks his chin down while he speaks. His blue eyes hold their sparkle.

Business. I figured it had to be something. All this talk of my beauty is just a farce, as is any trust I have in Dr. Jeff Curran.

"Tomorrow night, then." I give in, trying to avoid my father butting in yet again.

Jeff exits, and my father stares at me, disbelief covering his expression. "You're going out with the plastic surgeon? Poppy, are you feeling okay?" He puts his palm on my forehead.

"It's just dinner, Dad. I would think you'd like him. He's a doctor, corporate as they come, and would probably have me barefoot and pregnant in a matter of months."

My dad raises an eyebrow. "Doesn't he embody everything you think is wrong with the world?"

I nod. "Pretty much, yeah." But he's asking, and I have to learn why my friends think I can't date normally. *He's as good a place to start as anyone.*

Daddy just nods. If there's one thing he's learned with Sharon and me, it's that reason does not necessarily play a role in our romantic thought process.

As for me, I can't figure out for the life of me why I'm going out with Dr. Ken Doll except maybe I have some latent homecoming princess dreams that haven't gone away. But then again, he may hold the answer to my questions.. The spandex comment not withstanding.

chapter 5

Dinner with Daddy.
Desperation scale: 7

We walk into the dark restaurant. (Restaurants from my father's era are always dark; apparently, there is some peace in not quite making out your food, some sort of idealized romantic view. It's probably hiding a lot of saturated fat and hydrogenated oil as well.) We're led past the dining room down a long, dank hallway that reminds me of a scene on *Law and Order: SVU*. I can almost hear the music: *"Bomp. Bomp."* The waitress doesn't have our leather-clad menus, but she turns around and grins at us as we're led down the hallway. We're passing everyone eating, so where exactly are we going?

"Dad, what's going on?"

He nods. "Little surprise for you." He winks again. My dad seems to have something stuck in his eye constantly the way he winks anymore. I'll bet he gets to Arizona and gets a job selling golf carts.

I hate surprises. All control freaks hate surprises. You can't control surprises, and besides that, you generally have to fake happiness. Another gift I completely lack. I try to call up a good memory in the recesses of my mind—"A mohair sweater? Wonderful!"—in case I need to use it.

This back end of the restaurant is perfectly still, and I have to say if I was on a date, I'd wonder if the guy wasn't in the mafia. But as it is, I know my father has no such relations. He just thinks dark restaurants equal class.

When we get to the end of the hallway, the first thing I see is a sign draped across the back wall: "WELCOME HOME!"

I'll admit, this sign sends a surge of fear through me. *Who are we welcoming home?* And of course, I can't help but think this has something to do with the decrepit house in Santa Cruz that has just come into my possession. I walk a few more steps and quickly gather the mohair-sweater smile. Underneath the sign is a smattering of friends from my former life in Santa Cruz. A life I might remind my father that I left for a reason. I always had the sneaking suspicion my dad was a bit "touched," but this sort of puts the suspicion to rest with absolute certainty. Santa Cruz doesn't exactly hold the warmest memories for me, and this conjures up the nightmare in the present.

Santa Cruz is a city from days gone by. People never have to actually conform to live there, and the sixties—its clothing, its artwork, all of it—are alive and well. My skirt is perfectly at home there, and though that might be clichéd, it's very true. The university's mascot is the banana slug, and that sums up my childhood. Slow and blissful, among the magnificent redwoods and the majestic Pacific.

More mohair smiling. I notice with a tinge of regret that none of my current friends are here. Only the people I left behind—and forgive me for adding this, but I think I left them behind for a reason.

This is your life: Birkenstock style.

My high school boyfriend, Jed Pierce, is there. With his

wife. He rolls his eyes when he sees me as if to tell me this wasn't his idea. *Don't be under the impression that you were ever good enough for me,* his eyes seem to say. I wonder what my father said to get him here. And if Daddy has an effective sales pitch, maybe I could use it to meet Orlando Bloom.

My pediatrician, Sally Amos, who saw me through all the stomachaches (that were purely psychosomatic, but there just the same) smiles at me through a thin veneer of confusion. She doesn't know what she's doing here either. There's nothing like seeing how little you truly mean to people in your past, and I suppose I should just be thankful this isn't my funeral.

My childhood neighbor, who didn't have any other friends: Kate Lockston. Kate lived with her mother Eloise (who's here also). Mrs. Lockston never worked, never left the house, and clothed Kate in boy's plaid snap shirts and corduroy. My own mother forced me to play with her, and let's just say, neither one of us is all that fond of the memories. There's emotional baggage that comes with being forced to play with someone. Even if you actually might have been friends. With the pressure comes a little resentment. I can see it in Kate's eyes even now.

And there's my father, smiling broadly with his arm around his lovely Sharon. He's grinning at her as though he's pulled off the Olympics. He's proud of his accomplishment, and I grin to acknowledge that, *Yes, Daddy, you do have a talent for surprising me. I'm surprised. Can I go home now?*

"Surprise!" They all yell in unison once they've noticed my presence.

Bigger mohair smile. "Hello, everyone," I say barely above a whisper because I can't find my voice. With that, they all come towards me and I am surrounded by the reality that was my childhood. And trust me, they're as thrilled as I am.

"Dr. Amos," I say before clutching her like the anchor she was for me. "I'm so glad you're here."

"I wouldn't have missed it. Your father says you're thinking of moving back into the house." She lets her voice fall to a whisper. "I'm not sure that's a good thing, but I'll be there to support you. And if you ever decide to have a little one of your own—" She pats my stomach. "—I'll be at your service." She goes back to her wine, a habit she always had. I remember the scent at ten in the morning and suddenly wonder if my pediatric experience was all that healthy.

Next up: my first boyfriend. First sloppy kiss, first breaking of my heart: Jed Pierce. *I loved him*, I think to myself. *Really loved him.* Granted, I also wrote in cursive *Mrs. Jed Pierce* over and over on my notebook and really loved George Michael, too, so I'm not completely sure I was capable of real love. But here he is, as if to remind me all over again how he never really loved me back. He's accompanied by the real Mrs. Jed Pierce. She's a little blonde thing with a jealous eye and a vice-like grip on Jed. It's really odd to see what attracted you as a high school girl. Something makes me wonder if I wasn't just attracted by everyone else's opinion of Jed, because I'll tell you, I can't see it now. He's still so basketball-star-looking, the complete opposite of what I would find attractive.

"Hi, Jed. Allison," I say, acknowledging his wife. He gives me a simple nod, making me wonder why the heck he bothered coming. His wife only looks me up and down, as though I want her husband with a passion that is worthy of a Shakespearian tragedy. And you'll just have to trust me on this one: I don't.

Jed awkwardly gives me a kiss on the cheek. Check that. The ear. I think he was going for the cheek, though. We smile at each other, shamed by the horrible experience of being placed in the same room as though we have missed each other one iota since we saw each other last. I've thought about "Now & Laters" more than I have Jed Pierce. Yet, another reason I think *love* was a bit overzealous a word for my emotions.

Finally, my old neighbor Kate and her mother come up and stand uncomfortably and I extend my arms for them. "It's so good to see you!" I say with my most enthusiastic squeal. Seeing Kate's brown eyes, I remember times when we waded into the creek to pull out frogs and tadpoles. History can't be undervalued.

Finally, Kate puts out her hand. "Poppy, good to see you."

"You, too, Kate. You're looking well."

She takes an abrupt turn on her heel, followed by her mother, who never actually said hello, and finds her way back to the table. I'm beginning to wonder if my father didn't offer up a bribe for my so-called "friends" to be here. As reunions go, this couldn't be more pathetic. I like to think I had some dignity before college and that my funeral wouldn't be this pathetic. I did have friends, after all, and this is what he dredged up?

My dad grabs a wineglass and dings a fork against it. "Thank you. Thank you all for coming all the way over the hill for our precious Poppy. Please, find a seat and we'll get started with the festivities."

Festivities? My stomach is in absolute knots. I cannot imagine why these people, this odd collection of history, is here. Nor why my father lied to me about dinner alone. Though I must admit, there's a relief factor that our shopping spree is cancelled. It's not all a loss; at least my stepmother is ignoring me. Usually, by now, she's commented on my clothing and offered to take me out with a stylist.

My dad clears his throat ceremoniously and continues, "As you all know, Sharon and I are leaving California." A round of half-hearted gasps here as though they aren't all thinking, *Maybe that house will finally be landscaped and our property values will rise.* "But what you don't know is that we've been living in Poppy's house all these years. Her mother left her that house long ago and it's time it returned to its rightful owner." Dad looks at me. "And that its rightful owner returns to the house. She's going to fix it up or sell it, so it won't be the neighborhood eyesore anymore."

A few cheers here.

I'm just counting the moments until I can run screaming from the room. I have my first and third fingers clasped together, trying to find a little peace meridian energy. As one might guess, it's not working.

"What you don't know," my father goes on, "is that Sharon's sister is in rehab in Arizona, and we'll be taking custody of her children."

I feel my smile fall, and I try to force it back, but it won't come. I don't want to put my father down, but I think I did a little more parenting in that house than he did, and I can't imagine what he's thinking.

"So it's with great pleasure I hand Poppy back the keys to her home and kiss my daughter farewell. Into the future. If she were a ship, I'd break a bottle of champagne against her. This is where I send her off into the great world on her own."

I'm not exactly sure what planet my father is currently inhabiting, as I've been a working chiropractor for three years with my own practice, my own condo, and even a cat to call my own. Where exactly am I being launched? I don't know if he actually remembers this, but our past hasn't exactly been the stuff of gumdrops. I mean, if he's going to give me a gift, couldn't he pass on the Lexus? It's probably worth more than the house in its current condition anyway.

It's everything I can do to stand up for my father's "ceremony." I can't reach out for the keys. I look to Sharon, who is smiling as though to tell me she's won. And I know it's true—she has. She'll take my father away, leaving me with a rundown house near the ocean to console me. And my father will parent her relatives—who I'm sure need it, but all the same . . .

Excuse me, I think. But what I actually say is, "This is too much excitement for my bladder." Then I jogged towards the restroom in my own live commercial for an incontinence narcotic. *I should have gone to dinner with Jeff.*

Looking in the bathroom mirror, I'm struck by my wan appearance. The grown-up, Christian thing to do is be happy for my father starting the second half of his life—even if I do think it's repeating the first half, which he wasn't all that adept at. When it comes to parenting, my father is the weekend Disneyland dad.

Lord knows Daddy deserves some joy in his life at this point, but the small, little, whiny girl who seems to be so prevalent is upset that my other parent is riding off into the sunset. Captured in the clutches of a disease called Sharon and her do-gooder future. Of course, he wants to do a good deed, but he has no clue what his weaknesses are. And stability is definitely not a trait he embodies.

My cell phone is trilling again, echoing off the tile in the sickly-sweet-smelling bathroom. I find the little bench and slide down onto it, my legs no longer strong enough to hold me up.

"Hello?"

"Finally. Poppy, it's Morgan."

Just the sound of her voice makes my eyes well up. "I need help, Morgan."

"What's the matter?"

"I can't begin to explain. It's everything, and it's nothing at all. How soon can you get down here?"

"I was on my way when you hung up on me. I'm almost there. Where are you, the condo?"

"I'm in Jackson's. It's a restaurant on Steven's Creek by Vallco."

"I'll be there in five minutes. Lilly wanted to come, but she's so tired at night with the pregnancy. She stayed home. I'll be there soon. We knew you were having a bad day when you hung up. And you took the wedding stuff so badly and asked for Spa Date. Hang on, Poppy, I'm coming."

I sit on the bench, drumming my fingernails along the fake leather and wondering what it is I should do next. I mean, it's not like those people out there don't know me. It's not like they haven't watched me run to the loo. At some point, I have to go back out there, plaster the best mohair smile of my life on my face, and tell them that under no circumstances am I coming back to live in Santa Cruz. My dad is the only one being launched at this party. I'm a grown-up. This shouldn't bother me, and yet I'm completely annoyed at myself that it does. I want to believe my father's dream of an Arizona orphanage is a good idea. Of course it is. Unwanted children need homes. *What kind of Christian am I?*

I love Santa Cruz, I remind myself. I grew up there under the blanket of fog and sunshiny days. I took hikes in the nearby redwoods, and I embraced all that was Santa Cruz. For crying out loud, look at my clothes. If that doesn't tell you I have enough of the beachside city in my heart, I don't know what will. But I am not going back to that house. I am not going to grow old beside Eloise and Kate. I am not going to run into Jed's wife at the grocery store. Just because my father is leaving doesn't mean that I'm stepping into his role. We should have sold that house a long time ago.

The bathroom door swings open and Sharon stands in front of me. "What are you doing?" she asks. "Your father is throwing you a party." She says it with a warmth in her voice that reminds me she is not always the monster I make her out to be.

"Hello, Sharon."

"Your father planned this party for you, and you're the guest of honor."

"I know that, Sharon. I went to Stanford," I remind her. It's my way of saying *duh!* without being rude.

She sits down beside me and sighs deeply. "You don't have to live in the house. Is that what this is about?"

I look at her, totally shocked she has any clue what's going on inside my head. "Sort of," I say, keeping the truth close to my heart.

"I imagine it doesn't bring up the best memories for you. You can get a reverse mortgage on it and take care of the financial effects that way. It needs a lot of work." She pats my leg. "Your father isn't into the maintenance side of things." She laughs. "But I guess you know that."

I shake my head. "I'll figure it out." With this statement, I succumb to the knowledge that I am, indeed, getting stuck with the house.

"Do you want me to put the house on the market for you? I have a friend in real estate."

"I don't know what I want to do." I look at the keys in my hand. "Why does Daddy want me to go back there?"

"He thinks you need to break free of your childhood." She pauses for a moment. "Trauma. He thinks going back will help."

"It won't." I feel that familiar knot in my stomach and I wish with everything in me that I could run right now. I wish I had my workout gear, which I usually keep in my car, and could just run until I couldn't go any farther.

She pats my leg again. "I've waited a long time to get out of that house, Poppy."

I nod, thinking that perhaps, just perhaps, this woman hasn't been quite the vixen I've created her to be in my mind. I still don't like her, and it's so much easier to believe my father was duped than that he actually left our lives and my mother in the recesses of his mind. But still . . . "You've been more than patient, Sharon."

She smiles. "Come out and mingle with the hodgepodge of weirdos your father assembled. He went to big trouble."

We laugh, and I catch a glimpse of myself in the full-length mirror. Who am I kidding? I look like that group's leader. There's no getting around it. Suddenly, Morgan's words today don't seem that far-fetched.

As I follow Sharon out the door, Morgan is there. She's wearing diamond earrings the size of peacoat toggles and is dressed to the nines. Her blonde hair is up in a perfect swirl.

"Wow, you look great."

She smiles at me. "You're not mad at me."

"I'm a little miffed, but I have bigger fish to fry. Come smile with me." I give her a toothy grin. "Like this."

"I set up the spa weekend," Morgan says as we walk the hallway. "We're all set and Lilly's coming too. I brought you a picture of your date." Morgan looks down at the floor. "If you're interested in meeting him. Otherwise, you come alone or with whomever you please. All right?"

I smile at her and put my head on her shoulder.

"You know, I've never heard you mad like that. Well, maybe that one time when I wouldn't drink that orange slop you were giving me. But I realized I overstepped my bounds. I'm sorry."

"I'm glad I got mad. It helped me know what I want out of life, and being set up is not that thing. Come meet my other weirdo friends." I pull her into the room of my history, where she is greeted with sheer astonishment. To say Morgan is beautiful is a vast understatement to her presence. She gives off an aura that acts as a magnet to all around her. You're drawn to her like a lighthouse on a stormy night. "Everyone, this is my friend Morgan Malliard."

Jed looks for a little too long, and I think his wife kicks him under the table, "What?" he asks in all innocence and I have to muffle my giggle.

I find us seats next to Dr. Amos. "Morgan, this is the woman who encouraged me to be a doctor. She was the only female doctor on the coast at that time, and I just worshiped her." I smile at my mentor, and she speaks to Morgan.

"Poppy was always an interesting child. Interested in what everything did and how you diagnosed all the different diseases. I think she had the medical dictionary memorized by age twelve."

Interesting. Now there's a word I've heard to describe me for years. I believe it's a thesaurus word for *weirdo*. Not that I shun that title, either, but if you look around the table here, everyone's a weirdo. Even Morgan's a weirdo, though no one can tell because they're too blinded by her beauty. But I've been one of her best friends since college, and trust me: she's a weirdo too. She just dresses better. I wonder if I let my girlfriends dress me I'd hear the adjective *interesting* less often.

Morgan is laughing. It's her *Get-me-out-of-here-now* laugh. But we still have dinner to sit through. A long and uncomfortable dinner. Full of my childhood foibles and quirks—and let me just say, I hardly needed to be reminded. I look at Sharon and suddenly see her as my alibi instead of my enemy. Get thee to a realtor. Poppy Clayton is leaving her shell, and her childhood, behind!

chapter 6

Home.

Desperation scale: 4

I get home to the condo and drop my keys into the basket at the entry. Some days, it just feels better than others to be home. I flick on a sunlight lamp, and the house is illuminated with low-end energy and all the brightness of natural light. My answering machine is blinking, but the last thing I need is more negative energy, so I let it blink. I take my sweater off and with the recessed light overhead, it's like I'm about to be beamed up. And when I go? I realize that I'm in a really bad skirt.

I wonder if aliens would notice.

I scan my outfit in the mirror, looking at the tinged, wild colors of the worn cotton, which I've taken to hand-washing so it won't fall apart, and it occurs to me my statement is getting old. It used to be that I felt different, set apart and unique in a look that brought me joy. But tonight, being around my past, I see I'm really not all that different. I'm just your average product of Santa Cruz and a mother who loved all things natural. I am a human banana slug. Loveable, but a loner.

For a brief second, it dawns on me that perhaps I don't want to look like my past anymore.

Morgan parks her car and follows me into the house and Safflower, my cat, goes straight for her nylons. Morgan is all politeness, but she hates that cat. Morgan sees me eyeing my skirt, and I know what she's thinking, but she says nothing, like the loyal friend she is.

"Are you going back?" she asks me, meaning to my childhood home.

I shake my head.

"Your father thinks you should. At least for a little while. I've never known your father to ask you to do anything, Poppy. Maybe he's on to something."

"My father also thinks I should have five children and be homeschooling them on the beach in a jumper. Any questions?"

"I'm inclined to agree with him on this one."

I look at her like the traitor she is. "You think I should go back to that house and drive the long commute over the hill? For what reason exactly?" I put a hand to my hip. *This I have to hear.*

"Seriously, Poppy, you want to help everyone but yourself." She looks at my skirt again. "I think it's time you helped yourself. No offense, but you date weirdos. You dress like a beatnik in the Silicon Valley. And you know, Poppy, I'm beginning to think it's all an act, quite frankly. No one who cares about her body-fat percentage as much as you do is oblivious to her body's affect on men. I just don't buy it. And I've seen the plastic surgeon. You're blind, deaf, or dumb on him because he is hot. I know you believe in all things natural, but love chemistry is as natural as it comes and—"

"I'm a runner. I run to be healthy, not tease men. When have I ever been a man chaser, Morgan? Going back to that house will not help me. There's so much negative energy there. I'll bet even you could feel it. My father should have sold it a long time ago, regardless of what Mom said. My mother would not have wanted me to live there with all the ghosts of history. She would have wanted my father to handle it for me."

"If that were true, she wouldn't have left it to you, but to him." Morgan flicks her hair triumphantly.

"I'm going on a date tomorrow with someone you would call normal," I say out of the blue. When in trouble, it's always best to avoid the conversation.

"What?"

"Is that so shocking that I have a date?" I ask.

"Not that someone asked you out, but that you said yes. Does he wear sandals in the winter?"

"No."

"Parachute pants from 1984?"

"No!" I say with a little more force.

"Does he color plants for a living and call it art?"

"That was one date I went out with that guy. One date. You don't need to keep bringing it up, do you?"

"But you can't expect us to forget it," Morgan says coolly. "He's an adult who uses crayons and calls it a vocation. Me, I think of a vocation as something you actually make money at. How can you not see the humor in that? It was one for the ages, truly."

I purse my lips at her. "Someone *you* would call normal asked me out and I'm saying yes. I just decided right now." I glance again in the mirror. "I sort of already said yes, but now I know I'm going."

"Who asked you?"

"The plastic surgeon who works next door. There's no chemistry, so let's not go there. It's just a dinner with a colleague in the medical field."

"You're going out with Dr. Nip/Tuck?" Morgan laughs. "Poppy, I don't know what's going on with you, but you need to sit back and light a candle or sip an elixir. You're not thinking clearly." She pauses. "And I like it. You're doing something that just isn't right. There's hope for you yet."

"I have always thought that people who aren't afraid to be different are mavericks." I punch my fist in the sky, "Mavericks! So now, I'm just saying that I'm going to try out one of the drones and see what life is like on the other side. Maybe I've been missing something."

"I'd hardly call Dr. Nip/Tuck a drone. *Drone* implies boring, one of the pack, the worker bee. Not a real hottie with a medical degree." Morgan shrugs. "Maybe it's just me." She shakes her head. "No. You're human and you're female. You're so not immune. But if you can get me a discount on a facelift when I get older, I'm all for it!"

I head over to the stereo and turn on a little light jazz. "There will be no facelifts in your future. I'll buy you a lifetime supply of *La Mer* before I let that happen."

Morgan shrugs. "I'm just keeping my options open, is all."

"Jeff and I are both in the medical field, so maybe we have more in common than I've allowed myself to see." Granted, a little pathetically hopeful, but I don't think I knew how desperate I was for companionship until the possibility of this date opened up.

"But what about 'Plastic surgery is a tool of the devil' and all that talk? You're telling me that you're going to sit all night and keep your mouth shut on your opinions to show you're not a bigot?"

"I'm not a bigot!"

"Oh, but you are. If people don't believe in the natural way, you're a health bigot. The worst kind—the kind that tells other people how to live."

"Based on scientific research and centuries of study, I tell people how to live. It's not like I'm just talking out of ignorance. I have thousands of clients who have benefited and been healed the natural way."

"Still a bigot."

"Will you help me find something to wear?" I ask, hoping to put an end to this conversation.

Morgan's smile disappears. "You're serious. You're going to get out of that skirt for this man?" She crosses her elegant arms and leans back on her heel. "Well, I'll be."

"I just want to know what it's like for a day, that's all. You can rest assured I'll be back in gauze come Wednesday."

"We should start simply. Do you have a black skirt?" Morgan asks.

I shake my head.

"A pair of slacks that aren't too colorful?"

Again, no. "What's wrong with color, anyway?"

"I'll call Lilly."

I grab her cell phone. "It's not an emergency or anything. I'll find something." I walk to my closet with Morgan. There has to be something in there.

"I'd say it is an emergency if your date is tomorrow night. You can say whatever you want to make yourself believe, Poppy, but don't lie to yourself. If you're going out with Jeff Curran, it's because you think he's hot and you want to get rid of that emotion. You want to prove to yourself you're above the fray."

I swallow hard. Her assessment is probably closer to the truth than I'd like. Jeff is indeed hot, as she calls it, but when has that ever affected me? I am living, breathing proof of the necessity of mercy dates.

"I don't want to go overboard," I tell Morgan. "If I suddenly change everything, he's going to think I have feelings for him.

Trust me, this guy has enough ego for the two of us. I can't up and change my style. I just want something subtle that says I'm open to the possibility, but not that open."

"Give me a T-shirt." Morgan starts unbuttoning her blouse.

"What are you doing?"

"Get me a T-shirt."

I grab her a running T from one of my races, and she puts it on, handing me her creamy button-up blouse, which I'm sure is some designer label and is probably worth more than my futon. In her job as the assistant chief of protocol for the City of San Francisco, Morgan has made dressing an art form. When she quits after her marriage and becomes a stay-at-home mom to George's son, her clothing tastes should get interesting. She'll still probably be one of those mothers with perfectly-pressed slacks who sits on the ground at the park.

"Put this on."

I pull off my black Lycra shirt and put on the cream. My hair likes the cream; it doesn't clash at all.

"Come on." Morgan starts rifling through my closet. She pulls out a skirt with the tags still on it. It's an aubergine/eggplant color and Sharon bought it for me last Christmas. It fit me perfectly, but I just didn't want to wear anything she bought me. Of course, she would want me out of my mother's clothes. Out of the reminder of her sin. Now I'm beginning to see that life does indeed go on, and it was very thoughtful of Sharon. I must learn to appreciate the way life is in the here and now.

I pull on the skirt, not explaining its origins or the negative energy it creates in me, and it fits like a glove. "Dang, the woman really has good taste." I twist and turn in front of the mirror.

"What woman?"

"Sharon bought this for me."

"Of course she has good taste. She picked your father, didn't she?"

"Touché." Naturally, Morgan would see my father as such a catch. She's having him as her stand-in daddy. As far as fathers go, he *is* a good daddy. I imagine to Morgan mine is the cream of the crop.

Once in the skirt, I realize that in this you can actually appreciate my 14-percent body fat. It's not sleazy, it's not too clingy, it just says, *I'm a woman and I have curves, but I'm not going to flaunt them freely for you*. I catch my breath at the sight of me. Not because I think I look so fabulous or anything, but just because I look so completely Silicon Valley and non-natural. If I walked out tonight to a restaurant, no one would ever know I'm Dr. Poppy Clayton, chiropractor and Chinese medicine practitioner. They wouldn't have any idea that I could talk intelligently about immune disorders and their relation to environmental allergies.

"You look gorgeous." Morgan takes off her long strand of pearls and starts to place them on me.

"No. No pearls. Pearls say I made too much effort. I don't want Jeff to think I made too much effort. Any effort, really. It's just dinner between neighbors." I smooth the shirt a bit, still a bit taken aback by the image in the mirror. Clothes hold power if you give it to them. I immediately turn away from the mirror and my vanity.

"Fine. Then we're having Jacob—you know the runner Max met on the beach?—we're having him over to the house, and you two can meet and get acquainted. You don't have to wear the pearls that night. I think the wedding would be more fun for you if you found someone to enjoy it with."

I love how she tries to convince me this is for my benefit.

"We're going to the spa." I clap my hands at the thought, ignoring the talk of Jacob and the pearls, which are now clasped about my neck. I'm sure Morgan owns several strands, but their iridescence is hypnotizing.

"We can go to the spa first thing Saturday morning."

"Regarding Jacob." I broach the subject casually, fingering the pearls as I do so, to remind her of our unspoken deal. "I think one date this week is quite enough. I don't want to implode or anything." I focus on my appearance, smoothing the skirt down. "I have no shoes to match this."

"Cinderella *must* have shoes," Morgan says, climbing out of her shoes, which read Donald Pliner. I can only assume they cost money. They look like they cost money. I slide into them, and I have to say for heels, they are very comfortable.

"They're a little big," I say, looking for something negative to offer. I can't very well say I like them. Me, who is always touting the benefits of comfort and cushioned soles. It's heresy. But as I glimpse my calf, I have to force down a smile.

"Quality footwear that looks that good is never too big or too small. You *make* it work. Didn't you learn anything from Cinderella's stepsisters? They just didn't try hard enough, I'm telling you!"

"My mother wouldn't read me that story. She thought it was sexist and would force me to wait on Prince Charming rather than determining my own destiny."

"Poppy, you were thirteen when she died."

"I was six when she taught me that. My dad reiterated it all those years. Once brainwashed, always brainwashed."

She just shakes her head. "Do you hear what I'm telling you?" She pulls off her knee-length nylons and stuffs one into the shoe I'm not wearing. "Try that."

I nod, sliding my toes in, feeling their grip tighten. "Perfect."

"You're going to wear a little makeup, right?"

"No. Definitely no."

"Just a little lipstick, nothing that makes you look like a fashion model. Just something that shows you put forth a tiny bit of effort. Every date deserves at least that much." She starts to take out her compact. "He's buying dinner, right? He shouldn't have to look at any skin flaws." Morgan looks closely at me. "Not that you have any, but still. It would even you out." She comes towards me with the compact puff.

"No." I move out of range. "I thought you said my date was a joke. I believe 'deal with the devil' were your exact words."

"I said *you* think that about his being a plastic surgeon. No normal red-blooded American woman is going to turn down a date with a fine specimen of Christian MD. All I know is that if he's got something that made you say yes, there has to be something there. Who am I to question? And quite frankly, it's good to see you looking forward to something besides a 5k in town or hand-washing your skirt.

I purse my lips at her. "I have to admit, I am a little excited. I think part of it is knowing that I can't blow it, or I won't be able to show my face in the office. I have to learn to be nice and accept his wicked job. It's the chance to practice my multiculturalism. Some people have a problem with racism; I have a problem with mixed-medicine marriages."

"I guess," Morgan says as she walks around the room, sniffing all the candles. "I don't think you need to put that much thought into dinner, but maybe that's me."

"San Francisco's assistant chief of protocol wouldn't need to put in any effort. But I am not you, and I'm going to prove to Jeff that the natural way is best."

"No, no. You are not going on this date to evangelize your nutty health stuff. Give me my shoes back."

"Not on your life." My phone rings, and I answer it, feeling like . . . well, like Morgan. "Hello!" I say silkily.

"Poppy?" It's a man's voice.

"Yes." Again with the low rasp. I could make a decent living at this if I wasn't a good girl.

"It's Simon."

"Simon?" I'm embarrassed to say my stomach does a complete somersault.

"I'm sorry to call you at home—"

"No, that's fine. Is your back all right? Did you throw it out again?"

"No, nothing like that. I just wanted to apologize for my behavior today. I felt like I got off to a really bad start with your dad, and that wasn't the impression I wanted to leave him."

I stammer for an answer. It's not like Simon to care what anyone thinks.

"Poppy, you still there?"

"Yeah, I'm here. I'm just trying to figure out why you felt the need to call." I look at Morgan and shrug.

"Because it's been gnawing at me all day and I had to make it right. So you'll apologize for me to your dad? I don't want him to think I'm harassing his daughter."

"You are harassing his daughter." I laugh.

"But not in the way he thinks I'm harassing you."

"Oh," I pause for a minute. "You're not?"

"You sound disappointed," Simon accuses. "Did you want me to harass you in *that* way?"

Maybe a little.

"No, of course not."

"Good, so I'll see you next week and your father won't have a heart attack at the sight of me."

May he never get sight of Simon again. The last thing I need for business is my father standing watch. "I'll let him know, Simon, but it's no big deal. You didn't have to call. I know who you are."

"Just tell him for me, all right?"

"It's as good as done, Simon."

"Bye, Poppy." Simon hangs up the phone, and I stand there with the receiver in my hand.

"Poppy, you all right?" Morgan asks me.

"Huh? Yeah . . . Yeah I'm fine."

"Then hang up the phone."

I do so, but not without a moment of melancholy. Simon has never made any sort of gesture to impress me before, and it wasn't until right now that I realized how much I wanted him to.

"Ahem, earth to Poppy." Morgan makes sure the phone is back in its cradle correctly. "Let's get back to this."

I stand tall, admiring how the heels make my calves look strong once again. "I'm going on a date," I say aloud. Disaster will probably ensue, but it is moving forward. At least from the Spa Girls' point of view. They've been trying to get me out of gauze for a decade.

My heart starts to pound as I think about being able to control my mouth tomorrow night. Is it actually possible for me to sit across from a plastic surgeon and not tell him he's the devil? "You know, Morgan, I think I need to run a few miles. I didn't get enough in today."

"Right. Because it's probably been a good five hours since you did a few miles." Morgan pushes me down on the sofa. "You are not running. It's ten o'clock at night. You're going to bed, or reading a book, like normal people. It's just a date. I'm spending the night on your couch so you're not going anywhere. I'll head back to the city in the morning."

I light a candle, flick on the news, and try to slow my surge of adrenaline. But Morgan, unable to withstand the question, presses the answering machine button.

"Hey, nosy!" I tell her.

"Poppy? Listen, it's Simon and I just want to talk to you for a minute. Call me. It's 555-5414."

"Who's Simon?" Morgan asks. "Is that the guy who just called?"

I feel a smile develop. "Just a client. A wealthy client with more time than purpose." Even as I say the disparaging words I know they're not true. Simon did not get where he is by being lazy. "That's not true; he's a great guy. Invented some widget you and I will never understand."

"He sounds like a nice guy," Morgan says.

I roll my eyes. As if she'd know the difference. Until she found George, Morgan was the poster child for "Smart Women, Foolish Choices." But I know why she said it. My friends, as wonderful and selfless as they may be at times, have one motive, and that's to find me a husband before I get too weird to find one myself. Unfortunately, I think I've already passed that threshold and no one wants to admit it. My dad's party tonight told me that much. I am merely a younger version of every oddity he invited. I still have the original, vintage skirts to prove I am a card-carrying, native Santa Cruz girl. Normal need not apply.

Sorry I bothered you at home last night." Simon is lying face down on the table when I get to work, and he's been here for awhile according to Emma. He doesn't look up.

"How do you know I'm not Emma?" I ask.

"Emma doesn't smell like mint. You do."

I bite back a smile. "It's my bath gel."

Oversharing.

"I'm glad to know you're always clean," he jokes.

"While the world resorts to quick showers, I luxuriate in a scalding tub filled with rosemary-mint-scented bubbles. Generally before prayers, I read a waterlogged *Daily Bread* and get ready to start my day."

Once again, judging by Simon's silence, I'm going to a place no chiropractor has gone before, so I clamp my freshly cleansed mouth shut.

"Sorry, Simon, I got carried away. What are you doing here so early? I didn't know the retired folk got up so early."

"Are you kidding me? I already played the back nine at Deep Cliff." Simon sits up on his elbows. "And I threw my back out on the sixteenth hole. I thought if I got in here early enough, you could take me before your first patient."

"The sixteenth hole. Let me guess: that didn't stop you from playing the last two holes."

He looks back at me and grins. "You're beginning to understand the mindset of a golfer, Poppy. I'm proud of you."

"Well, I can't say the same for you." I push him back down on the table. "Listen to your body, Simon. You'd be much healthier if you did so. And I've told you, you can't throw your back out; that's a figure of speech."

"Just work your magic, my love, and save your definitions for someone who cares." Simon turns his head towards me. "I hope you're not angry I called you at home. Did you talk to your dad yet? No, I suppose you wouldn't have. But you know, he really has no reason to dislike me, do you think?"

"Put your head down," I order him. "You were making a pass at me in front of him. Dads sort of have a thing about that." I feel down Simon's spine until I get to the misalignment. I just shake my head. *This guy's back is the plague of spines!* "My dad doesn't bite. Besides, since when do you care what people think?"

"He may not bite—AHHH!" Simon yowls as I adjust him. "Gentle. What are you trying to do, beat me to a pulp? You can be sadistic, Poppy! Everyone else comes in here and gets this little gentle push, and I get beaten."

He turns over and props himself on his elbows. His eyes are warm brown and when I look him in the eye, I forget that his back is a textbook case for the Palmer School. He's just Simon, the handsome face I look forward to once a week. More, if he's playing a tournament.

"I'm sorry, Simon, but you're really out of order today, and I do adjust you differently, you're right. It's because you're special to me."

"Well, I pity the man who marries you."

Our eyes catch again at the comment. "Do you?" I hear myself ask.

"I mean, I don't pity him, I just think he's marrying a tough cookie. No, I mean I think he's—"

He's nonexistent is what he is.

"You need to work out the muscles in your shoulders to carry the weight of your head. Your ears should be behind the shoulders at all times. I think if you got your posture and stance in order, you might have fewer misalignments. You should think about ballroom dancing. It's excellent for the posture."

"Are you telling me I have a big head?"

"No, I'm telling you that your rather large cranium is not in the right place." I'm laughing. How completely unprofessional.

"All right, tell me what other patient has to suffer this kind of abuse."

"What other client puts his body through the abuse that you do? Hmm?"

"You tell me I have a giant cranium, and you're not abusing me?"

"I said rather large."

"Which could be construed as ginormous and you know it. Call me crazy, but big head doesn't exactly ooze warmth from you."

I don't know how he always manages it, but as bad as he must feel when he comes in, I have never seen him unhappy. Not once.

"I don't think your head is ginormous, Simon." I try to busy my hands with rosemary-mint hand lotion. The accompaniment to my bath oil. Simon inhales deeply.

"Oh, you're bringing out the hard stuff now." He raises an eyebrow.

"Do you want some?" I ask him lamely.

"You don't think it's hard enough on the ego to have a

beautiful chiropractor? I'm now supposed to live with the fact she thinks my head is huge? I have to get one of those hats like that kid always wore on *Fat Albert*. Maybe it will be less obvious. He drops his head in his hands. "Oh my poor, aching, large cranium."

"Simon." I wipe my hands on a paper towel to remove the excess lotion. "Statistically speaking, men in Hollywood have larger heads than regular Americans. Maybe it means you're destined for the large screen," I offer hopefully, trying to dig my way out of this.

"But don't quit my day job, is that what you're saying?"

"You don't have a day job, Simon."

"That's where you're wrong. I just do it at night when I can talk to China and Taiwan and help them with manufacturing. I'm consulting lately. I got bored, you know?"

I step back, shocked by the news. "So when do you sleep?"

"When I'm tired." He shrugs. "Is that a trick question?"

"I didn't mean anything by the head comment. I was concerned with your posture after golf. You're Tom Cruise, all right?"

"Do you like Tom Cruise?"

"Not really. I'm a Johnny Depp girl."

"And how's his head?"

"I think it's huge, Simon." I start to laugh, having no idea if Johnny Depp's head is huge or not. I start writing in his chart. "I appreciate your lovely conversation, Simon, but you're not working to get any better here. Your back is a mess and if you're going to come in here to sweet talk instead of icing your back when I tell you to and—"

"I'm sorry. I lost my big head. I really do have something to tell you, and I think it would be mutually beneficial." He sits up and makes a concerted effort to place his head in proper alignment. "I didn't want to talk in front of your father."

"I'm listening," I put the chart next to him, cross my arms, and give him my full attention until another client comes and gets on the second table. "Good morning, Mary."

"Hey, Doctor Poppy."

"Let me get Brian started on working your neck." Brian, the office masseur and physical therapist, hears me say this. He walks in with the neck massager that's nearly as big as him and starts the vibrating machine so that Simon and I once again have privacy while Mary vibrates with vigor.

"So what do you have to say?" I ask Simon, still fixated on those brown eyes, which, as a chiropractor and professional, I shouldn't be noticing. After three years, I've only just noticed them and learned that Simon actually works. I wonder what else he's kept close to his heart. Or in this case, his spine.

"It's more of a proposition, really. I've been thinking a lot about my future and what I want to do with my life—"

"You proposition me every week, so what's special about this one?"

"I'm serious." As I look into his intense eyes, I see that he is indeed serious. Naturally, I know he has to have this side of him. He would not have been able to retire at his young age without some intensity, but I usually don't see that side of him. I have to say, *I like it*.

"You're serious about something other than your golf game, I'm assuming."

"I'm serious about changing the shape and scope of your career."

"I thought you were thinking about your future, not mine."

He looks around my office. "You're bigger than this, Poppy. You have healed more people than your walls will even hold. I think it's time you thought bigger, dreamed broader, grabbed the golden ring. You're not just a chiropractor. Your care goes deeper, and I think you should too. Why settle for mediocrity?"

I laugh, but he doesn't join me. Simon is the type who can't help but think big, but not all of us are meant for that lifestyle. "Now I'm mediocre? Let's see how you feel when I go on vacation."

"You know that's not what I meant, but everyone is capable of going bigger, doing more with the gift God's given them. I just see how easily you could make that step if—"

"I love my career. I don't really have that corporate drive you're describing. Look, I employ the three of us—Emma, Brian, and me—and that's major success to me. No, I haven't invented a widget I can live off the rest of my life, but I have a daily purpose, and I love it."

"You may not have the corporate drive, but I've got enough of that, Poppy. I just see a need here, and that's my passion—to streamline businesses and make them the most efficient they can be. If I had your gift I'd want to help more people."

"I'm efficient," I say.

"I can help you make more people healthy."

"I have as many clients as I can handle, Simon."

He grabs my hand in his own, and without thinking, I grasp his. I look into his deep brown eyes, and I forget where I'm standing. It's like the entire three years of our knowing each other has suddenly flashed before my eyes.

"I'm not joking, Poppy."

He's talking with such passion about my career, and I'll admit work hasn't entered my mind for the last moment. I've only seen something I've missed. Something that was right in front of me. And quite frankly, I don't like it. Not one bit.

I pull my hand from his. "Thank you, Simon. It's just not my thing."

"I'm moving to Hawaii, Poppy."

"What?"

"I have some family business to take care of there. It's the perfect setting for you to have a health spa. People are relaxed and ready to be healed; they're ready to leave the stress of their lives behind and focus on their future."

"*Hawaii*?" Even the word makes me laugh. "No one actually goes to Hawaii to work, Simon."

"People work there all the time. I've already helped two people with businesses there. Hawaii: where the running is good and the usage of natural medicines has been practiced for centuries. Hawaii is the *Aloha* of the natural health realm." Simon grins, and I can see where his charm has gotten him far in the business of persuasion.

For a brief moment I allow my imagination to float to Hawaii and its lush greenery and gentle ocean breezes. I imagine Simon in a Hawaiian shirt and me busily working in a spa and running all the triathlons that go on throughout the year. I find myself completely whisked away at the images. But admittedly, it's not the only place my mind goes—and Simon isn't offering me that kind of deal.

"Simon, it takes years to build a practice and a reputation. I'm just getting this practice off the ground. I don't want to start again."

"Poppy, I can get your business off the ground easier than you did it here. It's my gift."

"Your back is going to be a royal disaster when you move." I try to busy my hands, but inside I feel the immediate loss. Simon was one of my first patients. He got other men to come from his office, and he preached my abilities like an evangelist.

"Poppy, it's a great place for a runner too."

"You already mentioned that."

"But I can see you need more convincing."

I clear my throat. "If you need help finding a chiropractor,

I'd be happy to get you a referral to someone who uses the same method I do on your spine. I can forward your chart, and they'll be able to go right to the problem. You won't have to start over with someone new if that's what you're worried about."

He lifts up my chin with his thumb. "I don't need help finding a chiropractor. I want to bring one with me. One who knows my back and all its foibles. You can tell another chiropractor all your secrets, Poppy, but they don't have your touch."

I step away from him. Inside me, I want him to be saying so much more than he is, but he's not saying any of that. He's looking to make as few changes to his life as possible while at the same time inhabiting an island across the ocean. "I'm flattered, Simon, but that's hardly realistic. I can't leave the rest of my patients for one." *Even my favorite one.*

"In business, it's all about matching the right person to the job. That's why CEOs make what they do. It's why some companies are going private again, after being public. To get the best CEOs, they want the freedom, and it's driving the new business trend."

I shake my head. "I hardly see what that has to do with me. I couldn't be any less corporate if I'd never entered a Starbucks."

"CEOs make what they do because of their track record. A good businessman is only as good as his last deal. His record is based on substantial success."

"Again, I don't see what that has to with me."

Brian looks over at me and sees I'm still talking. Mary's massage is coming to an end, but seeing the depth of our conversation, he continues to vibrate Mary's back with vigor.

"You, Poppy, have that same track record in your field and that's what I want in Hawaii—the best. It's not simply a matter of my being spoiled; it's about taking you to the next level. You can be here and be ordinary, but you're not ordinary."

"Simon, I'm not moving to Hawaii. And trust me, I'm as ordinary as they come." One only has to look at my dating résumé to see that.

"What's here for you? You can run every day of the year, swim, bike ride. You were made to live in Hawaii, Poppy. We can chop that skirt of yours off above the knee, make it a mini, and you're ready." He looks at my aubergine skirt. "Speaking of the skirt, where is it?"

I don't want to admit it's gone missing because I have a date and I'm trying my hand at normalcy. Simon would see it as selling out. "It took me a long time to build up a clientele; I can't just leave them to move to paradise. What kind of healer would I be?"

"There're sick people in Hawaii, and you could sell the business to another chiropractor and we'll find some Hawaiian locals to work with over there. You can have an entire clinic. A health spa, if you will. I'm willing to fund it, Poppy. Not because I think you're a charity case, but because I know what you're capable of and that's what I do. Invest where I'll get a return. I believe in you wholeheartedly, in case you're not hearing that in my tone."

When our eyes meet again, I know he truly does believe in me that way, and it's just too much weight on my shoulders. "Simon, oh my goodness, what would I do without you and your positive energy? Not all of us were meant to be moguls like you and have everything we touch turn to gold. Some of us have to be the average folks, you know? I'm just a worker bee."

He lifts my chin tenderly once again. "Are you?"

I catch my breath. "I have average things to do. I have my childhood home to clean out, patients to see, a bridesmaid to be, a run to train for. I'm average, and I'm happy with that. Not that my own natural spa isn't extremely tempting, Simon." *And those brown eyes asking me—not that that isn't tempting.* I pause for a moment. "What's this about Hawaii anyway?"

"I just have family business there, and there are a few opportunities I want to pursue while I'm at it."

"Right." Is it just me or was there really no answer in that? "Simon, I'm not buying a car here. Answer the question."

"Well, I'm bored, Poppy. A man cannot live on golf alone. I've dabbled here and there with a few start-ups and helped them get moving, but I just want more. I went to Hawaii a few weeks ago, and I met with a local whose golf business was failing. Poppy, I knew exactly the problem, and I knew how to solve it. This is my gift. And like I said, there's the family issue, but I'd rather not go into that."

"It's a nice thought, Simon, but my friends are here, for one thing. My Spa Girls are fabulous, and they're not in Hawaii. I don't just up and make friends. I like the old ones. If you think I keep my clothes a long time, you should really hear about my friends."

"Your friends are in San Francisco, an hour away, and they're all getting married. Your father's leaving town and leaving you with a house to be fixed up. Poppy, you don't have as much keeping you here as you think."

"Do you listen to everything that goes on here?"

"Well, it's not exactly private here."

Mary looks up from the massage table. "It's really not, Poppy."

Simon ignores her. "So you don't even like the spa." He looks down at me as he stands up, and I swallow hard at the accusation.

"How do you know that?" I ask him. I notice Brian asking me with his eyes if he can finish. He's battering poor Mary and she's looking wan. I hold up a finger. *One more minute*, I plead with my eyes.

"Because you can't sit still. You complain about Lilly being like a hummingbird, but I know the truth. I know that the entire time you're getting smeared with facial creams, you're thinking about the run you should be on, or how many laps in the pool you could have done. I bet your leg jiggles like a nervous rabbit."

My mouth is agape. Simon is truly a mystery. Part businessman, part engineer, and a huge part observer. Like a lion waiting for its prey, I feel as though I've been ambushed by him, that he's seen way more of me than makes me comfortable. All those years, I let my guard down because he diverted me by the simple act of asking me out each week. I cross my arms across my chest and look at him with new eyes. I am completely exposed: the good, the bad, and the anal.

"You're quiet," he says to me, and just as he says it Brian turns off the massager beside us. The silence is deafening. "To be continued later then?"

"You have my answer, Simon." I feel the sudden urge to escape and run, but Mary has been pummeled with the massager until she looks unable to stand.

Simon shakes his head, ignoring Mary and Brian's weary looks. "I don't think I do have your answer. I have the answer you *should* give me. The one that good-girl Poppy will always render first. Go home and obsess a bit like you do, and come back to me. I can wait."

I step back. "I should have known better than to call my girlfriends with you in the room. You've been spying on the Spa Girls for years, haven't you?"

He raises his eyebrows and offers a sideways grin. "*Spying* is a strong word, Poppy. You overestimate my fascination with the Spa Girls."

"You're just nosy is the fact of the matter."

He's laughing now. "When can we discuss this further?"

"I think you already know enough about my friends and me."

"That's not what I meant and you know it." He raises his eyebrow in that oh-so-charming way he has, and I purse my lips before speaking.

"Simon, please don't do this to me." I whisper at him. "These are my patients. I can't have them thinking there's even the possibility I will walk out on them. Alternative medicine in Silicon Valley is finally happening. I do maybe 50 percent chiropractic and the rest is my allergy-clearing treatment. I'm hardly going to walk now."

He gives me one last puppy-dog look. "Please think about it."

I'm not made of stone. It's a ridiculous notion I'd never consider, but Simon's smile forces a nod to indicate I will think about it. Realistically, I'll think about Simon, and that's not good. Simon couldn't commit to playing golf on the same course two days a week, much less a woman. What kind of man makes a woman an offer like her own clinic anyway? I think he's been watching too much reality television.

Mary, my other client, is more than done with the massage portion of her treatment. She sits up and pushes away Brian. Her eyes laser at me as she awaits her adjustment. Simon notices too. "She'll be right with you. This is important."

Simon takes me into a corner by my private office. I can smell the light scent of his aftershave. "I've known you for a lot of years. You used to have a smile that brightened the entire office, but it's wearing down. You're taking on too much of this place. You need to get out more and be with other natural health people to encourage one another."

I feel hopeful at his words. The romance of being taken away from all this is every girl's dream. The reality, my nightmare.

"Simon, enough of this, all right?" I say it, but I don't move away and our proximity stirs something within me that I haven't wanted to admit. So I go straight back to business, the safe topic. "I believe in this mind-body connection, but I'm not a New Ager and nearly everyone in my field is. I am a Christian and I believe the energy of the Holy Spirit is the most cleansing type of energy. Where are you going to find people like that in my line of work? On a little island no less. You may be good, but you're not a miracle worker."

"Are you trying to convince me or you?"

"I dance to the beat of my own drummer. I don't want a health spa."

"Your own drummer? Then what's the purple skirt about?" he asks, looking at my trendy, Sharon A-line skirt.

I feel myself starting to get hot. Why has everyone taken to analyzing me? Fixing me? *I'm* the one who offers advice. *I* fix people. This is *my* gifting. "Simon, I have to go to work."

He waves over his shoulder without turning around. "Think about what I said; you won't get a better offer or an easier shot."

I don't answer him. I just change the paper on the table and motion for Mary to lie down, awestruck at how small she feels after Simon's muscular frame. I suck in a deep breath and get her in the right position for her adjustment, but my mind wanders into the lush greenery that is the Aloha Spirit.

The bell rings in the foyer and I look over the swinging doors to see the blonde I saw in the convertible yesterday in the parking lot. "I've got to run," I hear Simon say to her. He kisses the blonde on the lips as he walks outside. I flinch at the image. Naturally, with his money, he'd be toting a trophy woman to his events. An elegant lady like Morgan who could hold her own at all his business events. (Well, like Morgan except for the screaming into the cell phone part and the public discussion of divorce. Morgan would never resort to such commonness.) I try to focus on Mary's back and swallow the lump in my throat.

"Simon really does want a personal chiropractor," I whisper aloud. The revelation is like a cold shower on a brisk day. *And that's all he wants.*

She's not good enough for him, and she's not even divorced yet. *Why are men such idiots?* How can they start huge companies and yet succumb to something so common as a blonde in a convertible? I wonder if Simon neglected to tell me she was coming to Hawaii as well. She'll probably get one of those quickie foreign divorces with a man like Simon on the line. A girl like that doesn't catch and release.

"You know, there's nothing wrong with telling the man how you feel. The worst he can say is that he's not interested. He's leaving, so what does it matter?" Mary stands up and slings her large handbag over her shoulder. I start to comment on how bad that is for her back, but I quickly clamp my mouth shut.

I shake my head. "It's not like that."

She pats my shoulder. "Whatever you say, Poppy. See you next week."

I follow Mary into the foyer and watch her leave. "Poppy? You all right?" Emma asks while munching on a wheat-free bread stick. "What'd you do to Mary? She didn't even pay."

"Huh? Oh yeah, I'm fine. I probably made Mary run late. She'll pay next week." I point back at the tables. "Send in the next patient."

When I get back into the examination room, Brian is just finishing up with another patient's warm-up massage. "I'm here," my patient, Claire, says. "You're running late; that's not like you. I'm feeling neglected."

Claire drips with diamonds and high-end clothing. She'd

feel neglected if her Visa bill wasn't ten grand this month. Besides, *neglected* is a strong word for your chiropractor. The expectations for any kind of service here go well beyond the call of duty. They want me to be their savior.

It's only nine a.m. and I need to run—at least ten miles. Wait. I've been made an offer and dissed by the same man in the space of thirty minutes. That's at least another mile.

chapter 8

It's the end of the work day, and tonight I get to play princess. Or as my case goes, the closest thing to it: Morgan Malliard. Although I've worn her blouse all day, there's something special about climbing into her heels. I received the extensive "talking to" about my Clarks clogs with the outfit this morning, but I can hardly be adjusting people or manipulating masculine bodies like Simon's in spike heels. So I spent the day half Morgan, half me. I was the fashion "Don't" half that might have appeared in *Glamour*. Morgan's own assessment was reserved. She gave a light cluck of the tongue followed by the words, "It's a shame. Really it is."

It still makes me laugh. The things my friends value have absolutely no bearing on me. But after the long day, and Simon's proposal and announcement of his departure, I am nervous about my date with Dr. Jeff. If you can call this farce a date. I'm wringing my hands as I pace the office floor. I have plenty of office busywork to do, but my mind is preoccupied—and I didn't want to run and shower for fear my hair wouldn't dry in time and I'd look like something the cat dragged in. Tonight, I'm going to do Morgan and Lilly proud if it kills me. Or Jeff, as the case might be.

I don't know why I'm nervous; I actually go on a lot of

dates. Perhaps not a lot of second dates, but I do go on quite a few first dates. It's just I can't help but see the guy as a potential mate. And there's the health factor. Simon's back has nothing on some of my past escorts:

One guy's eye whites were yellow (bad liver function).

One guy's face was pocked red, and his nose was bulbous (too much alcohol?).

One guy's tongue was white (oral yeast—not enough good bacteria).

One guy had a lack of appetite and fatigue through dinner (adrenal insufficiency).

I don't know why I look at men like gene pools, but it's part of my health fetish. I can't help myself. Lord knows someone like Simon will give his next generation a spine from the Dark Side, and yet I can still be tempted, so there has to be more.

With Jeff Curran, MD, my fears are different. First of all, a person could never tell if his health wasn't perfect, because he'd just cover it with the plastic version. Then, there's the whole beauty issue. What exactly does a plastic surgeon find beautiful, and is it attainable by anyone? I mean, he deals in perfection all day long, and I've changed my skirt. Not that I'm thinking romantically. I'm just thinking of how I can practice for Morgan's wedding. If I can be "normal" with Jeff Curran, I can take on the world.

My ego's already taken a hit today. All these years, I thought Simon had a crush on me. In fact, I thought the Hawaiian idea was his way of making one final attempt at a future with me. Then, he kisses the blonde bombshell in my foyer, and here I'm thinking he's propositioning me two minutes earlier. It's the ultimate in rejection. It's been my job to reject Simon. Couldn't he just leave with that image intact? Was it so hard to spare my ego?

"You're wearing heels?" Emma asks me as I come into the foyer.

"What are you still doing here?"

"Are you kidding me? You have a date with Dr. Dreamy and expect me not to watch? This is better than *The Bachelor* and Dr. 90210 all wrapped into one delicious package."

"It's a dinner between working companions. Trust me, you're better off with reality television at home."

She crosses her arms and eats another bite of a protein bar. "Whatever. I'm still sticking around. I wouldn't miss this for anything. You never go on dates with anyone who would tempt me. This should be good."

"You really don't get out enough," I tell her.

"Look who's talking."

I breathe in deeply and open a vial of eucalyptus oil and suck in the cleansing fragrance. Now that will clear your lungs. "Do I look like I'm walking okay in these heels? Or do I just look stupid?" I ask Emma.

"You'd never know they weren't attached," Emma says.

Months ago, when Lilly, my fashion-designing Spa Girl, talked me into modeling for her fashion show, I thought I would turn into Lot's wife pillar of salt right on the stage. I move like a penguin on a Habitrail in heels.

"Did you see Simon's girlfriend today?"

"You mean that blonde?"

I nod.

"She's not his girlfriend. Simon's an intellectual, Poppy. You know that much."

"Didn't he kiss her?" I ask.

"He didn't really *kiss* her. Why do you care?"

"I don't. I've just never seen Simon's type before. I was surprised."

"You see Simon's type every morning when you look in the mirror." Emma rolls her eyes. "You two are pathetic."

"What does that mean?" I know I said Emma sees a lot and

watches my patients like they were her own private reality show, but she's wrong on this one. Simon does not see me that way.

"Jeff's nurses just left. I imagine he'll be over here any minute. I'm going to warm up my tea before he gets here."

"We're not your nightly entertainment, Emma."

"Oh, but you are."

I feel my heart pounding a bit harder thinking about my first date with an actual employed person in . . . well, in some time. The differences between us are huge and now's as good a time as any to obsess about them. Jeff's all about the exterior, but I'm about the interior. The daily cleansing of the heart, body, and soul. He just wants to suck it out and make the world look like Paris Hilton. I hate to admit it, but I take on a little air of superiority here and feel ready to meet him, as the bell jangles at my office. If I can survive this, I can survive anything Morgan's wedding throws at me.

"Wow," Jeff says, blinking several times. "You . . . look . . . great."

Darn. Too much. But you can't trust the word of a plastic surgeon either. They get paid to lie to you.

"Thanks. So do you," I say, pointing at his suit. "I don't usually see your clothes. You're always in that white jacket."

"So this is a truce evening, right? No talk about work?"

"That's a good idea." Which begs the question, *What on earth will we talk about?* But I'm not going to say it.

Emma comes in and sits at her desk staring at both of us. "Emma, shouldn't you be getting home?"

She just shakes her head and takes a sip of tea. I see her snap her fingers as if to say darn, she missed the show.

"Hi, Emma." Jeff smiles before looking back at me. "I made reservations at a sushi restaurant. Do you do sushi?"

"I do," I say. *Not my favorite*, I add silently. Jeff harbors an ability to make you believe you're the only woman in the room when he speaks to you. I'm sure it's a practiced art, but it's effective. He can make my stomach tingle at the sound of his voice and I watch him with the same inquisitive skepticism I'd have for a childhood magician. As far as endorphins go, Jeff is as good as three miles or so. Which makes me wonder how truly shallow I am.

He's the Tom Cruise in my life. For instance:

1. Tom Cruise jumped on Oprah's couch like the ape in the Samsonite commercial.
2. I know Tom dumped two perfectly good wives to find himself. (I believe he's still searching.)
3. I know he's with a girl young enough to be his daughter.
4. I know he bought his own personal ultrasound machine upon learning of his young girlfriend's pregnancy.

In other words, I *know* better than to find Tom Cruise attractive. Logic tells me to steer clear, to seek higher ground. But then, I see him in *Jerry Maguire* again on TBS at night, and I'm charmed senseless just like the next girl (Renee Zellweger in this case). I'm continuously reminded that I'm not superior, I am not free from his charms. Tom says, "You complete me." And I don't laugh at that ridiculous line. I cry—sob actually—falling for it every time.

And don't even get me started on my illogical crush on Johnny Depp—especially dressed as a pirate. Not healthy, I'm certain.

I am average, one of the crowd, and Dr. Jeff Curran knows it.

My point is there are some people with entirely too much charisma, and Tom Cruise and Jeff Curran are two of them. Perhaps Jeff's fake white smile sets you aback slightly, but when he flashes that grin, I feel myself smiling. Even though I know better!

"Bye, Emma."

"Bye," she waves, like a seventh grader about to write in her diary.

"Are you sure you're all right with this?" Jeff asks me, sensing my pause at the doorstep.

I just nod. "Two associates having dinner, am I right?"

"So will you still hate me in the morning?" he asks.

I stumble for a moment. "I think so, yes."

"Then we're good."

"Fantastic." I smile at Emma before we exit my office. She appears duly entertained, so I guess we did our job.

Outside, Jeff opens the door to his Lexus convertible, and I nearly turn back to my office. This is normal for Silicon Valley; I understand that. I look the part, I can act the part, but what I find myself thinking is *Do I really have to get into this car?* It makes such a statement. I'm a snob. And not even in the right direction. I'm humiliated to get into a car that's too nice, not too dumpy.

I wiggle into it like a sardine into a can. *This is so not comfortable.* Why would anyone spend an inordinate amount of money to be uncomfortable? It's not like you can floor it on the freeway and feel any sense of freedom. There's far too much traffic here. If anything, I would think having a powerful car would only frustrate a person. I will say that the cream, calfskin leather is nice and the car smells good—a mixture of new car and Jeff's aftershave. But he's got to be six foot two, and he looks ridiculous driving this well-constructed, finely appointed roadster.

"Tiny," I say about the car.

"What?"

"The car. It's tiny."

"It's a Lexus," he reminds me. "Nothing about it is tiny."

"You don't think it's too small for you? You're a pretty

big guy. It's not good for your back to scrunch in this bittie car."

"I thought we weren't talking about work."

"I'm not talking about work, just telling you that your spine gets a workout each day. When you go home, you should tuck your hands under your knees and roll your spine on the floor. It's a self-massage that will keep you limber enough to drive this."

"My spine will be fine, thanks for the professional opinion. These seats hold my back like a luxury glove. Besides, I like my car. Worked hard for it." He looks over at me, and I figure another one of my opinions is not going over well. From here on out, I'm going to practice keeping my opinion to myself.

"It's a beautiful car," I admit.

There is a definite something between us. I close my eyes and try to focus on the energy aspect of this emotion I'm feeling and all the reasons I should know better. It's amazing to me how someone completely wrong for you can stir your heart by the simple chemistry God created. This is where I don't know how much brain to use and how much instinct. This is why I should date sensible men. Men who eat their oats, and don't sow them.

"So, I miss your skirt."

"No, you don't."

"You're right. I was trying to be pleasant."

At least I know he's a terrible liar.

"So I've always wondered, does it have some sort of significance? Or is it just comfortable?"

"I have more than one."

"Really?"

"They look alike," I admit.

"I like them, actually. They're very retro and anti-establishment. When you see women put together all day, it's nice to see someone who feels at ease in comfort."

"You're saying I don't look put together?" Granted, I may not, but do I need to hear it from him?

"No, I'm not saying that. I'm saying that you're your own woman, and it shows. Fashion gets to be like a uniform. I admire your spirit, Poppy."

"Is that so?"

"So what was so secretive about your dinner with your father? I've been in suspense all day."

I can't quite tell if Jeff is making fun of me. I suppose it's all those years of being the odd man out at Stanford. I never really cared if someone made fun of me; I knew I was different. But this is a date. I didn't come out to be ridiculed. It's like signing up for the privilege.

"My father's moving to Arizona," I answer. "He's leaving me the house in Santa Cruz."

"You're not going to commute, are you?" Jeff acts as if I've just told him I'm moving to Mars.

"It's over the hill, Jeff. It's not in Timbuktu."

"It just doesn't seem like your kind of place."

I raise my eyebrows. "Now that is the first time someone ever told me that. Usually, people across the country would think it's my kind of place. I grew up there."

"I don't know. I think crystals and moon worshiping. It doesn't seem like your Christian heritage to me."

"There are Christians in Santa Cruz!" I say, sort of offended.

"I'm just saying you don't seem to fit there. Why are you getting so upset? I thought it was a compliment."

I gasp. "Because obviously, I *do* fit there. My father seems to think I fit there. He handed me the keys himself."

Jeff stays calm, which I credit him for. I'm clearly not doing as well. "Sometimes, Poppy, our parents don't know who we are when we grow up. We're still the colicky baby, or the child who couldn't make friends with other children, to them. But you know, if you want to go back to Santa Cruz, I think you should. Maybe start your practice over there?"

"My father knows my passion for pushing the human body to its peak. He has always encouraged me in that, whether in track in high school or bowing out of medical school. But none of this is an issue, because I'm not moving."

"Right. Of course you're not. Wait a minute—you were in med school?"

I shake my head. "No, I was just accepted. I didn't go."

Jeff lowers his brows, and for a moment I want to tell him my whole sordid past and why I turned on the medical establishment, but I don't, and for that I feel a brief moment of bliss. I don't say anything anti-establishment or what Lilly might deem kooky. I just act as though it was the right choice for me. I am, for the first time, politically correct. *Call CNN!*

"Listen, I don't think this is going well. You're establishing motive in my comments," Jeff accuses, like a lawyer. "I didn't mean anything by my Santa Cruz comment. I was just trying to be supportive. If you want to go to Santa Cruz, I think you should."

"What about Hawaii? Do you think I'm the Hawaiian sort?"

He shakes his head. "Nah, I think you're too obsessive for Hawaii."

"Obsessive?" I squeal. I'm not liking the word *obsessive*. Sure, I'm motivated. I'm ambitious. But obsessive?

"I mean detail-oriented," he corrects.

I look at his profile, which is lit by the dwindling sunlight and I'll say one thing for him, if he's not sincere, he does a really good job of pretending. His deep brow is furrowed, and though I know better, something deep within is thinking that making this guy mad is a little hot.

"My mother died in the house," I explain, unable to fathom why I've overshared this with him.

Jeff stops the car at an intersection; he has no idea where to go with this information. His expression is just like my cat Safflower when she got caught up the tree with nowhere to go. "That's awful. I'm sorry about that."

I shrug. "It was a long time ago. But that's just one reason why I'm not going back."

"Right. Right."

I'm afraid my Zen personality has sort of left me momentarily because even though I know I should just shut up, I find the need to explain. "She didn't really die in the house. She went into a diabetic coma. She died later at the hospital. But it feels the same."

"Right."

"I was thirteen. Things had been bad since I was nine, though; that was just the culmination." *Shut up, Poppy. Shut up!* There is absolutely no hope for me. I've brought up my mother's death before we've even made it to the restaurant. That's worse than calculating my biological clock for him.

No wonder Morgan fears me at her wedding. Not only am I an oddity of the peacenik, health sort, but somewhere along the line I've become a full-on train wreck of a conversationalist. It's like I'm on the *Oprah* show reliving all my nightmares in this moving truth-serum mobile. *Maybe it's the leather off-gassing from the seats*, I try to rationalize.

"You probably should go back. Maybe you never really had time to grieve. I won't operate on patients if they haven't dealt with some of the emotional things in their history."

"I'm not looking for plastic surgery, Jeff." Maybe it's my paranoia, but Jeff seems awfully interested in where I live.

He laughs. "No, I know that, Poppy. But you asked me about Hawaii, and . . . I don't know—I just thought if you're still upset about your mother and the house . . . maybe . . ."

I just smile at this. He's trying to understand my manic behavior, but I'm sure he's over there thinking, "*Fatal Attraction II, here she is!*"

"I can't have you being high maintenance, you know," Jeff guns the motor and we take off from the stop sign with a start. "That's what I deal with all day. What happens if you suddenly start becoming self-absorbed and stop trying to prove to me my Lexus is a waste of my existence? You can't upset that balance. I need you to be the stable one, Poppy."

Jeff makes me laugh. Even though I don't have pearly whites the color of tic tacs, he still makes me grin. His boyish charm is undeniable. Of course, I'm more than curious why he's asking me out for any reason, neighborly or otherwise. But I remember this is about Morgan's wedding, and if I can do this, I am ready. Well, I mean, I just screwed up big time here, so I don't have to do it at the wedding.

"I would think a plastic surgeon likes a high-maintenance girl. It keeps you on your toes and provides insight into your patients."

He shakes his head. "I don't think I want any more insight into that or I'll never get married."

"That's a bit cynical."

"I know you think I waste my days, but if you had crooked teeth and braces would fix them, would you do it?"

"Not if it meant slicing me open, no."

"Well, what if you'd been sliced open a few times for a cesarean birth, and the results left your stomach looking like a minefield?"

"We're not supposed to be talking about work. But I don't think I'm ever going to have children." Yeah, me and the procreation thing—not happening. But I've already brought up my childhood nightmares; why not go right into baby making? *Ugh.*

"You're like Mother Earth herself. You mother everyone, and you're telling me you don't have aspirations for motherhood." He stops to laugh. "And you expect me to believe it."

"No, really. It's not that I don't want them, just that I don't see them in my future." I don't mention this has a lot to do with my assessing the gene pool or thinking about my own. Which would be better termed a cesspool.

"I want four," he says.

I laugh out loud. "Is that your way of avoiding second dates? I've heard some good ones, Jeff, but that's pretty fantastic from the unattainable standpoint."

"No, really, I want four."

"All men who work twelve-hour days say that. Of course, they want four; they're not going to be there to deal with the long days and the diapers and the food on the wall. They just go to the office and boast about all their kids."

"Is that what you think? Who has to earn the college money for those four kids? Who has to romance his wife when she's grumpy at the end of the day? That's right, the man."

"How do you know so much about this?"

"My mentor. He had five kids. I'm lowering my expectations to account for the busier pace of homework and expectations of the workplace now."

Aren't you generous?

"And men have to be responsible for everything that goes on in their home. They have to manage it, according to the Bible."

"You're talking about pretty straightforward roles."

"I am. Call me a Neanderthal, but I like roles. I'm comfortable with roles. I want my future wife to stay at home and spoon-feed our children and sing lullabies to them, work in their classrooms, and bake cookies in the afternoon."

"How romantic," I purr. "Good luck with that. My mother

always worked. My father stayed home with me and worked on his art. I survived."

"I'm not putting anyone down, Poppy, only saying I like traditional roles. Like I said, call me a Neanderthal, and perhaps God will set me straight, but it's what I know. What I want. I set my expectations high."

Always a good way to be disappointed.

We arrive at the restaurant, and there's a long line out the front door. It looks like we're going to be waiting regardless of any reservation, and I worry that our conversation starters may have run out—I mean, we've already dealt with death, pregnant women, and that I'm obsessive. What else is there? We're going to have to fall back on work, unless we can stretch the menu items into two hours of conversation.

Jeff helps me out of the car and, one good thing about having Morgan's shoes on, I don't feel like running. But I do feel like my shoes might turn into ratty moccasins at midnight. In fact, I'm hoping they will.

"We've got a table in the back. I hope you don't mind removing your shoes."

I think about Morgan's nylon socks stuffed at the bottom of the toe, but I mention nothing. "No, of course not."

"Welcome, Dr. Curran," the mâitre d' says. And we're led to the back without another word. Lord willing, I'll be in running pants in less than two hours. *Just don't bring up Mom or babies. Or health— Oh my goodness, I've retired my entire repertoire and we're not even sitting yet.*

We're led to the back booth, where Jeff opens a paper wall door for me. There are pillows to sit on. As I slip out of the shoes, one of Morgan's nylons sticks to my nylons as though they're breeding, and I've got this bulbous balloon of stocking at the end of my toe. Jeff notices, but he says nothing, and I just reach down and pull it off with an awful Velcro sound. It wouldn't be noticed if it weren't for the quiet back room. I should probably explain why my shoes don't fit, but why bother. This is the last time I'll have to endure dinner with someone like Dr. Jeff. Besides, he seems to like his women barefoot and stove bound.

As we're seated (not so easy on a pillow in this tight skirt, I might add) Jeff looks at me, and I meet his gaze. In another lifetime, I might think he was incredibly adorable. All right, the truth is I do think that. But it ticks me off.

"So I imagine you're wondering why I brought you here to this quiet little restaurant."

Actually, I wasn't. Which may only prove my naïveté. I just lift my eyebrows in answer.

"It's about your office."

I feel my stomach drop. "M-my office?"

"I'm sure you've seen just how many people our office is accommodating right now. It's crazy." He slaps his forehead as though he can't imagine how this happened. Naturally, I can't help but think of the myriad of color ads with his beaming, fake smile in every city magazine within the fifty-mile radius.

"That's great. With all that business, you'll soon be able to find your surgical building," I say brightly. Jeff is a nice man. I'm certain he's a Christian, but his way of "helping" the world is beyond my reach. He plays on women's deepest fears, and I can't help but be reminded of this as he puts on the innocent act. *Spare me.*

He clears his throat, "Like I say, we're expanding and could really use the space next door, and I wanted to find out just how long you plan to stay there."

My thoughts are abruptly cut off. Nothing comes out of my mouth. It's open—I can feel the cold air rushing in—but I have no words. This is it? This is what this dinner was about? Just like the great pharmaceutical conglomerate, Jeff

Curran is determined to put the body natural out of business. And me dressing for the occasion, in fancy shoes like a bad Cinderella rendition. No wonder he was anxious to get me back to Santa Cruz and let that do his dirty work for him. *Well, I don't think so.*

"Poppy, you're not upset are you?" He asks with that fake-doctor concern. The one where they rip off the prescription and send you on your way.

My mouth is still open. I realize he's trying to upset me, and so I will not give him the satisfaction. But really, can he be this clueless? Can he think one dinner in a sushi restaurant is going to make me hand over my lease? I mean, I know it's crowded here and all, but come on, even he can't believe his charm is that effective.

"Upset? Why would I be upset?" I finally say. "You're welcome to ask anything you'd like. But then again, I'm not apt to give you the answer you'd like."

"Poppy," he says again with his hand on my own. This is like a high school guy trying to put his arm around me in a movie.

In my most calm voice, I continue, "I've spent years watching the medical establishment do more harm than good for autoimmune issues and allergies—in my opinion, naturally." I add the disclaimer just so he doesn't latch onto that and try to start up with the charm again. "I live to heal people, to seek out the true source of their problems. I don't believe you can heal issues like childhood tauntings with surgery." I fixate on a koi picture on the wall. "So you see, Jeff, not only am I not closing my practice anytime soon in that space, but the idea of you expanding the plastic business is never going to be something I help along."

I turn back towards him and watch his Adam's apple bob nervously. "Irregardless of how you feel—"

"*Irregardless* isn't a word, but go on." I say calmly. Thinking to myself, *People are letting a man who uses bad grammar slice them open like a vegetable!*

"Your lease is up next year, and I plan to take over your space. I thought this was an act of friendliness by telling you ahead of time, so that you might plan."

Just like that he says it. Like he's saying "Um, you have a little smudge on your face." I exhale and don't allow any expression to come across my face. I imagine he's already taken care of these arrangements with the landlord, and I know the income he generates would make my offer, and even my legal lease, a joke. So I stand up. In the land of the lease, money always takes precedence. While he may get away with this garbage, I don't have to be nice to him while he does so just to eliminate the guilt he should feel.

"I see."

"You're mad." Jeff says, still looking handsome, albeit slimy as all get-out.

"You have to answer for the things you do in this lifetime. If this is what you want to do with your career, you go right ahead. I'll leave without any trouble once the landlord takes action, but any guilt you feel is not my problem. I'll find another space. My patients will follow me because they embrace real healing. Not a temporary stab of Botox to make their wayward husbands stay a bit longer." I don't actually have this confidence, but I think it's great practice for the wedding because I am sounding very convincing.

"That's really what you think I do." He moves his eyes to the cushion to tell me to sit down. Apparently he's afraid I might make a scene.

"I'm sure that at some point, you've helped a child with cleft palette, or you've removed someone's painful extra skin. There are always excuses."

He stands up himself and I think he'd slam the table if it wasn't resting a good four feet below him. "You really think you're a better cut of Christian than me, don't you?"

Of course, his show is just for me. We're in this room ourselves. I look around, wondering if somewhere his cheering fans will appear. "Does it matter what I think, Jeff?"

"I need that building for my expanding practice. This is what I was called to do." Again he looks towards the table as if he wants to inflict violence upon it. *Ah, our caveman appears.*

I nod. "So then why feel guilty? If this is what you have to do, do it. You obviously don't need my permission anyway. Do you want me to be happy about this, Jeff? Do you not see what you're asking me?"

"You should congratulate me that I'm in a place to grow my business in such an overcrowded field."

This makes me laugh, but he's completely serious. I know men are on a constant search for significance, but at some point Jeff's got to think about others in business as well. And now would be a good time. "So I should thank you for trying to destroy my business. Is that your take? Perhaps you're waiting for me to turn the other cheek and prove to you I'm a Christian?"

"I'm not going to destroy anything." Jeff slowly sits down, but his jaw is still clenching uncontrollably. "Your granola-crunching fan club will follow you. I'm sure the scent you put out over there will lead them like the breadcrumbs for Hansel and Gretel."

At this point, I feel the first sting of tears. I know Jeff feels desperate, but he can't possibly be this selfish, this cruel. "As if the Botox crowd won't find you for their next fix." There's a mirror on the wall, and I walk to it. "Oh my goodness, oh my goodness, is that the beginnings of a . . . gasp . . . wrinkle!"

"This is all a big joke to you, isn't it? You are the most maddening— Why don't you fight me, then?"

"Because I don't have the money to fight you, and you know that, Jeff. So why even bother with this ruse that we can still be friends? That's what this is all about, right? You destroy my business, and don't have to feel the guilt? If you're doing what you have to do, why bother with anything as mundane as guilt?"

"I don't feel guilty, but my practice is too successful for you to make fun of me."

"Like you're making fun of me, you mean? Plastic surgery is epidemic in California. Probably across the nation." I shrug. "There are physically healthy people out there who want to be more beautiful. That's your gig. I'm not looking for those patients, and you're right—mine will follow me because they need help. I'm realistic, and money always wins, and since I'm not in it for the money, we know what that means."

"You're saying I am, I understand." Jeff is a subtle blend of red and orange. If he believed in auras, his would be on fire at the moment and emanating from his ears.

"Jeff, I'm not going to apologize to you while you try to shut the doors of my business, nor am I going to give you the kudos you want to hear for how successful you are." The waitress comes to the room but hears our raised voices and quickly retreats out the paper doors. "You're scaring the staff. Can we have this conversation later? I'm hungry and you're buying." I'm not about to storm out and let him off the hook for dinner. I deserve that much. I wore heels.

I wonder if there's lobster sushi. I peruse the menu.

"All the more reason you should just walk from the lease. You're happy with the size of your business, and I haven't yet begun."

People and their quest for money puzzle me. What more

can you do with it? How much more can you buy? It's disgusting, quite frankly. I sit back down and gaze around the paper room. "So is this where you bring women to break up with them?" I ask, taking note of the waitress's strange retreat. "What do you do, pull a *Bachelor* on them?"

"A *Bachelor*?"

"It's a reality show where a guy who's supposedly a catch makes out with multiple women, usually in a hot tub so the network can get the obligatory plastic surgery work on camera, then picks a woman at the end, and the rest go home angry and meowing, only to find out later he was macking everything in a skirt on national television, and it wasn't really true love after all."

"And you watch this?"

"Sometimes. It's like a car accident. I can't help myself," I admit. "So you're not answering my question. Is this where you cut the ties?"

"I'm just not buying this calm, cool, and collected bit, Poppy. Tell me how to proceed with this."

"I think that's a conversation for your lawyer. They do have lobster sushi!" The waitress comes in and starts to back off once again. "Wait." I tell her. "Can you get us some green tea? He's trying to break up with me, but I want to eat first." I giggle as she retreats.

"That wasn't nice."

"Neither was telling me you were bringing me to dinner with no discussion of work, when your goal was purely to have me shred my lease."

"That wasn't the reason I brought you to dinner. It just seemed convenient."

"Of course it was. You got into the restaurant where you dump your girlfriends, and you thought it would be just as easy to dump me here too. Understandable."

"Only once did I break up with anyone here. You're right, she got a little hysterical." He shrugs and his face contorts as though he had no idea she would lose it in this way. Obviously, he had some sort of idea or he would have done it privately. He was hoping for her fear of humiliation to save him. At least, that's what I'm guessing.

Granted, I know we're all sinners, but I would have thought dumping someone painfully yet publicly would be reserved for the heathen. A guy who would do that deserves hysterical. It's sort of the ultimate battle of wills.

But then my mind drifts to Simon leaving and I don't feel as strong as I thought. If Jeff really is the type who would see an end to my lease, maybe I have the excuse I need to follow Simon. And the blonde. I have to remember the blonde is coming too.

I focus on Jeff again. "I hope you dumped her *after* she ate. You owed her that much."

"It was after she ate. Things don't necessarily work out, you know." He flips open his menu and his blue eyes drop to read, thus avoiding anymore prying on my part.

Granted, breaking up is never fun, but doing it in a restaurant is so tacky. It's like your last meal and very hard to enjoy knowing what you do. Even though Jeff won't look at me, I stare directly at him. For someone who claims to have it all, and gaining more by the second, he sure doesn't feel all that confident to me. It's probably just the sports car and the virginal teeth.

"So let me ask you, did you think you could just sign me up for a free pair of implants and I'd go away quietly?"

This makes him look up from his menu. "I know your stance on natural. That most certainly wasn't my plan. I thought you'd be loud and vocal. That's why I brought you here." He says this matter-of-factly while continuing to peruse his menu.

"Fair enough. Sorry I couldn't help you out on the hysterical." Actually, I could, but I'm practicing for Morgan's wedding.

"So, you'll discuss relocating with me? Calmly?" He gives me his full attention, raising his eyebrows. His warm gaze meets mine, and even though I know the form of snake that lurks within, he really is a joy to the eyes.

"You'd be perfect."

"What?" he asks.

Yeah, it sort of scares me too. But before I speak my brilliant plan out loud, I really have to think about whether I could spend another evening with Dr. Jeff, his blue eyes notwithstanding. A girl can only hold in so much for so long.

So I'm still staring at Dr. Jeff. Still imagining his gorgeous exterior and European suit with the personality of Jon Stewart, and I'm like Frankenstein. I have created the perfect wedding date. (Insert evil laughter here.) He's a doctor, he's intellectual, and he doesn't even know what an adrenal dysfunction looks like. If I can simply ignore the fact that he injects poison into women and makes Mr. Cunningham from *Happy Days* look forward thinking, I have myself an answer.

"I have a proposition for you, Jeff." I sit forward in my chair, trying desperately to hide my true emotions of what I actually think of him and his ever-expanding shallow, plastic world.

"Should I be afraid?" He narrows his eyes at me.

"I'm just a natural healing chiropractor, hardly anything worth a wave of your flyswatter."

"A mosquito with the personality and effect of a mountain lion."

He so owes me this. I can still bring out the big guns, the threat of a doctor's worst fear: a lawyer. "I'll go quietly from the building, let you have my space at the end of the year with no lawsuit or rise in the sublease, on one condition."

He drops his menu, and I can see he trusts me about as

much as he trusts a malpractice attorney. "I'm not sending my patients to you."

I ignore his inane suggestion—as though I'd want his patients. I'm just going to blurt it out; there's no easy way to say it. "Attend my best friend's wedding with me. As my date."

He laughs. "Poppy, have you looked in the mirror? You hardly need to settle for me on a date. We all know your opinion of me."

"Don't flatter yourself. I can get a date. Just not necessarily one who will mingle with the San Francisco society crowd with ease. That's your specialty, isn't it? Feeding on the froth that is idle conversation."

"If this is your idea of charming me into it—"

"I have no such intention of charming you into anything. Morgan Malliard wants a certain kind of wedding, and I just think you'd fit in perfectly. They'll probably wonder why I'm an attendant when you're the actual guest, but I'll deal with that in time."

"You know Morgan Malliard?"

"My best friend."

"You're telling me if I go to a high-society wedding with you, you won't sue the landlord or me for your early-exit lease."

"That's exactly what I'm saying." I don't mention I wouldn't sue him anyway. Life is too short, and life's not fair. If there's anything history has taught me, that's it. Besides, after the dot-com bust, office space is plentiful.

"What's the catch? Do I have to dress up like a piece of broccoli or something?"

"You have to get a tuxedo and look like a respectable San Francisco socialite." Again, I notice how handsome he is, and I get another troubling thought. "Oh, and you can't pick up women in my presence, nor can you give medical or plastic surgery advice to anyone in attendance. It seems that's what I'm in trouble for." I figure Morgan won't appreciate that type of guidance any more than she will the mind-body-spirit counsel.

"And that's it?"

"That's it. I promise."

He reaches across the table and shakes. "Done."

And with that, I make a deal with the—well, never mind. It's one I'm comfortable with, and I've just eliminated stress from two aspects of my life. The Spa Girls will think I'm entering into normalcy, and I can start the search for new office space without a fight. Neighbors. Sometimes you just can't get the fence high enough.

It's an odd world we live in when a man who puts plastic breasts in women for a living is a respectable date. I know, he does more than that. But he does that, too, and it's just odd to me that I, a chiropractor who has studied the art of natural healing—and how the body is designed to heal itself if given the proper tools—am the weirdo. But a man who blows women up to look like Barbies—he's the epitome of normal. I must be missing something. I really must.

I suppose it's money. Money is respectable in this world, and plastic surgeons make money hand over fist. I suppose the one thing we have in common is that we both loathe the insurance business that tells doctors how to run their practices.

"I guess I don't really understand you, Poppy Clayton. You're so anti-establishment, anti-plastic surgery and you could date anyone you want with that fiery red hair and those blue eyes from heaven, so what's up?"

"You know, don't snow me, Jeff." I roll my eyes. "Spare me the Hollywood screenwriting, and just ask your questions."

"Why me for the wedding?" This time, there's no smile. He's dead serious. When he relaxes the sales pitch, he's really a decent human being. I wish I could see that side of him more often. It's the facade I can barely tolerate.

"I told you, you're respectable in that crowd, and right now, I need respectable." I gaze down at my respectable skirt and think about how long I have to be respectable. *Morgan is worth it*, I remind myself.

"It's just odd you see me as the respectable date, because you don't respect me."

"So you're going to grow a conscience now, is that what you're saying? You want me to respect you in the morning?"

"I just don't necessarily want to be used. Maybe you'd like to go with me to the wedding because you find me handsome and an interesting conversationalist." He cocks an eyebrow.

"Nah." I shake my head. "That wouldn't be it. You owe me, and I just find it easier to collect where I see a need."

"So you're saying you don't necessarily find me attractive."

"Oh, no, I didn't say that." *Like George Washington, I cannot tell a lie.* "You're handsome, Jeff. But you know that." I wrinkle my nose. "But I'm just really not into appearances."

"Except when it comes to finding a respectable date for a wedding."

"Right. You act like there's something wrong with that?"

"What? Being shallow for an occasion? Not at all. Let's eat. All this arguing has made me hungry." He buries his face in the menu again.

"I'm glad I could be of service. Haven't you decided what you want yet?"

"I have. I'm just trying to find some of my dignity down here."

This makes me giggle against my better judgment. As much as I want to, I can't despise Dr. Jeff. There's a heart in there somewhere.

He puts the menu down and stares at me with those

sparkling eyes. How is it I can still see him as gorgeous when I know all he is about? When I know he only brought me here to indicate moving offices is a good idea. I try to decipher this great mystery of chemistry and energy when he speaks up again. "Confession time: I did need to discuss the lease, but that's not why I asked you out. It was just an excuse."

I cross my arms waiting for the next half of his so-called confession, which is clearly meant to charm me into who knows what kind of game. But the waitress isn't here yet, so I've got nothing but time. The fact is I will eat at his expense no matter how many hours it costs me.

"I want to deny it, too, Poppy."

"Deny what?"

"You don't feel this?" He points to me and then himself. "That thing between us."

"No," I lie. So much for George Washington's morals.

"You're telling me I've invented this emotion that's passed between us. There's nothing on your part."

I read *Smart Women, Foolish Choices*.

"I think you're good looking," I admit to him. *Hot*, I admit to myself. *But a jerk.* "You can find someone attractive, but still understand they represent everything you loathe in life."

"I can't. I see something more in you, Poppy. I think this homeopathic wall you put up is not as sturdy as you might think."

"Well, that's where you're wrong. We're human, we find each other attractive, let's move on, shall we?"

"Fine."

Oh my goodness, I am mortified. I just admitted I find Dr. Plastic attractive. And worse yet, it's completely true! I am an embarrassment to my trade.

By his shade of pink, I'd say he's tasted enough humiliation for the evening. It's now time for a confession of my own.

I figure I have to give a little now that he's at least admitted what neither of us wants to. "You know, Jeff, if it makes any difference to you, I've seen a lot of the good things you do over in that office. Just in the last day or so, I've been watching." I smile at him, hoping the tea arrives soon and gets me out of this most uncomfortable situation.

Truly, I am at peace about the building. I don't like smelling the Greek food every day anyway, and the truth is I could use more space myself. Plus, I have a date for Morgan's wedding. He is not a running nudist from San Francisco. I feel good. Let's not push it.

"I have a leasing agent who's going to help you find a space. A better space—maybe something near Whole Foods or that vegetarian restaurant, or maybe a yoga studio."

"Thank you, but I'll get Simon on it before he leaves. He's one of my patients with a head for business." One deal with the Dark Side is quite enough for me.

At this point, the waitress comes back in and whispers in Jeff's ear.

"Excuse me," he says, while getting up quickly. He tosses me his keys. "Would you get my doctor bag out of my car?"

I catch the keys, wondering what's going on, but I do as I'm told, snaking my way through all the throngs of waiting customers. Opening the trunk of the Lexus, there's a small black bag, which I retrieve and walk resolutely back into the restaurant. The same waitress meets me at the door and pulls me to the kitchen, where I see a lot of blood.

"Little accident." Jeff says, reaching for his bag. My stomach lunges as I see the chef has sliced more than the sushi. Jeff has wrapped the man's forefinger in gauze and asks me to get things out for him as he intends to sew the man back together.

"Shouldn't you just call 911?"

"I can save the finger faster this way." Jeff digs into his bag and pulls out a series of things, including surgical gloves. "Where's the sink?" he asks the waitress, and he starts to clean his hands, lifting them to the sky while he scrubs.

Suddenly, I'm not as hungry as I once was.

"No 911," the chef orders from the chair he's sitting in. "Customers won't come back if they see 911. Jeff will do it." He nods at Jeff, showing complete confidence in his regular customer.

Jeff looks up at me and smiles apologetically.

The restaurant continues to work with the one remaining chef, and the waitresses exert extra energy to maintain a sense of calm that there's nothing whatsoever going on that's out of the ordinary. If they get tired of sushi, they'd make excellent airline attendants.

I sit beside Jeff and hand him things as he needs them, watching him sew the portion of the finger back on with the skill of a master seamstress. "Forty-eight stitches," he says when he's done. "Impressive." He wraps the finished product in gauze. "It's going to hurt for some time. You keep it on ice, and no more work tonight."

"How long?" The chef holds up his finger.

"At least three weeks. You come to my office tomorrow, and we'll clean it up and redress it."

The man sighs loudly and resigns himself to the healing process.

"You're not squeamish," Jeff says to me as he puts things back into his bag. He has a plastic bag and he places the dirty needle and scissors into it and puts them in the side pocket of his attaché.

"No," I admit. "I was giving my mother insulin shots when I was nine. She didn't like to do it herself."

"It's a surprise you didn't go to medical school after seeing all that. Not even a flinch. I watched you."

"I'd hope you were watching what you were doing." He zips his medical bag and I think we've found the one area we might respect each other in. "What drew you to medical school?"

Jeff laughs. "My father didn't actually give me a choice, and by the time I knew I had one, it was too late. I was already in love with medicine, and surgery especially. Once the fight was on for surgical time during my residency, it was over. I'd found my calling."

"You have warm eyes," I hear myself say. "I don't know what to believe about you. You're half car salesman, half competent doctor. I'm not sure which one I trust." We share a smile, and I'm not sure it matters. One thing is certain, Jeff is as serious about what he does as I am about what I do.

He coughs. "You just don't hold back, do you? Is that perhaps why Morgan Malliard is uncomfortable with your dating choices at her wedding?"

"That's none of your business."

Jeff stands up and helps me to my feet from the nearby chair. "You should have gone to medical school, Poppy."

"I beg your pardon. I do what I love, and I heal people."

He just nods.

"What is that supposed to mean?"

"Nothing. It doesn't mean anything. Why do you assume everything I do or say has motive?" He pauses for a minute. "What I meant is that your natural health mantra might have a little more credence with a medical degree behind it."

"Like chiropractics?"

"Touché."

"Silicone stops the flow of energy, you're right. It's not a conductor." It's an attack and totally ill timed. I feel guilty after I say it, but it certainly didn't stop me from saying it, did it?

"We both want people healthy and happy. Can we agree on that much?"

But I don't quit here. Something within me keeps attacking. "Don't you ever feel sort of like Frankenstein? You know, '*It's alive! It's alive!*'"

"I don't, actually. If you stepped outside that peaceful place you inhabit and smelled a little smog, you'd know there are people who carry lifetime pain in the words of some childhood taunt. I can take away what's stopping them from moving on—at least the physical aspects. I had a patient today who underwent gastric bypass. All her life she'd been known as "Fatty Patty," but she's not that person anymore. She's the person she's felt like her whole life, locked inside a body that was just hers since childhood."

Is it just me or does this sound like a lead-in on *Extreme Makeovers: Home Edition*?

"She only has to undergo this last step—removing the excess skin—and she leaves those taunts in her past."

"Do you really believe that, Jeff? That she can just look better and it will fix everything?"

"I don't think it fixes everything, but I do know it makes them feel better when they have confidence. To become who you feel like on the inside is powerful."

I look at the sincerity in his expression and it's clear he believes it. I'm sure his work does help people, but I'm living proof the exterior means nothing. Childhood taunts are never forgotten, only dulled by time and circumstances.

"It's a journey. Life is a journey. The physical may help, but it's not the core and looking good on the outside doesn't fix a thing."

"I imagine you're not in the mood for sushi anymore?"

I laugh. "Oddly enough, I'm not. I doubt I ever will be again."

He slides his hand down my back. "Let's go. My work is done here."

This is such an odd night. I'm with a man I have nothing in common with, he's told me he's stealing my office space for all intents and purposes, and yet I feel no anger or strife. Just a small thrill that I have acceptable date material for Morgan's wedding. Perhaps I don't set my standards in life high enough.

"I have to say, you do know how to show a girl a good time, Dr. Jeff."

"No one's perfect." He winks.

"Until they come to you?" I grin.

"At all. No one is perfect. I'm well aware of that fact." Jeff lifts his bag to say good-bye to the waitress, who is clambering to see us fed. Jeff is shaking his head, and that seems to satisfy her. "So I know that no one is perfect, Poppy. The question is do you? Miss Triathlete?"

And what I'd do for a run right now. Jeff is much more perceptive than I've given him credit for, and it's unnerving. I'd give anything to be under my eucalyptus trees stretching and running until I forgot this conversation ever happened. I got what I came for, and I suppose he did too.

"I don't know why you want to expand anyway," I say as he opens the door to his little can-opener car. "Everyone in Silicon Valley expands, and then they work more, and then they have even less of a life, and they pay people to have it for them. It's all so blasé and expected."

He laughs. "It's blasé to succeed?"

"No, what they call success here is passé. You know: nannies, maids, trainers. Gourmet kitchens for resale value, but no actual usage. It's like we build the perfect habitat, but no one's actually living in it. Like hamsters on that wheel. We just live in a constant hurry, going nowhere."

"You, who run everywhere, are telling me I live too fast?" Jeff asks.

I draw in a deep breath. Slivers of serenity rain down

upon me. "I live slowly and methodically. I may not get ahead, but I don't get behind either."

"I see," Jeff says.

"So tell me, is there a method to this expansion? Or are you just watching Dr. Connors up the street?" I see by his flinch that has something to do with it. "You already work fourteen-hour days, at least. What happens with a bigger patient load? What happens when you can't give them the care you think they deserve? The care you always told yourself you'd give them. What can more building bring you?"

"Security. Reputation. Don't you want to be the best chiropractor there is?"

"I am the best chiropractor there is."

"And so modest too. I mean, don't you dream of leaving a legacy? Like the Dr. Poppy Clayton Center for Alternative Health Clinic?"

I look at him with my face crinkling. "Why would I want that?" I allow him to shut the car door and wait while he puts the bag back into the trunk and reappears in the driver's seat.

"I admire you for knowing yourself so well. It surprises me, though, for someone who is so goal oriented that you're so content with a simple office. I see them lining up over there, waiting to get their herbs and back crackings."

I think that's meant to unnerve me, but it doesn't. "I don't use the cracking method. Well, except on one client who needs more force. I believe in gentle chiropractic and acupressure, using the body's own energy meridians."

My mind drifts to Simon, and how I wish he was here to defend me. I know it's all so Neanderthal to think of a man rescuing me, but just by his mere size I would think he'd be able to speak for the attributes of chiropractic. And if he couldn't, he could at least intimidate Jeff. It might not help my cause, but it would make me feel better.

There is a chemistry with Jeff that is undeniable. But like I say, lesser living through chemistry. Sometimes, it's just best to ignore what you can't explain. That goes for UFOs and attraction to the wrong men.

chapter 10

Miles run: 6
Laps swum: 20
Desperation scale: 7 (*Date with Devil, the Sequel*, pending)

Natural medicine is like an onion. You have to peel away the layers of troubles to get to the core or central issue. Medical doctors generally treat the symptoms, drugs generally treat the symptoms, but with alternative medicine, it's all about the root and digging it up as one would pull a carrot from the soil. Like a treasure hunt, I know with each layer I get closer to the cure.

Once upon a time, when I dreamed of going premed, I found my fascination with the natural side of healing had become my passion. It was probably my mother shoving all that organic, free-range chicken soup down me as a child. How I wish she'd done the same for herself.

I turn on the blender in my small staff room and whip myself up a grass-green superfood shake, but when it comes time to drink it, I can't swallow it. Not today. I don't know what's wrong with me, but I am craving a chocolate shake. Which would probably make me sick, and yet, somehow right now, it all seems worth the risk.

"How can you drink that stuff?" Emma asks.

"I can't today. There's some kind of blockage I'm having." Which is, of course, my body speaking to me, so I put the shake down.

"Taste buds, maybe? Yours might have started working again. What did you eat for dinner last night?"

"Very funny."

"No one but a rabbit should eat something that color. It's the color of baby grass. I don't think of that as edible."

"You eat healthy," I accuse.

"I do. I eat healthy. I don't force inhumane substances down my system and expect it to be happy like you do. That will make your nose twitch."

"So it will twitch," I tell her while I plug my nose and try to gulp the shake. I can't let it go to waste.

"Your dad called while you were in with the last patient. I told him you'd call him back."

I sputter and smack my tongue to get that taste out, drinking an Odwalla orange juice to cleanse my palate. "All right."

Of course, Emma has more information, being the encyclopedia on my life that she is. "He told me that if you couldn't find a date, your high school boyfriend said he would go with you—that you'd gotten hot in your older years."

"The married one?"

"I wondered. Your dad didn't sound too thrilled about it. Maybe it was a joke."

I just shake my head. "You know, I love my father, but sometimes, he's just not aware of normal-people emotions. He is like the relationship Rodney King: 'Can't we just all get along?' Rachel didn't get along with Leah, and I don't think my high school boyfriend's wife is going to be particularly fond of this brilliant idea. She already looks like a direct descendant of Lizzie Borden. Anyway, could you type up these reports?" I hand her several folders.

"Yeah. Morgan's on line one. She wants to know how the date went."

I sigh aloud.

"That's what I figured," Emma says. "It didn't seem like an exceptionally good idea. You both looked like you couldn't wait to get it over with last night. Even if you do want each other."

"What?"

"You both can't stand your weakness for each other. It's obvious." She lowers her voice to barely above a mumble. "And don't even get me started on you and Simon."

I just roll my eyes. "I'll take the call in my office." I sit down at my desk. "Hi, Morgan."

"Well?"

Well? How do I answer that oh-so-simple question. "I looked good, but Jeff was more interested in my office space than my own personal real estate. So the good news is that my reputation is intact, and the bonus was that I got to see what it's like to sew back on a body digit. Other than that, Mrs. Lincoln . . ."

"So was it worse than the guy who bragged about never once cleaning his bathroom and it still being clean?"

"It was better than that," I admit. "But I never really got the point of the date."

"Does there have to be a point?"

"If it's to decide if you want date number two, I guess we did accomplish that much. He's coming to your wedding."

"Why?"

"I thought you'd be proud of me. I secured my own respectable date."

"You and the plastic surgeon." Morgan starts to trill her light, dainty laugh. "No, really."

"I'm serious. I made a deal, and Jeff is coming to your wedding, and he has agreed to your no-health policy and we will not be discussing any surgeries, cures, or ailments that day."

There's a box of chocolates that someone gave the office as a gift, and I open it, tear through the packaging, and start munching on a dark chocolate caramel. I feel guilty immediately, but I don't stop eating. Chocolate is good for my endorphins, and baby, they're singing.

"So you do give in now and again." A man's voice interrupts my chocolate binge, and I turn to see Simon with his hands on his hips. I try to wash my teeth clear of the caramel, but I'm like a dog eating peanut butter. I just keep licking and licking and it won't go away.

"Simon," I say with a full mouth. "Morgan, can I call you back?" I don't wait for her answer and hang up on her.

"Dr. Poppy has her vices. It's good to know. I knew that perfect exterior had its Achilles heel."

"Simon, what are you doing here?"

"I came to harass you about Hawaii." He holds up a string of freshwater pearls and dangles them in front of me.

I cross my arms. "You think I'm crossing the ocean for a trinket."

"Trinket? These are certified, gen-u-ine freshwater pearls." He wiggles his eyebrows. "There's more where this came from."

"Ah, the dreaded pirate Simon is going to see to all my needs, is that what you be saying?"

He drops the pearls on the counter. "It was worth a try. I knew I should have brought the bikini. But I thought you'd read too much into it."

"A bikini? For you or for me?"

"Very funny. You don't want to know my body-fat percentage, and you most definitely don't want to see it in skimpy swimwear."

Simon is self-deprecating, but he's got the barrel chest of a linebacker and the charm of a classic movie actor. I imagine in Silicon Valley, the width of his wallet doesn't hurt either. I'm sure that's what Blondie is thinking. He does seem to date rarely, though, as he was dumped pretty harshly when his fiancée requested his net worth before their marriage. He refused to give it to her, and in return she refused to marry him. A decision I silently cheered. *Bimbo didn't deserve him.*

Simon said it wasn't her interest in the money, but her lack of trust in him. Personally, I think it was a sixth sense kicking in for him. Little did she know, Simon would have kept her in diamonds and caviar for a lifetime if that's what she wanted. He's one of those men who has a gift for paying attention. Too bad she didn't.

"What would you do if I actually said yes to Hawaii? What would your girlfriend think of such an arrangement? And what's with the new girlfriend and you not flaunting her in my face and telling me it could have been me? You must truly like this one."

He shrugs. "I don't have a girlfriend."

"Then who was that woman who kissed you in my office the other day?"

"The blonde?" He laughs. "I'm flattered you noticed."

"She kissed you in the foyer. There's not a whole lot of PDA that goes on in chiropractic offices, but maybe you haven't noticed that. So, who is she?"

He chuckles in his amiable way. "I don't know who she is. I met her in the parking lot and paid her fifty bucks to pose as my girlfriend at 9:07 a.m. She did a good job and she was right on time. I didn't think you'd buy it. I should have given her seventy-five."

"I suppose this is a crazy question, Simon, but why on earth would you do that? If you're looking for a good charitable cause, I can set you up with a natural health fund for patients who can't afford it."

He walks into the backroom of the office and sits on the table. "Have you got time for an adjustment?"

"Simon," I say, in my deep, mother voice. "You just walk in here any time you like?"

"That's right. Being first has its privileges."

"So are you going to answer me about the blonde?"

He shrugs. "I figured that if you erased the thought in your head that I was making another pass at you, you might reconsider Hawaii as the best thing for your career. I wanted to prove to you this wasn't about my crush on you, but a solid business arrangement."

I stuff another piece of chocolate in my mouth.

"That's what I figured, but really, Red, I don't know what my back will do without you, and I want to play golf year-round. I need the Aloha Spirit in my life. What good is it to retire at thirty-five if you can't do it in style?"

"Retire. How many companies have you helped start since you retired?"

"I'm only doing what I like, and I need a good back for that. Golf and business when I feel like it, that's what it's all about."

"How spiritual."

"You know the truth of that, Poppy."

And I do.

"People who have private chiropractors turn into weirdos, like Michael Jackson. I can't do that to you. I care too much for your mental health. Besides, I don't think I could be owned like that. It's too much like slavery."

"I'm not moving to Bahrain like Michael. I'm moving to Hawaii. Slavery in Hawaii?"

"I can't respect a man who retires at thirty-five."

"Spoken like a true workaholic." He leans in close to me and he smells heavenly. A touch of outdoors with the indoor clean of expensive aftershave. "I used to be just like you until the fourteenth fairway called my name. You want true natural healing, Poppy? Follow me to Oahu and get in touch with your inner golfer."

I stare into his eyes. He played me with the fake girlfriend. He doesn't work for a living—although, granted, he could still buy and sell all of us—and he wants me to leave everything for him. And the really pathetic part is that I'm considering it. I close my eyes and inhale. Somewhere along the line, I stopped being a professional with Simon. My heart is indeed involved here, and that is not good for either of our health.

"You can play year-round in California, and I'm here." I open my eyes to see if there's any reaction on his part.

He looks at my green superfood drink and comes towards the counter. He turns the cup over and empties the contents down the sink. "Why do you do that to yourself? That's why you're sneaking chocolates. Let's go to lunch."

"I don't go to lunch with patients. It's not appropriate."

"That green gunk isn't appropriate. Poppy, you're not my math teacher in high school, you're my chiropractor. Who is going to care if we go to lunch?"

"It's not right," I maintain, though inwardly, I want him to fight me. I want him to tell me it's all right until I can't help myself.

"Come on, Poppy. You need me. You're far too serious. I'll show you how to have balance in life." He winks and for the first time, it doesn't feel like an inside joke. It feels like it has meaning.

I raise my eyebrow at him. If there's one thing I'll say about Simon, he could truly sell me on most anything. There's a reason this man is successful in business. He seems to have all the answers. Don't we all want to believe someone will take care of us? But then I look at Simon's back, and I see that golf reigns in his life, to the point where he doesn't think clearly.

"Simon, did you need an adjustment?" I put a fist to my hip, trying to look annoyed.

"Don't blow me off, Poppy."

"You're a good man, but I'm not going to Hawaii for you. If it makes you feel any better, I'm not going back to Santa Cruz. So you're in good company. I'm refusing my father as well." I look at the calendar and thumb through it just to keep my eyes busy and free from Simon's boring gaze.

"What's wrong with me?" He asks and I look up at his big, brown, puppy-dog eyes. "Besides the obvious. Haven't I sent all my golf buddies to you? Come away with me, Poppy, and I'll make you a fisher of bad spines." He groans. "That was terrible humor, but my heart's in the right place."

"Nothing is wrong with you, Simon, but I'm not changing my life for you." *Not without more than being your chiropractor for life.* But as I look into his tender eyes, I have to admit if one's going to change her life for someone, it should be a decent man like him. Of course, why I don't fall is probably buried in my mother's house somewhere.

Before I asked Jeff to the wedding, Simon was my number one choice, but I worried he'd read something more into it, so I refrained. Now I feel like a complete idiot. I can't help but wonder, if I did actually risk something, might there be a lifetime to gain?

"Are you really here for an appointment?" I ask him.

He shakes his head. Emma peeks around the door. "Morgan's on the phone again."

"I have to go, Simon." I pick up the phone, pulling my hair behind my back. "Hi, Morgan. Sorry about hanging up on you." I shove yet another piece of chocolate in my mouth.

"Do you mind if we invite Jacob to meet you at the spa? He's down there for business. He grew up in Aptos. Isn't that right next to Santa Cruz? I'm telling you, Poppy, he's perfect for you."

I look at Simon and his sorrowful gaze at being ignored, and I vow to stand strong with Morgan. Whether Jacob is perfect for me or not is a moot point. Simon's expression is my first concern. I can't stand to see someone hurt, and my most loyal customer is certainly not one I wish to upset. "Yes, I do mind, actually. I found a respectable date. Let's leave it at that, shall we?"

"Oh—you were serious about that. All right, I'll make other arrangements."

"What would be the point?" I ask her.

"The point is that maybe Jacob is the one for you. He loves to run and scuba dive, and all those adventurous, outdoorsy things you like."

There's something about being forced into something that automatically makes you retreat. I mean, if he were so wonderful, he would be taken by now. Of course, he probably could say the same thing about me.

"I'm not feeling him, Morgan."

"Didn't you *feel* there was going to be a major earthquake last year on the San Andreas and the Hayward faults too?" Morgan asks with a hint of sarcasm in her tone.

I shake my head, even though she can't see me. "I just got the wrong signal that time. My emotions were off from too much work and not enough running."

"Jacob really wants to meet you, Poppy. He's a hippy, Christian, fitness boy. You have to at least meet him. I won't be able to live with myself if I don't at least introduce you two. What if he's *the one*?"

"You make him sound so attractive. Will he bring a gift of yogurt when he comes?" I see Simon move towards the door. "Simon, wait!"

"You're not listening to me," Morgan pouts. "I want you to have what Lilly and I do, Poppy."

"I want that too," I say, gazing at Simon.

He gives me one of his trademark grins. There's a cloud over his usual demeanor, and I look to the phone wondering if he heard or cared about the wedding. As Simon heads towards the door, I realize all the constants in my life are going away. Simon is only following suit, like Lilly and Morgan.

I grab his arm before he walks out the door. "Wait," I repeat.

I don't remember ever standing this close to Simon, and if energy were measurable right now, I think we'd have our own Richter Scale.

"Why?" He strides out of my office, as I listen to Morgan ramble about her impressive guest list and how her father's sins seem forgotten by her wedding responses.

Why, indeed?

"Morgan, I have to go. I have patients backing up." I hand the phone back to Emma absently, and just as I'm about to catch Simon, the door closes.

"Poppy, you've got patients," Emma reminds me. I pause at the door, but I turn around like a good girl should. One of my toughest patients awaits me, and right now, I relish the challenge. Need it.

As I was saying about natural medicine, it's a much slower process, and hence in this corporate, dog-eat-dog world where time is money, the patient loses. The symptoms are easier and far more profitable to treat.

It's not that natural medicine is more costly, it's that the time involved will never interest the insurance companies. It's a much slower process, made for my methodical mind, and it's like playing my own game of *CSI: Cupertino* with each patient. Discovering is about listening, about hearing what the patient is undergoing, and trying to find out where the symptom starts. With each treatment, each answer, you get closer to the cure. That's the beauty, and unfortunately what is so difficult for medical doctors. Maybe it was too many *Scooby Doo* mysteries as a child, but I was a meddling kid and I wanted to rip the mask off the symptoms.

Working for a doctor and filing insurance bills didn't help my disdain. All the free stuff sent to the doctor with the name of a pharmaceutical didn't help me. I'd seen what the "cure" had done to my mother, and no way was I going to be involved in that kind of business.

"Hey, Doc," Leslie, one of my first Chinese medicine clients, says as she bounces into my office. "You're not going to believe this. I'm getting married!"

"Married?" I give her a great big hug, but I'm really thinking, *Oh please don't invite me, so I have to get a date. I already ran six miles today and I'm so very tired.*

"We're getting married in Mexico this fall."

"Fabulous!" I squeal. "What's he like?"

Leslie herself is very masculine in nature. She's built like a linebacker and has blonde locks that I swear are never without black roots. I don't know when she actually dyes it, because I've never seen it fresh, or all blonde. Which of course makes me wonder why she bothers rather than keep it natural.

"Well," Leslie says. "He's a software engineer and really kind and good looking and gentle. We both love bird watching out on the Baylands and communing with nature. We're going to Mexico to rescue sea turtles, and then we're getting married afterwards on the beach!" Leslie squeals the last part.

Admittedly, my thoughts are with Simon walking out the

door. I would never hurt him on purpose, but I can't have him be my only patient either. No matter what type of future he promises for my Hawaiian spa. Usually, men just promise marriage. Not Simon; he puts his money where his spine is.

I focus back on Leslie. "Why haven't you talked about him before?" I ask. Leslie is here every week, and she is the picture of health now that I've treated her for a litany of liver-related dysfunction. She's purified herself of the damage, and she'll look like the gleaming bride she's meant to be.

"Well . . ." She looks hurt. ". . . I just met him two weeks ago, Doc. I didn't know it was going to come to this."

"Oh," I say, trying to hide my shock. The way she talked about their love of the Baylands, it sounded like they'd been together for an eternity. "You're getting married?" I try to feign my joy. But it's obvious I've just nullified a bit of her joy. Two weeks! What is this world coming to?

"I know, I know, it sounds crazy, but both our grandparents were married within a month of meeting 'the one' and we just know. So what's the wait for?"

Security.

The knowledge he's lacking mental illness.

The time to check his credit report and wedding history.

Peace of mind.

"Well, I wish you every happiness."

Leslie has the glow of a woman in love. And really, they've got bird watching in common. What more is necessary?

"We are already happy. We moved in together last week."

Lord have mercy. I am living in the wrong era.

"Well, let's get your spine set up strong for the wedding, shall we? We don't want you slouching the day of your nuptials."

Slouching while saving turtles and marrying men you barely know is definitely not a good idea.

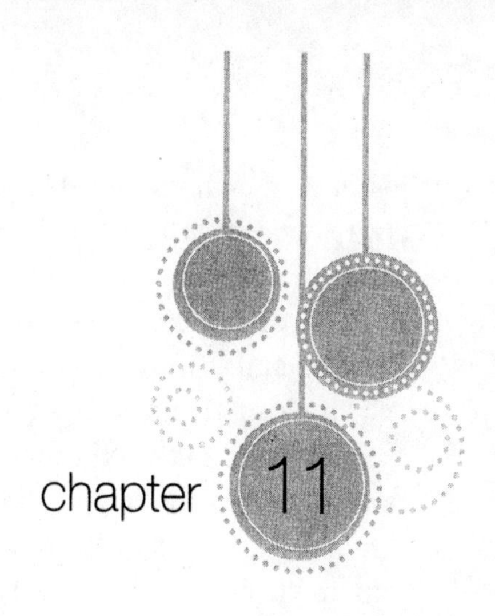

Spa Del Mar sits nestled in Central California, away from the coast but within breathing distance of the moist, salty air off the Pacific. With the stand of eucalyptus that surrounds the spa, one can just imagine the legend of Zorro come to life. It's California as it should be: pure and untouched by long expanses of concrete. This place is the antonym of Silicon Valley's hectic pace and forces me to slow down and forget the race I must complete. It reminds me that the tortoise got there eventually.

I suppose these days are coming to a close. With Lilly married and Morgan on her way to the altar, I know my Zen days will be fewer, which will be good for my spiritual life (I'll be in church more!) but bad for my workaholic side (how much easier to spend a little more time in the office!). Sure, there's something perilous about being the last one left standing. But while all my best friends have husbands to take care of, and new lives to forge, I am happy with my old one.

I stay the same.

Why can't everything else?

Morgan and Lilly enter the hotel room first with their myriad of suitcases. Apparently, Lilly is working on the wedding designs over the weekend, and Morgan . . . Well, Morgan is just a clothes horse. I bring my scrappy carpetbag that Lilly always makes fun of and drop it on the floor. Admittedly, I enjoy her reaction each time she sees the bag. It's sort of a mixture of curiosity and disgust, all rolled into one magic Elvis-lip smirk.

Plunking their things on a shared bed, my Spa Girls clear a path for me to the other one—my own private bed. In their not-so-subtle way, they're reminding me it's my turn for it. I'm the pathetic one, so have at it. It used to be a privilege to get your own bed at the Spa. Reserved for the one whose life currently sucked the most. I guess we have our answer.

"What?" Morgan asks in all innocence, noticing that I drop my suitcase with a little too much force.

"I get the bed?" I want them to tell me, *Yes, your life is the most screwed up*. "I thought you'd want it with all the wedding stress, Morgan. Or you, Lilly," I say, looking directly at her bulbous belly.

"What wedding stress? You think this is more stressful than my father going to jail? And almost taking me down with him?" she asks. "It's planning a party. I did that every week of my life. I could do this in my sleep."

"It's not like I still have any girth," Lilly comments on her oh-so-meager size.

Their sense of calm bugs me. *I'm the calm one. Don't they know that?* I'm telling you, the world has turned upside down.

"Fine, I'll take the bed." I toss my bag on the bed while Lilly opens the balcony doors and lets the smell of sulfur into our room from the steaming redwood hot tub below.

"You don't *have* to take the bed," Lilly yells over her shoulder. "We were trying to be nice. What's with you? Since when are you wound so tight?"

"Since you've both been trying so desperately to get me a date to the wedding. Since you think I need to move back home and fix some unknown issue. Since you're just not being honest with me and you suddenly think I can be fixed with the right clothes."

They both sigh like two balloons flying across the room.

"I've always thought you could be fixed with the right clothes," Lilly says with a shrug.

"So what, is this like an intervention?"

Morgan and Lilly look to one another and then back at me. "It's just that the running, the exercising, the natural food intake—it's all become a little overwhelming over the last year. You used to be the most caring person I knew, Poppy," Morgan says, with a hint of a tear in her eye. "Now, it's like you're so obsessed with the health stuff. I miss the crazy Poppy who made me laugh and didn't care what people thought. Now, it's become—well, it's almost become your religion and you're trying to convert everyone."

"I've got news for you," Lilly says. "Doritos aren't going away. They'll be like cockroaches, around long after us. Face it: preservatives taste good."

"I still don't care what people think." I unzip my duffle, pulling out my running gear. "And I haven't changed."

Lilly says. "You're different now. It used to be cute how you bucked the norm and danced to your own tune, but now it's sort of a defiance. Not sweet and appealing like it used to be."

"Maybe I'm just getting older. Maybe I'm just not sweet and cute anymore. Maybe I'm entering middle age and bitter. Did you think of that?"

The two of them laugh out loud and Lilly shoves me on the bed. "Thirty is not middle-aged, especially with 15-percent body fat."

"Fourteen," I correct her.

"See, that's what I mean. Do I walk around telling everyone my weight? Where did that come from, Poppy? You didn't have a prideful bone in your body, and all of a sudden we're getting regular updates on your body-fat ratio. What if the girl with the most hair was fabulous?" Lilly asks. "What if I came to you and told you what my head count was on a daily basis? Little strange?"

"So my body fat is the reason you want to set me up for the wedding?"

"No, that would be the intestinal talk," Morgan clarifies. "When Lilly wanted to date Colin Whatshisname in college, didn't you fix that?"

"You helped," I say. "He was only after one thing."

Morgan continues, "When my father was not acting in my best interest, didn't you scout me out and find me? I believe you even went to my church and my gym and interrogated people. Double-O Poppy, I called you."

"You were being an idiot," I remind her.

"So we're returning the favor, Poppy. When friends don't see things clearly, their best friends tell them the truth. We're telling you the truth, even though you don't want to hear it."

"Meaning what?"

"That you're getting a little odd. We think you've been inhaling too many herbs. We just want you to know up front that your fat ratio and people's organs are not wedding conversation," Morgan purrs with an up-voice at the end, as though she hasn't just been completely rude.

"And you're going to dress in the gown I've designed for you. If you stay at that weight, it's going to fit perfectly. So quit running, or eat some chocolate. I did thirty-two measurements, if you'll remember, and I don't want to do them again!"

"You're like a fashion Hitler, Lilly."

Okay, so I'm a weirdo. I'd like to say this acknowledgment bothers me, but it really doesn't. I've always been a weirdo, meaning different from the norm. My parents taught me to embrace it, and I do. But for my best friends who've seen me through the worst of life, I can keep it at bay. For one weekend, anyway.

"All right. You want me to fall in, I will."

I'm having the yin-yang balancing facial this weekend, just because I liked the sound of it. It lacks conventional wisdom, and if my friends won't let me be my true weird self, my aesthetician will. For a price.

"Very good," Morgan says. "That's all we ask. We want our friend back."

I take out my energy bar, and unwrap it, holding it up. "Want some?"

Judging by their looks, no.

I will be the perfect friend at this wedding. I will be Molly Ringwald in *Pretty in Pink*. This weekend, I want to enjoy a massage and a clear head. I'm going to try and not run every time I get nervous, and I'm going to forget there's a small exercise room downstairs. This weekend is to reconnect with my friends and God. I brought my Bible, and I'm going to forget the urge to fix everyone else's life for the next two days. This weekend is mine. I will be a selfish pig, just like any good hedonist should be at a spa. With a dash of Christian on top.

I can't stop Americans from downing Big Gulps, brimming with excess sugar the body can't tolerate or create enough insulin for. The pancreas! Oh, my agony for the pancreases of America. I can't keep people from clogging their arteries with processed foods containing hydrogenated oils. I can't even stop Lilly from sneaking Diet Pepsi and truffles into the hotel room. (She gave up pickles when she got married and pregnant. For that, I suppose I should be thankful. With all that salt, her ankles would have been the size of tree trunks. Even her emaciated, little ankles.)

"Morgan told me you had a nice aubergine-colored skirt you wore on your date," Lilly says, starting a new conversation.

"It wasn't really a date," I clarify. "My next-door business neighbor was hoping I'd be moving my practice."

"Well, your business meeting, then. My point is why is *that* skirt back here?" Lilly looks at what I'm wearing—one of my mother's skirts—and wrinkles her nose. "You know, they make soft cotton clothes that are available in one color. Why is it you have to wear them all at the same time? You're like a Persian rug over there."

I cross my arms at her. "Why do you two care so much what I wear?"

"Because we all wish we had your body, Poppy, and you waste it. Why run like that if you're not going to take advantage of it?"

"I'm modest. That's a good thing. You want me hanging out of my shirt like Kayla Havens?" I ask, referring to a college coed who, we believe, spent more time in the men's dorm than classes.

"The Bible says nothing about modesty including ugly," Lilly says. "We don't want to tempt men, but must we completely discourage them? I mean, grab a burka, Poppy. You do want to get married someday, don't you?"

I set my chin forward. "The man I marry will have no problem with my fashion choices. I don't want to marry a man who cares what I wear. That's the first step. Next thing, you're in Dr. Jeff's plastic surgery office getting a nip here and a tuck there."

"All women say they want that kind of man, but you know you don't have to completely put them to the test, do you? Even God says not to put Him to the test."

"Except in the arena of tithes. He says He'll open the floodgates of heaven for that," Morgan says.

"Thank you, Billy Graham. You know what I'd like to see," Lilly continues. "I'd like to see the man who would make you buy Prada."

"I would never buy Prada. Unlike you, I don't care if something is stitched well and I could probably feed Mongolia for the price of a purse."

"Well obviously Prada was too big of a step," Lilly says. "But you could spend a little. Buy something, perhaps, without the word *vintage* in front of it."

"People barely wear stuff in the Valley, Lilly. You can get a lot of great stuff at the secondhand store."

Lilly holds up a palm. "No, I'm not going there. Your issue isn't money; those running pants you wear cost a fortune, and you buy them at Nordstrom's. I've seen the tags."

"You are so nosy, Lilly," Morgan says.

"Like you wouldn't have looked, Morgan. Look, it's expensive to go to Hawaii and exercise, Poppy," Lilly adds. "You spend money on some things. We're not saying you need designer gear. We're just saying get rid of your mother's skirts and stop trying to make the statement you're a weirdo. You're not and you know it; you're just trying to avoid dating."

"Hawaii is a triathlon, not just a trip," I explain. "It's pushing myself to my very limits and coming out victorious on the other side. It's that high of accomplishing what I've strived so long for. There's nothing else like it."

"There's lying on the beach. Same great taste, half the effort." Lilly unclips a barrette and lets her wild hair shake loose.

"Then she wouldn't have that body, though," Morgan says.

"True, but she'd still have that red hair and those blue eyes. When we went to your fancy gym, Morgan, she was like a man magnet. She was dressed in that skirt, with moccasin boots no less. I'm telling you, she doesn't want to get married.

Men look at her like she's a piece of art in the Louvre, and does she care? No, she's like Mona Lisa wrapped in gauze. Nobody get too close."

"Hello, I'm right here," I announce.

"So prove to us you want to have a relationship," Lilly says. "Besides with your trainer."

"How would I do that? Should I get engaged to the next man who walks through the spa?"

Morgan looks down over the sulfur-laden hot tub under our balcony and snickers. We join her to see a portly, bald man looking up at us.

"He probably wouldn't care about the skirt." Lilly shrugs.

I cross my arms and whisper at the two of them. "So rude. He could be to the soul what Brad Pitt is to the eyes."

"Was that on your SAT?" Morgan asks before looking over the balcony again and giggling. "Break out the truffles, Lilly. Poppy has a date in the hot tub."

"You used to at least sneak the garbage when I was getting my spa treatment. Now you're just flaunting bad behavior in front of me."

"I'm pregnant, Poppy. If I don't eat fattening now, what's the point?" Lilly asks with her lanky hundred-pound frame with the small bump in the front.

"It's not about the fat. It's your body-fat ratio. Your skinny little self could be 30 percent fat and that's not healthy."

Lilly stares at me with her mouth open for a moment before popping a truffle inside. Whole.

"There's nothing wrong with dark chocolate," I say over crossed arms. "Magnesium is great for the digestive system—a natural laxative, actually."

"Eww!" Morgan says. "Do you have to talk about such things, Poppy? It's so unfeminine. You manage to make chocolate unpalatable. How do you do that?"

"I'm just saying if she thinks that's entirely unhealthy, it's not."

"Yeah, well, don't say," Lilly says, spitting out the chewed-up truffle into a napkin. "You take the fun out of everything."

The accusation hits me hard, because right now, it feels really truthful and I can't help myself. There's this little voice in my head that tells me how to do health right, and I can't shut it down. But I think I *need* to shut it down. Just like a true Trekkie has to shut it down after age thirty to get a date.

"So what of it—do you want to be single forever?" Lilly asks.

"I never said that." I unpack my bag into the plastic dresser painted to look like wood. "Look, Morgan, I've done a lot of prep work for your wedding and my run. After that, you all can worry about getting me a date, all right? It's not like I'm going to dry up in the next month."

I came for this last, blissful weekend with my gals, and they're putting me on the battlefield. I mean, it's not like I haven't been avoiding serious dating for ten years. Why the fuss all of a sudden?

"Then what gives, Poppy? You've had more guys ask you out than I think Morgan or I had in a lifetime, and yet you're the only one who's never had a long-term boyfriend. Why is that?"

"I guess I just get a feeling on that first date, and I haven't been interested enough to follow through. I'm not avoiding relationships. Quit acting like I need to be diagnosed. I'm just single, that's all. I don't want to marry just anybody."

"So that means Dr. Jeff is a *why bother*?"

Is he ever. "I have no respect for that man or what he does. How desperate do you think I am? Jeff Curran is about as mainstream as a person can go. And besides, I think he might go to church to get business. My mother would be horrified that I even spent time with a plastic surgeon. I feel guilty still. And I even dressed up for the occasion."

"See, I think you and Dr. Jeff do have a lot in common and you don't want to admit it. You both think you're the answer to everyone's problems. He cares about his patients and their perfection just like you do. The only difference is he obsesses on the outside, and you go for the inside. And you were going to be a medical doctor until . . . well, you know."

"There's a reason I didn't become an MD, and therefore dating one has the same problem for me. Look, I know you both want to find me romance, but trust me on this, Dr. Jeff is not it."

"Okay, so no go on Dr. Jeff; we're good with that. What about one of these guys?" Morgan hands me a folder. "I printed out a bunch of men from the Yahoo! Personals that I thought sounded a lot like you. Look, this one is a runner and a swimmer and he's pretty hot."

"Online dating?" I push the folder back at her. *It hasn't come to that, has it? Now they want me to become so Silicon Valley that the only way I can meet a guy is through the computer?*

"Hey, the good news is that the guys over the Internet can't see the skirt," Lilly quips.

"So how will I know if they pass the first test?" I ask. "Maybe I want them to look past the skirt."

"Men don't notice clothes, anyway. They only care what's underneath them." Morgan shrugs.

"Morgan! That sounded like something Lilly would say."

"It's true. The men don't care if she wears that ugly skirt. They see her red hair, and they lose it. They always have. Even that senator's son at Stanford. He went crazy for beatnik Poppy."

"Morgan!" I yell again. "What are you turning into? Lilly?"

She pauses, smoothing her pretty blonde hair and blinking her wide eyes. "Well, Poppy, do you think that skirt is pretty? That you're adorning yourself in any way? Do you think it makes you appealing?" she asks.

I look down at my mother's dingy skirt and notice just how many strings are hanging from its hem. "I suppose not, but my mother thought it was more important to care about the earth and its inhabitants than arbitrary things like clothing. Daddy too. At least at one time." I think about my dad's love of Sharon and her well-sculpted over-fifty body, always dressed like a Christmas package. Neatly wrapped and with all the accessories to look special. "My father may have forgotten, but I haven't."

"She's impossible." Lilly shakes her head. "Poppy, our mothers are gone too. You can't keep her around with her ugly skirts. Morgan can't keep her mother around through her jewelry, and I can't keep mine around period. Your dad loved your mother. He didn't betray her by marrying someone different after she died. You need to get over it."

We all sit around staring at each other for a moment. We're probably thinking about our mothers, how Lilly's slipped off into a new life and left her with a grandmother, Morgan's succumbed to a horrible cancer after a horrific marriage, and mine slipped into a diabetic coma, never to wake again because of the dangers of sugar and insulin.

"Well, this is depressing," Lilly finally says. "Let's go shopping and get you some clothes. We'll burn that thing when we get back. It will be symbolic. Our new life starts now. We start our families, you start trying to not scare men."

For a moment, I'll admit I'm tempted. I liked the way I felt out the other night with Jeff. Well, except for the getting blindsided and the pantyhose stuck to my toes because my shoes were too big. Other than that, I liked the skirt and the heels. It was a good calf exercise too. It was a workout just to walk. A little yoga involved in keeping my balance, even.

I slip off my shoe and show off my neatly painted pink toenails. "I'm making progress every day." Generally, when we stop for our pedicures on the way to the spa, I avoid color. Today, rather than pearl, which Lilly calls wheat, I picked bright pink. I feel almost scandalous.

"We thought you were painting your toenails for a guy," Morgan says, her frown apparent.

I don't explain that I only get the pedicures for them. I personally could do without someone touching my feet and painting a toxic colored shell on my nails, but I know when to back down. Everyone seems to love pedicures, so I figure I should at least find a way to enjoy the experience. The pink was just one more way to show them I could play. Here I'm feeling like Gwen Stefani and they're disappointed.

"Would it make you two feel better to make me over? To know you'd done everything you could possibly do to get me married?"

They both nod.

"Okay, so the pink isn't cutting it. Go ahead, make me over. I have nothing to fear." I sit down on the balcony and cross my arms.

The two of them are like two plucky birds planning their next move and chattering excitedly. "First, we're putting you in makeup," Morgan says. "Just a little light powder foundation. Nothing heavy."

I sit in the chair while Morgan takes out a compact, hands me a mirror, and smothers my face with a pasty beige film. "See? Very simple, and you've completely evened out your tone." Then Morgan breaks out the mascara. "Your eyes are incredible, but they need mascara to stand out."

"Don't forget the eyeliner," Lilly adds. "Just think, if you weren't busy wearing that colored sack, people would truly see you. You might find someone like Max," she says about her husband.

"Or George," Morgan says about her fiancé.

I look into their faces, and I remember when they too had no hope and spent lots of evenings on bad dates, getting set up with old men and worse, but my current mood wins out. "But you know, the guy could be allergic to cats."

"Look up," Morgan commands while finishing my mascara.

"And you could fix that with your voodoo," Lilly says, referring to the allergy relief acupressure that I practice.

"All right, let's see what you've got." I laugh, reaching for the folder with the online dating possibilities, though my hopes couldn't be any lower. Computer dating? Where's the chemistry in that? I take a deep breath and force myself to think positively. My soul mate could be in this folder. "This is just like take-out. Only a guy comes with the pizza. I'll take tall, dark, and handsome with a side of anchovies."

"That's when you get one from Russia." Morgan says, and considering she was once engaged to a Russian consulate, it makes me wonder how much truth there is to her comment. "This is different. This is simply online dating."

"These guys are more afraid of commitment since they don't get a green card with each purchase," Lilly says.

My friends, helpful as always, have printed out several bios. I rifle through each page with a disappointed frown. "Every one of these guys says they want an athletic woman." I scrunch my face up at the sight of the word over and over again:

Athletic.

Must be Athletic.

Slender and athletic.

You: an athlete. Me: your partner in sports.

I'm into kayaking, hiking and conquering the next mountain. You're there with me.

Um, no. I'm not.

"So what if they want athletic," Lilly shrugs. "You're athletic."

"But you're not reading what they're really selling. Look at this guy, he must be 275 pounds. Bowling is not a sport, and he's not athletic. What he's saying is you must be skinny and look like a model, even if I resemble a human warthog. These men are single because they think they've bought the Cinderella fairy tale in reverse. Only they aren't Prince Charming, and they most certainly don't have a kingdom. But by golly, she better have tiny feet, fit into the glass corset, and worship the ground he walks on. They grew up on Bond, and they believe it."

"You're cynical," Lilly accuses. "And coming from me, that's saying something, because I'm cynical."

"Tiny feet are a qualification you still meet," Morgan offers. "What's the problem?"

"You don't get it—*athletic* is simply a thesaurus word for *thin*. No fat chicks need apply. And while I may not have that issue, I do not want to hook up with someone who values their women solely by the exterior. These men are shallow. These men are why Dr. Jeff has a practice."

"You don't know that; maybe they're just wishful thinkers. Come on, tell me if you made your list, it wouldn't say '*Looks like Johnny Depp and understands the way the intestinal system functions.*'"

"Lilly!"

"Look at this guy. He says he's a Christian and looking for his Proverbs 31 woman."

I grab the paper. "He's forty-seven, Morgan. If he hasn't found her by now, he may as well be looking for his Proverbs 54 woman because she's not out there."

She grabs the paper. "Sorry, I missed that. He doesn't look that old."

"He probably got the picture from the J. C. Penney catalog."

"Look, if you don't want to get married, that's fine Poppy. We respect that," Lilly says. "But what we don't respect is your spending every day running farther and faster to nothing. Your body-fat percentage is not a worthy life's goal; you're better than that, Poppy."

"But these guys are looking for *America's Next Top Model* while they themselves belong on *The Biggest Loser*. Men seem to have this special mirror. In it, they are all Bond, James Bond, and looking for their Bond girl. When they're Christian, make that the Proverbs 31 Bond Girl."

"Not every guy is that shallow. You're reading too much into that; you're not giving them a chance."

"Look at this. He says, 'No one under 5'3".'"

"You're five-nine," Lilly reminds me.

"This guy is five-six if he's a foot." I hold up the picture.

"But maybe he has the soul of the Christian Ghandi," Morgan says encouragingly.

I hand her back the folder. "I just think when I'm ready, I'll be ready. I'm not ready. Not for this, anyway. I'm still recovering from my so-called date with Jeff. Which cost me my office space."

She takes the folder and sighs. "So your life's goal is what? A clean digestive tract?" Lilly lifts her lip in disgust. "At least have a purpose. Then we'll leave you alone. If you want to go to the deserts of Africa and preach, we'll support that. If you want to straighten the most crooked spines in all of India, we'll support that, help you raise funds even. But if you want to hide out in that little office of yours and pretend the fun girl in college never existed, want to hide her away in ugly skirts so she won't get hurt again . . . ? Yeah, we're not into that."

"You need to go back to Santa Cruz and finish this," Morgan says.

I look at their sincerity and the depth in their gazes and I love these women. But I don't think Santa Cruz is going to solve a thing. I left that history there. Only the skirts came with me.

Really.

chapter 12

My favorite skirt disappeared this weekend. Of course, I have more than a subtle idea where it went, but it's missing just the same. In its place, Lilly left me something she made for me in hopes that my hippy style might disappear. I like what she left me. It's comfortable and fashionable. Apparently peasant skirts are back, and she made me one in a soft, buttery-cream cotton. Truly, I feel like myself with a touch of princess, and I want to spin like a little girl in her first Easter dress.

As I unlock the office door, I hear giggling and look at Jeff's office to see the blonde from the convertible exiting. That girl is trouble personified and she's everywhere. I let myself into the office and slam the door behind me. *Men are so clueless.* The last time I saw her she was kissing Simon for fifty bucks. In my day we had a name for that. Wrap something up in a beautiful package, and men's IQs fall to single digits. I'm not jealous, just sort of disappointed Jeff is no better than that. Now, not only is he missing fruit, but he's a little nutty to boot.

I sit down at my desk and hear a small knock at the door. Moving the curtain aside, I see Jeff standing outside. "Can I come in?" he shouts through the door. I open it, crossing my arms at Mr. Flirtation. And on a Sunday, no less. "I assume that door slam was for me?" he asks.

"Don't flatter yourself."

"So it's true what they say about the fiery redhead. You're a jealous one then? How exciting." He rubs his hands together.

"Jealous of what? I'm just mad you took my parking space. It's Sunday. Don't you ever go home? Get yourself a life, and all that?"

"I thought we agreed that it was *my* parking space. One blonde and the deal's off, huh? Women. I'll never understand them. You basically told me I was human vermin the other night. What do you want from me, Poppy?"

"I didn't know the parking deal extended to weekends," I say, trying to dig myself out of this hole. What is that little part in women where we take ownership of someone? Even when we don't really want them and when they're perfectly free to marry another? In the back of my mind I can't help but think he's my date for the wedding, and can he not be flirtation-celibate for a few measly weeks? I hate that I care what he does, but my mouth just betrays me when he's around. I say things I can't imagine myself saying and all sense of peace goes out the window.

"Are you going to church tonight?" he asks me. We go to a megachurch that has a huge Sunday night singles group. I go for the worship and sit in the back, sneaking out early before the migration to the hamburger and pizza joints kicks in, while Jeff seems to be right in the middle of everything, passing out business cards at after-church events and being as friendly as possible. He's a regular Mae West. *Come on up and see me sometime.*

"I'm going. After I finish a little paperwork," I say with as little expression as possible.

"Do you want to drive together?"

Why would I want to do that? "In that thing?" I ask, staring at his Lexus.

"It's my car. I don't have a glass carriage around the corner if that's what you're waiting for."

"Who's the blonde?"

He smiles slightly, "She's a pharmaceutical saleswoman who's selling more than the product. I'm not buying, in case you're interested."

"I'm not. She works on weekends?"

"But if you were interested in me, not the pharmaceuticals, would it bother you?"

I poke my hair behind my ear. "Why would it?" I ask, meeting his gaze.

"I don't know." His usual bravado disappears from his voice and he shrugs. "I was a bit hopeful, I guess. It's not everyday a redhead looks my way."

"We can be friends, can't we?" I ask, hoping to wave the white flag. I know we both feel this chemistry, but I'm also practical. In addition to finding him incredibly attractive, I also think he's the scourge of the earth.

"You know, Poppy, plastic surgeons aren't met with any more grace in church than an alternative healing expert. I know that you think I look down on you for what you do, and maybe I have had an attitude, but I get the same thing. It's no different for me."

"I think it is. You're a doctor, and therefore a catch at church, regardless of what you do with your day."

He exhales deeply. "I'd like to be respected for what I do, Poppy, not just looked at like a Christian wallet for someone."

"What about the four kids and the barefoot-and-pregnant thing?"

"I think you're remembering that a little differently than I might have said it," he laughs. "I want four kids, and I believe in traditional roles. I assume that's what you're speaking of?"

Something about the way he says this pierces my heart as I realize I have been aiming a spear straight at *his* heart. I've wanted to bring him down, put him in his place. In short, I've wanted to make him feel like others have made me feel.

Words elude me as I realize the truth. My life verse booms in my head: *the human spirit can endure in sickness, but a crushed spirit who can bear?* I can't speak as I remove the plank from my eye. *Is it wrong to want a woman to stay home and be a mother to your children? Or just to admit it in this day and age?*

Jeff continues trying to justify himself to me, and with each word, I feel its crushing blow to my own ego and the attacks I've made on him. "I have a calling, Poppy. Just like you, and it doesn't fit neatly into the puzzle. We're two leftover pieces. In a world of engineers and marketing experts, we're two freaks of nature trying to serve out our purpose here until the Lord returns."

I try to recover. "I bet you say that to all the girls."

He smiles widely. "I love surgery, Poppy. For a surgeon, it's all about the surgery. There's the paperwork and the set up and the consultations, but when I get into surgery, I come alive. Every time I want to do better than the last time. I want my patient to thrive after their procedure. I want each cut to be neater than the last, and each scar smaller than the first. You may not cut people open, but I know you understand the high that comes from fixing something a patient has struggled with. It's a triumph."

I nod in understanding. What he says actually makes sense to me, and suddenly, I hear his fruit. The fruit of the spirit I've been so quick to judge. "It *is* a triumph."

He grabs my hands, and I don't flinch or back away. In his steely blue eyes, I see the exact rejection I've felt myself.

"Finish up your work, and we'll head out and have some dinner after church. I've got a surgery to plan in my mind. I like to go through it in my head before I'm in the operating room and—"

"Jeff," I start to shake my head.

"So I'll be back. Don't say no, Poppy. I'm trying here." He slams the door behind him, then opens it up again. "By the way, I love your skirt. It's new again."

Lilly said men didn't notice clothes. I nod.

"You look happier in it," he says.

My head snaps up as he says this. "I do?"

"You do. Give me an hour?" he asks while backing away.

I nod. "That should work."

As he walks away, I lean against the door. I'm heading for a fall, and I'm smart enough to know it, and powerless to stop it. Three more weeks until the wedding, but how long can I play normal? And what if I start to believe it?

chapter 13

Miles run: 8
Laps swum: 0
Desperation scale: 9

I am a fraud. For someone who supposedly embodies all things natural, lying is a toxic emotion. And worse yet, I'm lying to myself trying to pretend I'm someone I'm not to please Morgan and Lilly.

I feel like I'm being picked up for my prom as I wait for Jeff to finish his work and drive us to church. I want to be as nice as possible to make up for my past behavior. His real estate issues not withstanding, I have my own conscience to answer to. My heart pounds when I see him come out of his office, and I fling myself in my office chair to act as though I'm working. There's no knock at the door, so I get up and peek out the curtains and see him letting himself back into his office.

Sigh.

My cell phone rings at this point, and it's a number I don't recognize. I think twice before answering, but my curiosity gets the best of me. Like curiosity did anything for my cat, Safflower, when she climbed that tree. It did get *me* a single date with a fireman, but it did little for Safflower. Come to think of it, the guy was a jerk, so it really did nothing for me either. But I digress.

"Hello," I answer.

"Hi, Poppy Clayton?" It's a man's voice. A deep and resonate voice. Definitely not the jerk fireman.

"This is Poppy." I fan my skirt out over the office chair.

He clears his throat. "You don't know me, but your friends Morgan and Lilly . . . They suggested I call you."

My stomach drops. Oh my gosh, they didn't give my name out to some "looking for athletic/skinny" guy online, did they? I'm not thinking of health at the moment. At least, not theirs!

But the voice continues. "I met Max while jogging on the beach—"

"Oh," I say with a sense of relief. "It's you." Running man from the nude beach.

"I hope you don't mind my being forward, but when I met Max, he just went on and on about you, Poppy. How much you loved to work out, eat right, and that you really enjoyed the beach."

"And I like piña coladas and getting caught in the rain," I joke. Badly.

"What?" he asks.

"Nothing." Morgan and Lilly are just asking that I be good for three days: the couples' shower, the rehearsal dinner, and the reception. I can do this. I can keep my mouth quiet about all things health. Even with a plastic surgeon on my arm.

"You're a drinker?" he asks.

"No, I'm not a drinker. What?" I'm confused.

"What's with the piña coladas?"

"It's a song. Piña coladas . . . getting caught in the rain . . . Remember?" He doesn't remember. He's probably twenty-two, but Morgan and Lilly are counting on me, so I push away any thoughts of doubt. Let their dreams of grandeur continue until they're both well married.

"Oh, right, that song," he says with false laughter. "Well listen," he continues. "I was sort of hoping we might get to know each other before the wedding. Maybe have an evening or two out. Maybe we could take a jog along the beach or I could come there, and you could show me where you run."

I'm not telling an unknown where I run. I don't care how well he knows Max. Suddenly, it occurs to me that Mr. Piña Colada is taking a lot of liberties with our future. And as far as I'm concerned, we have no future. I'll admit my mind goes back to Jeff "He's going to break my heart" Curran. And Simon "Already broke my heart" Jennings. But there it is. Apparently, Lilly did not pass on the information that I already had a date, and I have a feeling it wasn't a mistake on her part. It's her editorial on my choice.

"The wedding?" I ask. "You mean Morgan's wedding?" I clarify.

"I thought it would be nice to get to know one another before the wedding. They tell me that you're incredibly beautiful, so I hope you're not too disappointed meeting me. I'm not much of a looker myself."

This makes my face feel hot. "I think you're the one who might be disappointed. These are my best friends telling you that, remember." *Come on, Jeff, where are you?*

"They showed me a picture. I think that I trust them."

I feel my stomach tingle at the compliment. But that does not change the fact that I never agreed to any wedding date without meeting the guy—and where there once was none (wedding dates), currently there are two. I may not be a math genius, but this I know to be an issue.

Max jogs on Ocean Beach, the nude one near the zoo. I

have to make sure this guy was wearing clothes when they met. But of course, I doubt Max would jog willingly with a naked guy, so that's probably not a real issue.

"Uh," I stammer. "Meeting you. Yeah, that would be good. What's your name again?" I try to ask this as nicely as possible, but it's always a rude question when you should know someone's name.

"Jacob Frawley. I'm a scuba diving instructor. Lilly said she told you about me."

I can tell his voice is tentative, and I'm not putting him at ease, which makes me feel an inch tall. I want to put Jacob at ease, but blast it, I keep thinking about the house in Santa Cruz, the disappearance of my twenty-year-old skirt, and being a bridesmaid yet again. A girl only has so much capacity.

I finally find my voice. "Of course I remember, Jacob. It's sweet of you to call. I'm bringing a friend of mine to the wedding." I want to give the man a chance to get a date and not be bullied by Morgan and Lilly. I'm used to it, but this guy is fresh meat.

"It's not a favor, Poppy. Is that what you think?" he asks. "Does your friend want to come?"

"Jacob, you have a very gentle way about you." Unlike my friends, who seem to have as much sensitivity as a Mack truck. "Morgan and Lilly can be quite persuasive and I didn't want you to feel blindsided. I've asked a friend to come with me to the wedding and we're looking forward to it. I'm in the wedding, so I wouldn't be able to spend much time with you anyway."

"The truth is," Jacob says, "I've always had a thing for Maureen O'Hara, so for me, this night is like starring in a John Wayne movie. I get the redhead."

Well, he's brutally honest, I suppose. A little scary, but honest. And I must admit I've heard the Maureen O'Hara thing a few times before.

"So how about it? Running this Saturday, maybe? Then maybe a light breakfast afterwards? Your friend coming to the wedding isn't a boyfriend, I'm assuming."

Oh, that I had the ability to lie well. "No, it's just a friend."

I can do this, I think, as I frantically search for an excuse. Sometimes, there's just the knowledge that this isn't the future for you, and I'm more than confident of that emotion.

However, I can play normal for a Saturday with a friend of Max's.

Jacob's probably fabulous and he'll teach me to scuba dive.

I'm worrying over nothing.

"Sure. A run sounds great. How about a week from Saturday? I have a fitting up in the city this Friday night, and I don't want to be too tired." Well, actually that's not true; I'm actually hoping to find the perfect excuse by then.

"I'll get directions from Lilly and Max. I'm just stoked to find someone to run with. It's about time a girl was really athletic."

Stoked? Athletic? *Ugh.*

After the stoked comment, Sammy Hagar Jr. hangs up. Without a good-bye. I let my head fall to the desk and groan. If my friends think this guy is me in pants, they don't think much of me. I am more than the sum of running and a crush on Johnny Depp. *I am!* And I haven't used the word *stoked* since junior high school.

I barely hang up when my cell trills again. This time, it's Lilly.

"Hi, Lilly."

"Did he call?" she pants.

"Yes, he called," I deadpan.

"Did you *love* him? He is so sweet, Poppy. You're going to love him. You two can eat at those sprout places you like. It's going to be perfect. He can teach us all to scuba dive, and we can vacation together with the kids in Hawaii. Morgan and I can be cows on the beach while you see how far you can run. It's going to be fabulous." She starts to hum "The Wedding March."

"Okay, Lilly, you're scaring me. I agreed to one running date with Nudist Man because you two are nagging, but this is scaring me."

"Nudist Man?"

"Didn't Max meet him on Ocean Beach?"

"People aren't nude there anymore, Poppy. When's the last time you were there, 1984?"

"Maybe. Regardless, he's really not my type, Lil. I can tell."

"How can you tell on the phone?"

"He used the word *stoked*. And he didn't know that song 'If You Like Piña Coladas.'"

"You know, I'm not even going to ask."

"That's fine, but do I have to go running with this guy? He creeps me out. Like those guys who drove Camaros in high school."

"He's not like that."

"What does he drive?"

"I don't know. You're going running; what does it matter? May I remind you that you're driving a Subaru? Just have an open mind. You can trust Morgan and me."

"Can I? Tell me this much: do you think he's handsome?"

"Since when do you care about a guy's looks?" Lilly asks.

"So I take it that's a no."

"He's not my type, Poppy."

"Is Dr. Jeff in the office next door your type?"

"No, too pretty," Lilly says.

"Do you think *he's* handsome?"

"That's not a fair question. That was a trick."

"You set me up with a dork, Lilly, who still uses the word *stoked*. Come on. Isn't it enough I have a chaperone for the wedding already?"

"Max likes him. We're thinking about long-term. And quite frankly, we know you and Jeff will fight. He'll say something about Botox, and you'll go into your botulism mantra, and it will be worse than if we let you loose on the wedding's general population armed with probiotics and green elixirs."

"Did I miss something? I'm agreeing to one date with Scuba Doo before Morgan's wedding because, apparently, you don't trust me to mingle. This way I'll have a date and a spare. People come to my office, Lilly, and they pay perfectly good money for my expertise. You think I can't mind myself for four hours of my life."

"Well, you and Jeff fight a lot, Poppy. This guy is really open to all that natural stuff. We know you'll like him, Poppy. We don't want to make you miserable. We want you to enjoy yourself. You need to get out more, have more fun, start dressing like you're friends with a popular San Francisco designer," she says, referring to herself. "Wait, what do you mean you have a date?"

"I told you I'm going with Jeff."

"But you weren't serious."

"Oh, but I was."

"Poppy, he's from the Dark Side. You said so yourself."

"But I also dress in a twenty-year-old skirt, and you take what I say seriously? Why?"

"Not anymore, you don't."

"Yeah, about that. You stole my skirt, and I want it back, do you understand?"

"Listen, do you know how long I've been wanting to do that? You never take it off."

"Lilly!"

"Do you ever wash that thing? I mean, I know you're all anti-detergent and everything."

"I am not anti-detergent. I just believe in using environmentally responsible detergent."

"I like bleach myself. Sucking in that smell . . . Ah, it's better than Lysol. When the whole house has the aroma, it announces clean to your neighbors. My Nana would clean the day she made sauce. Now that's Pavlovian—bleach and spaghetti sauce. It makes me hungry just to think about it."

"That's not good for you, all that bleach. You probably made your hair curlier with all those inhalants."

"Yeah well, the baby doesn't like all those smells, and I don't want to hurl every five minutes, so I've given up my clean scents, okay? Now I go for manageable. You'd be proud of me. I'm using organic cleaners because I can handle them."

"I've told you a million times, the reason smells bother you is an overgrowth of bad bacteria to your good bacteria. You need more yogurt or probiotics. The baby will probably need them too. You should start now so your baby isn't born with a sugar issue."

"And you, dear Poppy, need a life. Which is why I took the skirt. I'm holding it hostage. You go to Morgan's wedding with said plastic surgeon and you're a nice girl and you don't tell the mayor that he needs liver support or that his wife shouldn't bleach her teeth, we'll give you the skirt back."

"Blackmail. And after all I've done for you."

Lilly is a walking bag of insecurities and yet she has the nerve to touch on my confidence. I'm slightly annoyed, but she's not done yet.

"You stopped me from dating the infamous Colin in college. I'm only returning the favor." Lilly goes right back to her current favorite subject: my future with Mr. Piña Colada.

"Did you have a lot in common with Jacob? Besides the running and health stuff?"

"Well, I don't know, really. I mean, maybe we both had salmon for dinner once. But I didn't see a lot connecting, you know? I learned he has a John Wayne fetish and he likes to run. Other than that, I can't really say I learned a thing about him. I don't think you should be thinking of designing my bridesmaid's dresses just yet."

"Wasn't he sweet, though?" Lilly asks.

"He was . . . sweet. Sure. But what makes you so sure I want to date myself? You keep telling me he's just like me. What if we're both bad wedding guests and he scares off my normal date, and then we're left on our own? What if you're only squaring my attendance and he's weird cubed? What then?"

"Poppy, you promised."

I did promise. And I wouldn't do anything to hurt my Spa Girls. Even if it meant allowing someone's liver to go unchecked when their coloring is yellow. I can do this. "I gotta run. I have to get some work done before I head to church, and then over the hill."

"You're going to Santa Cruz? Tonight?"

"My dad said the house is empty, and I want to see how much work there is to do before I put it on the market. If I know my father, it's plenty. I'm thinking I'll sleep there, train in the morning, and work during the evenings until it's done."

"You're really going to sell it?"

"Why wouldn't I? Listen, Jeff's going to be here in a few minutes. I have to go."

"Jeff? Dr. 90210 from next door?"

"Yes, the plastic surgeon. My appropriate date."

"You're not going alone with him into that house?"

Her fears make me laugh. She's not worried about me

facing my history. She's more worried I'll do it with my complete and utter opposite. "No, we're just going to church together. Relax."

"Poppy."

"I'll be fine."

I hang up the phone, thankful, actually, that the trouble of finding a date for the wedding is gone. I mean, what does it matter? No one cares. There will be all these San Francisco socialites, and their tongues will be wagging about Morgan's father in jail, her dead Hollywood B-star mother, and of course her early entry into motherhood with George's Downs Syndrome son. There won't be anyone looking at me. I'll be that one line in the society page: "Morgan Malliard with attendants fashion designer Lilly Jacobs Schwartz and an *unnamed friend.*"

So this is it for me. This is my stop. Where I get off. Just me and Safflower and a house that haunts me like an unseen heartbeat.

chapter 14

I miss my favorite skirt. Not just a little bit, mind you, but as though a piece of me is missing. As I wait for Jeff, I realize I'm not in my comfort zone here. That skirt was like a second skin. But more than that, it's who I became. I saw myself in that skirt. Even now, looking in the mirror, I see a mirage of the colors, though I'm clearly wearing the cream skirt Lilly made me. The longer I wait for Jeff, the more I realize this facade isn't working for me. I slip out of the skirt and step into my running pants and Stanford sweatshirt.

Coming out of the office and knowing I look like I'm headed for the trees, I refuse to look into a mirror. There's this niggling within me that reminds me I don't want to send Jeff any type of message that I care what he thinks. I'm glad he's going to the wedding with me; I'm glad we'll be a desirable couple by all outside appearances. But truthfully, I wonder if my friends aren't starting to reject me already. They've always known how I dressed, how I dated, what was important to me. Why all of a sudden do they expect me to bend to their idea of normalcy? As if Lilly's hair fetish and Morgan's princess ways were ever normal to begin with.

My spa weekend has only served to stress me out further. Spa Del Mar's new masseuse didn't know her acupressure points and kept pushing all the wrong spots. I wanted to grab her hand and show her the right way, but I refrained. I seethed silently instead. Well, I mostly refrained, after I corrected her a few times. She got annoyed, and all I could think was, *Honey, think about the poor clients who are paying for the yin-yang massage with neither the yin nor the yang!*

I look at my watch, and Dr. Jeff is definitely late. He said an hour, it's been ninety minutes, and while that may not seem like much in doctor time, to me, it's made us late for church. Well, not exactly late, but later than I want to be to get settled. I glance at my watch one last time and become disgusted with myself. *Like I need some big, strong man to rescue me. Please.*

I open the door and look both ways. Jeff is nowhere to be seen, so I sneak out into the dark night, locking my office door behind me. I climb into the Subaru and start it up, noting that Jeff's office light still burns bright. I'd feel rejected if I wasn't so relieved.

As I'm pulling out of the parking lot, a dark shadow crosses the darkness before my car, and I slam on the brakes. My heart is in my throat as I see the muscular frame of Jeff, mere inches from my front bumper. I've killed my car from letting out the clutch so suddenly, so I start it up again and roll down the window.

"Are you crazy?" I yell out the window. "You about gave me a heart attack."

"That's guilt, not your heart, and that's a medical opinion."

"You should know," I counter.

"You were going to be a no-show. Here I was going to drive you to church, even treat you to tofu after the service, and you were just going to dismiss me. Like we never even talked earlier. Do you think the blonde would do that to me?"

"Where did you come from?" I ask through ragged breaths,

my hand still clutching my chest. *Sheesh, he scared the daylights out of me.*

"I was just locking up the front door when I saw you get in your car." He pushes a button, lighting up his watch. "I was a half an hour late. Why didn't you just knock on the door, Poppy? I know you have an idea what that time means in doctor time."

"I figured you had better things to do. Doctor time being so valuable and all. I'll bet you're ready to bill me now, just for waiting."

He walks around to the window that I'm yelling out of and puts his hand over the window's ledge. "Park your car. We're going to church in style, which unfortunately rules out the thought of a fake SUV in most people's mind."

"This is a nice car. I got it for a great price from some skier who took it to Tahoe twice a year." I pat the steering wheel. "Yes sir, great deal and it's all mine."

"I'm sure there's a jealous cross-country skier out there somewhere."

Looking up at him, I can feel his warm breath, he's so close. His expression makes me smile. Jeff and I may be an experiment in differences, but in a lot of ways we understand one another and can laugh at our opposite natures. Of course, I question if peace at any price is really peace. "I'll meet you there, all right? I don't want the singles seeing me drive up in a fancy sports car. They'll get the wrong impression of what I'm about."

"I don't think they will, actually. I think you're just afraid you might get attached to luxury. Do you get some sort of high from standing out in a pseudo SUV in Silicon Valley?"

I rev the car's engine to show him I'm ready to leave, and he laughs.

"It's a Subaru, Poppy. It lacks the effect you're going for.

Come on over; I'll show you what really revving an engine should sound like." He laughs, and I rev my engine again. It's a perfectly reasonable sound. My car rocks, thank you very much.

"Do you know," I ask him, "that a bigger engine puts more smog in the air? With global warming—"

"Poppy, you're freaking me out. Go park your car and let's go." He motions towards my parking spot. "We're late as it is. I got wrapped up in work, but sitting here arguing isn't helping the matter."

"We? There's no we. And we're late because of you. I'll meet you at church."

"I thought you said there was no we?" He laughs at me. "No," he says, opening the car door. "We're going together. You have to practice being with me for the wedding dates, anyway."

I thin my eyes at him. Since when has a guy ever wanted a practice date? He thinks I was born yesterday. "I'll meet you there." I try to wrestle the door from his clutches and finally pull it shut.

"Now who's bad for the environment? Two cars to the same church? *Tsk, tsk.* Those toxins are on your head. What is that? Two acres of rainforest?"

"I'm going to Santa Cruz after the service. I have to check on something, so it's a matter of practicality. I wasn't thinking ahead earlier."

"I can go to Santa Cruz tonight. Katie is always up for a trip to the ocean. She purrs like a kitten over that hill."

"Katie?"

"My car."

"You *named* her?"

"People understand me better when I say that Katie needs a checkup. It's a built-in excuse. They don't know if I'm getting my daughter to the doctor or my pet to the vet. It's a great cover."

"And you think *I'm* weird?"

"I do, actually. But I like you, anyway, Poppy, and I always have. Even when you were mean to me and pulled my hair—I mean, parked in my spot. There's something intriguing about a woman who never changes her clothes. Think of all the money a guy could save with a girl like you. Doctors appreciate practical women. I assume you just have to feed the cat. You do have a cat?"

"I change my clothes!" *They just all look the same.* "And yes, I do have a cat. Her name is Safflower and when she graces me with her presence, she's fabulous."

Jeff leans in on the window frame, "So what's going on in Santa Cruz? Do I get to see the house that Dr. Poppy grew up in?"

"Jeff, let's keep this business shall we? You get your office space, I get my wedding date. My friends are happy, you're happy, everyone's happy."

"Except maybe you."

Truer words were never spoken. "Global warming can wait." I gun my engine, which sounds plenty powerful to me, and pull away from Jeff, leaving him standing in the parking lot alone. I catch a glimpse of his outline, with his arms open to the sky in question, in my rearview mirror. But I feel no guilt. Well, very little guilt, anyway.

As I leave, I reassure myself I've just escaped a bondage of my own making. Jeff is one of those temptations a woman over thirty just shouldn't trust herself with. He has all the right words, makes all the right emotions bubble up within me, and I think a healthy distance is my way out from under a disaster in the making. With Jeff's charm, and those devastating blue eyes, and me in yet one more bridesmaid dress, there's no telling what could happen.

Arriving at the church, there's a line waiting for parking spots, and I take my place in it, putting in an Enya CD and trying to retreat to my place of peace. Someone pounds on my window and about knocks me into the backseat. I push the window button only to be bellowed at. "You're in the wrong line!"

"For a parking spot?" I ask.

"Yes," he shouts. "Over there! Over there!" He's pointing and doing a little dance, to show he means it.

"Let's not get too excited, sir. This is church." And me, without my lavender spray. He could use a squirt.

"Move! You're blocking traffic!" he yells again.

Why this suddenly breaks my resolve, I don't know, but it does and I steer my car around the screaming man, who by now is red as a beet and still dancing. As I pull around him, I roll down my window. "Before church, you might want to consider anger management." *Sheesh, or a heaping helping of Prozac.* And this is from someone against drug intervention, unless chemically necessary, of course. With this guy, I'd write the prescription myself if I could.

I pull out of the parking lot, and for some reason, my childhood comes nipping at my toes like a rogue wave. Somehow I want to go home. I want to walk into my Santa Cruz existence and leave this one behind. Granted, it's just an idiot in the parking lot, but his energy has me unable to walk into church tonight. Seeing Jeff with his normal, Sunday-night harem of women who want to marry a doctor won't help matters.

I drive in a trance for forty-five minutes before my head clears and I can finally hear the music in my CD player. The CD must have changed several times over because Jeremy Camp's gravelly voice invades my thoughts vapidly. It's like I've entered my own Narnian wardrobe and suddenly notice all the dark canopy of redwoods over the roadway. As I hit the summit of this road I know by heart, my car drives on instinct, traveling the path back home.

This is for Mom, I tell myself about selling my childhood home. I can see its little beachside cottage siding in my mind, and it brings a smile when I remember the good times that once inhabited its walls. It's the painted version I see. Before I hit age ten and the house and my life started to dilapidate.

"I'm just going to look at the house and figure out what needs to be done." *In and out. In and out*, I repeat to myself. "I refuse to let a material thing have any control over me." At this, I look up through the sun roof. "But You'll help me with that, right?"

There are tragedies in life that play over in the mind like a recurring nightmare. I squeeze my eyes shut against the home movies. I hope for a new ending when they play, only to be disappointed that, in fact, I'm not dreaming, but reliving history I cannot change.

I can't swim fast enough.

I can't pedal quickly enough.

And I can't run far enough from those thoughts.

"Maybe my father is right. It's time to go home and finish this." The stars are blinking in the darkened sky. Parents certainly leave their mark. When you grow up and realize their flaws, it's but a moment before you realize you're left to clean up the mess they created. And then start one of your own in your own family. *Which is precisely why I don't have a family.*

The house, which I expect to find dark and eerie, is lit like a lighthouse when I approach the driveway, and I find myself blinking several times and looking at the surrounding landmarks to make sure I'm in the right place. I shiver as I think my father and Sharon are still in the house, not vacated as they told me. The last thing I need is to hear more about their move and their future as foster parents. Since neither one of them is the parenting sort, I can't imagine what that's about. If it wasn't Sharon's relatives, I'd wonder if they thought they might increase their income as foster parents. Once they find out it means less schmoozing and travel, I shudder to think what it will mean to the kids.

"What on earth?" I say, getting out of the car.

There are trucks along the street, and even one in the driveway, and I see a bustle of activity going on inside the house. My ears are assaulted with a constant, rhythmic banging.

I slowly make my way up the path to the house and find the door open slightly. I push it open, and see the house has been stripped down to the studs, and there's a strong scent of bleach.

"Excuse me," I call out to the workers. I step out onto the porch for one more look at the address. I am indeed in the right place. Each worker looks my way and then summarily ignores me. "Excuse me," I repeat. "Who's in charge here?"

There are men everywhere, some of them looking at plans, some of them pounding, and all of them ignoring me. It looks as though I'm employing the entire town of Santa Cruz, and on a Sunday night, this cannot be an inexpensive thing.

Oh, Daddy, what did you do? One thing about my father, he's usually very free with other people's wallets and I'm sure he thinks he did me a favor here—that the sale will pay for all this.

One of the workers looks at me finally, rolling up plans in his hand, and nods his chin towards the back of the house. "You need to see the man?"

I nod. I guess I need to see the man. Naturally, I imagine pulling back the curtain in *The Wizard of Oz* because I'm quite uncertain of who "the man" is.

As I step through the rooms, the house is nothing like I

remember it. It's funny how your childhood home looks in your mind—so much bigger. And all the things that made it home are now stripped and painted over. Gone is the musty scent from the ocean and decrepit carpet of various bacteria strains. UC Santa Cruz probably could have found enough germs for antibiotics research to last for years. The carpet is gone to reveal the beaten oak hardwood floors underneath, stained and tattered by ancient nail marks. A small portion of the floor is being stripped by a loud, humming machine, and there the floor looks like fresh, raw wood.

I walk slowly, looking at each and every change and meeting the gaze of questioning construction workers. *What could this be costing?* I'm drawn to the backyard and step out onto the evening porch, which still looks exactly the same. I hear the familiar roar of the waves in the distance as I close my eyes and allow the emotion to wash over me. It smells like the beach, and I feel the touch of my mother on my fingertips.

I look heavenward. "Why leave me with this? I was thirteen, Mom." Of all the things she could have done to finish off her will, this was a final slap in the face of my father. He never took it that way, though. For that, I'm grateful.

"Poppy."

I open my eyes to see Simon's hulking frame talking on a Treo. I blink a few more times, wondering if I'm seeing a Santa Cruz mirage of sorts. Which would never be too normal. Simon comes towards me, placing the phone in his pocket, and I just keep blinking, wishing I had my tryptophan supplements or ylang-ylang to dab behind my ears for calmness.

"Are you talking to yourself?" he asks.

"I suppose I am." I close my eyes once more, and Simon's still there when I pop them open. He looks good under the moonlight. His bulky, muscular frame is masculine and offers protection. I'm not exactly thinking like his doctor when I look at him under the moonlight.

"Poppy, it is Simon." He gives me his sideways grin. "Are you trying to decipher that? Or having trouble with those hallucinations again?" he quips.

I shake my head like a cartoon character. "I don't understand." I look back towards the house. "This is my house, right?"

He smiles and walks closer to me. He's so much younger than I think of him at the office. I think because he's been so successful and seems to have everything under control, I neglect to remember he's only thirty-five. He feels about fifty, and with the excess golf and time off, I think of him as more my father's contemporary than my own.

But here in the moonlight, I think perhaps I've only been protecting myself. Simon is the kind of man who tempts me because he knows who I truly am. Well, with the exception of the Hawaiian spa idea—that's all his own. Naturally, it's not odd I haven't noticed how truly attractive he is. He's my patient. It's my job *not* to notice him that way.

Seeing Simon under the familiar blue of my Santa Cruz moon, with the scents of the Pacific so nearby is like seeing my first-grade teacher at the grocery store: a mixture of awe and confusion.

"Simon, what on earth?" I ask, stepping back and looking again at the house. "Do you have something to do with all these men here?" Granted, stupid question, but I'm not feeling like myself here.

"What are *you* doing here, Poppy? I wanted to be done before you saw it."

"Done with what? Don't you have to have permission from the owner to rip a house apart? What is this world coming to? Where's my lawyer?"

He crosses his arms. "If I lived in fear of lawyers, I'd never get anything done in California, where they breed like rabbits. So your threats, while made in jest and pathetic at best, don't scare me one iota."

"Simon, I can't pay for this." But that's not really true. I'm *afraid* to pay for any of this. I'm afraid to be without the money I've put away for a rainy day—and my father's latest escapade. Which, interestingly enough, will now probably come in the parched dryness of the Arizona desert.

He smiles. "Did you think I would make you pay for it, Poppy?"

This raises alarm bells. "Simon, I don't want to owe anyone anything."

"I realize that. Do you think that's the healthiest of attitudes?"

"I'm not going to Hawaii. I'm not going to give up my practice because you went over the top. You have *too* much money." I use my hands to emphasize that fact. "You need to start a foundation or take care of an orphan. Anything but this." I point back at the house. "I would have managed this fine. Did you ever think I might have wanted to sell the house as-is? Or not sell it at all."

"No, I didn't, because you're a perfectionist, Poppy. Not only would you have not wanted to do that, but you couldn't have done it. It would have cracked your core." He laughs. "So you're not happy to see the house different?"

"No, I am, but—"

"It was crumbling on its foundation, Poppy. Cracks everywhere. I knew you couldn't deal with seeing it destroyed. We needed to reshore the foundation, and that took the longest. Some people have a hard time caring for what's given to them."

Feeling cared for is just not an emotion I'm comfortable with, and I sort of want to kick him. He knows this, and that's exactly why he did it!

"Simon, you still haven't explained what you're doing here and why you're in my house. Knocking it down, I might add, with no permission from its rightful owner."

He exhales, deeply, nodding his head.

"And don't pull that fake concerned look with me. Don't you think I know your tricks by now?"

"I'm not nearly as bright as all that. I'm thinking of how I want to say this. Relax a minute. You're getting to be completely non-Zen. If I didn't know any better—"

"You're stalling."

"My best friend is a flipper," he says

"A what? Is that some sort of fetish or something?"

"No, Poppy. My friend flips houses for a living. He buys garbage, run-down houses that people can't sell, fixes them up, and sells them a month later for twice the price. He buys granite and high-end products in bulk and makes all his places look the same inside. Always upper-end quality, just the same."

"So why is he here? And what are you doing here?"

"Your dad told Emma what he was doing with the house and Arizona. That he was returning the house to its rightful owner, and you were that rightful owner. Then, I heard him tell Emma that you needed to go back and face the past. All this Dr. Phil crap . . . I don't know—it just made me boil inside. You just don't leave this kind of work for someone else."

"And you heard this?" I really have to get an office with more privacy.

"I'm a business man; I pay attention and your office isn't exactly set up for privacy. Yet another reason I want to help you get a real clinic. Anyway, he mentioned the house was a little run down and hoped it wouldn't be too hard for you to fix."

I give him the look that says I want more information.

"Emma said you were already pushing it, with ten-hour

days, the carpal tunnel syndrome symposium, plus two hours a day of training for your triathlon. She didn't think you could handle it, and your dad shrugged it off, saying you always handled everything else."

"So why wouldn't you believe that?"

"I just thought I knew the right man to help you. Leif and I went to school together, and I knew he could flip this house faster than you could get a permit. I just saw a need and I filled it. That's what I do, Poppy. I'm an efficiency expert."

"Sometimes the most efficient way is not always best. Why did you think that any of this was your business?" It comes out harsher than I mean it to, but I can't quite grasp what I really feel. My heart is thoroughly grateful that this mountain doesn't lie before me.

He steps closer to me, and I feel a sharp intake of breath at his proximity. "Because, Poppy Clayton, in case you haven't noticed, I want to take care of you. I know you slap me back at every turn, but that doesn't mean I'm ready to stop just yet. How long did it take Edison to get that lightbulb right?" Simon towers over me and I want to step back, but my feet don't move. "You've taken care of me for three years, and now it's my turn."

I swallow my emotion. "Haven't you heard of this thing called women's liberation?"

"I have. I think it's all crap, actually."

"Well, you should meet up with the plastic surgeon from next door. He seems to think we should all be barefoot and pregnant. And then, of course, erase all signs of such commonness later with plastic surgery."

"You're rambling. I don't care what that mouse thinks."

"Mouse?"

"A man who has to drive a car like that has something to prove. I don't."

"So what are you trying to prove with this?"

"That a man takes care of things. Unlike Dr. Plastic. And—" He looks at me again, and we both know he wants to say my dad, but doesn't go through with it.

I nibble on my lip, wanting to laugh, but I find I can't. There's not a sense of mirth in anything he says, but maybe it's the way he's saying it.

"Simon, you could sell a shark on fresh water. Now, if you'll tell me who's in charge, I'll take care of getting payment ready and finding out what they're doing to this house." I start to walk away, but I feel Simon on my heels and turn to face him. "What?"

"You're telling me you can pay for this?"

"Well, not yet, of course, but when I sell the house."

"What happened in this house?"

"You know," I say, reminding him. "My mother went into a diabetic coma and I found her."

He shakes his head, "What else? There's got to be a reason you've avoided it. People die, Poppy, and I'm sure it was tragic to lose your mother at such a young age, but that doesn't explain everything"

"Isn't my mother's coma bad enough?" I try to laugh it off, but he never cracks a smile. He doesn't look away, and he keeps those brown eyes of his fixed on my own, challenging me with their intensity. Simon reads me like an X ray. With him, I feel transparent.

He drops his gaze. "I'm sorry, Poppy. I should have asked you before I just took over. What can I do to fix it since I've already screwed up?"

"It's complicated, Simon." I turn back toward the house, but I feel Simon's arms come around me. When I turn around and look up into his steady brown eyes, every part of me feels his presence.

I crave things that are bad for me, like my mother craved sugar and carbohydrates. Her addictions killed her when she couldn't resist. I should have never let myself get this far. I should have never treated Simon like he didn't matter, while growing dependent on his weekly presence in my office.

I close my eyes, waiting for his lips to touch mine. But they don't, and when I open my eyes his are clamped shut as though he's really wrestling with something emotionally.

"Simon?"

"I'm sorry, Poppy. You're right. Maybe I should have started a foundation."

chapter 15

A spring night in Santa Cruz is filled with wonder. The stars shine against the black sky and twinkle in their neon light. It's magical. I've often pondered how people can live without an ocean in their life. Hearing its thunder, watching its power, and knowing its all-encompassing consistency will be there night and day is a constant reminder of how we're nothing more than a grain of sand in life. Whatever happens in life, the tide will come in and the tide will go out. How do people in the Midwest know that they're small and insignificant? How do people in Hollywood *not* know?

"Simon." I force my gaze from the backyard sky, seeing the uncertainty I've brought to his life. It's interesting to see how unfeeling I can be on the face of another. I see it in Simon's eyes. He appears beaten and haggard. I know him—he'll pop out of it. But the realization that I'm capable of inflicting such pain is still there. Helping people, healing people, I'm in my element, but on the receiving end I manage to mutilate things every time. "Simon." I grab his hand between my own. "Thank you for this. It's too much, you know, and I just don't know how to take it."

He nods stoically.

"No, I mean it. I really am grateful. What you did for me is just beyond the scale of what I can imagine, and I'm overwhelmed, and frustrated by my response."

"The proper response is thank you." He starts to walk towards the back door. He looks towards me. "And you're welcome."

"You're not leaving?" I ask.

"You tell me I've got a charitable foundation to start. I'll need to get on that."

"Are you making fun of me?" I'm blinking back tears as I ask this.

"Lord forbid I actually give to a friend who deserves my money. Someone who makes my favorite thing—golf—possible with her gentle touch. There's no tax write-off in that." He shakes his head. "Shame on me for thinking like a man, instead of a like businessman." Simon stares straight at me . . . and winks.

"You're winking at me? This is funny to you? You're not really going to start a foundation, are you?"

"I thought maybe the 'Woe is me' act would work," he shrugs. "You can't blame a guy for trying. Someday, Poppy, you're going to see what you're missing in me, and I just hope I'm not doing the hula with a gorgeous *wahine* when you realize it."

"Simon, you can have any girl you want and you know it."

"But I don't want *any* girl. What guy does? I want the one I want. The one I know is wife material for me."

I gasp. "W-what?"

"You heard me. I said the word *wife*. I'll bet you're dying for a run at this moment."

"Simon, you only have to go as far as Lilly and Morgan to know I'm not marriage material. Don't you want to actually *date* the woman you say you want in marriage? I'll make my husband eat— Well, what if I took your steak away?"

"You wouldn't do that, and I'm not as easily frightened as you might think. I can order a steak when we go out to dinner. Do you believe in restaurants?"

"This is flattering, you know?" *But I don't believe a word of it.*

"I do know. I'm a great guy. What's not to be flattered about?"

I force down the giggle I feel. I don't think I've felt this lighthearted since I was twelve. I feel as though Aerosmith is bellowing "I Don't Want to Miss a Thing." "You're so modest too."

"I'll give you that: modesty is not my strong suit. It's from growing up as the mathlete in a sports-related environment. Then, when football got really important, I had to final in the national science bowl." Simon raises his eyebrow, to give me his best romance cover look. "Now one might think being a quarterback is cool, but the hot chicks know that real men compete in a verbal format to solve today's technical questions."

"So you didn't have many dates, I'm guessing?"

"Not one. But I knew how to create a really cool robot that turned on the vacuum cleaner. It couldn't actually push the vacuum, but it was a start. Great science comes from humble beginnings."

"Are you telling me you created the precursor to the Roomba?"

"Come again?"

"The little vacuum cleaner that goes by itself."

"No, I'm telling you I couldn't get a date to save my life, and now science has made me a wealthy man and I can't keep them away. But I don't want those women. I want the one who would have loved me despite the science fair. I want the one who would have danced with me to the Bee Gees long after it was fashionable. I want *you*, Poppy."

Every part of me tingles as Simon says this. The truth is I want him too. I never really thought of the possibility, but the reality is that I have a different course and I'll only ruin his.

"Well, you're barking up the wrong tree." I lift my chin towards the sky. "I would have thought you were a geek back then, too, just like the other girls," I lie. The idea that Simon was ever a geek is ridiculous. He looks like a big, hunky football player with a scientific brain. Bill Gates in a muscular, masculine body. Hardly a geek in anyone's book.

"Poppy." Simon crosses his arms. "You wear tie-dye and your Walkman—notice I said Walkman, not iPod—still spews Credence Clearwater Revival. You're not really in a place to judge geekdom. Just one of the reasons you're the girl for me."

I look down at my running gear. In this outfit it's not all that obvious that I'm out of touch fashion-wise. But make no mistake, if being friends with Lilly and Morgan has taught me anything, it's that I have no fashion sense. But again, this isn't about me. "Credence is timeless."

"You shouldn't listen to it so loud; it's bad for your hearing."

"What, are you the doctor now?"

"I think you're the most beautiful woman I've ever seen, Poppy." At this I turn away and look down at the overgrown grass my father probably hasn't cut in a year. I focus on it, rather than take in what he's saying, which is just too far from reality. "I know you understand what it feels like to be different, and I know you light up when I come into the office, whether you want to admit it or not."

I swallow hard at this, trying to will myself to believe he's making this all up. *I do not light up when he comes in. What am I, an eighth-grader? I'm just happy to see a consistent patient, is all.* I clear my throat. "That's not a reason to think you should offer marriage to someone, Simon—because they understand being a geek. That's like taking the runt in the litter and thinking it'll love you more because you rescued it. I don't need to be rescued."

"I do," Simon says low and pointed.

"I can't deal with this now," I say.

"Do you want to run?"

I sigh loudly. "I'm dying to run. How can you tell?"

"Your leg is shaking. Let's go to the beach. You can admit your weakness for me tomorrow. I'll chaperone you while you run."

"Who's going to chaperone you?"

"That's the beautiful part. I'm hoping nobody."

"Good thing I can take you." I ball my hand into a fist.

He grabs it. "Good thing."

"I'm going to pay for all this," I say as we walk through the house and the stench of bleach. Lilly would be like an addict in here.

"I don't think you will when you hear what it costs."

"Are you trying to tell me I'm indebted to you?"

"Forever. How do you feel about indentured servitude?"

"Is that like aromatherapy?"

"Sort of, only the cologne comes on a gift with purchase. Me." He grins widely, and I have to say, his grin warms my insides. *I'm home.* I hear the ocean roaring, I see the fireplace where my mother had fires before the environmental protection agency warned us against such ozone evils, and I feel truly joyous. I thought this would be the worst day of my adult life, and Simon made it completely fun and I forgot what I feared in the first place.

Simon shouts some directions at the builders and sends them home. "There's no use in paying them for Sunday night if you already know," he says to me.

"I can't believe you did this."

"Oh that reminds me, I stored all the furniture in a storage unit up the street. You'll have to go through that."

"Furniture? My dad left the furniture?"

"Honey, your dad left everything. Not really a compulsive man, is he? When I saw him in that suit, I thought certainly his house would be like an Armani closet. It looked like a well-stocked secondhand store."

I laugh. "Actually, my father has more taste than cash. His house was almost like a hideout; he always met people at fancy restaurants." I stop on the front porch and hop one step down from Simon, turning to look at him. "Do you remember in *The Cat and the Hat Comes Back* how there's this one red spot and the cat destroys everything to clean that spot? That's sort of how my dad leaves the house looking. Everything around him is painted with the memory of his being there."

I laugh, but I can tell Simon isn't fooled. He doesn't laugh, and he doesn't comment. I can only imagine what my father left this house looking like, and I'm mortified that Simon saw my childhood in full bloom.

We walk arm in arm down the sidewalk to the beach, and I try to imagine what life would be like if I could submit to my emotions. The waves are lit by a tourist beacon for the restaurants nearby, and my feet are itching, they are so ready to take off. *I will finish two miles in seven and a half minutes*, I think to myself, and I have to hold myself back and not just take off. The surf is calm, and I just want to run into its embrace and feel its power and the sting of salt against my legs.

Simon lets go of my arm and looks down at me from his tall stature. "Just go. You're like a hummingbird that I'm clinging to."

"I know. I'm sorry. My body just wants to run. I can't help it; I'm like a greyhound that's seen the bunny, you know?"

His brown eyes crinkle in amusement. "I don't know, but I'll be here when you get back."

I take off as though I've just heard the starting gun. Oh my gosh, there's nothing like running on the beach. Tomorrow, my thighs will feel like wet noodles and the next time I run, it will be like my muscles are on fire, but it's worth every pain.

"Oh Lord in heaven, this is what I live for! Praise You. Praise Your holy name!" I shout to the sky with my arms lifted up. Sure, I look like an idiot, but sometimes that moment with God just hits you, and you can't help your gratitude. It's like that when I run.

As I get farther up the beach, the lone beach light begins to dwindle and there's only the moon. My heartbeat drowns out the waves in my ears. Something makes me stop. Right there in the middle of my run, with point-seven miles left to go according to my time. I turn around and look back up the beach where Simon ponders the stars. His masculine frame looks different here as he plays protector and stays close enough to get me at any time. He's standing still, but he must have run to keep up with me. Now he's casually looking towards the ocean as though he has no idea how he got there. His hair is lit blue from the moonlight, and just the sight of him makes me smile.

Simon is definitely the marrying kind, and it's just too bad he doesn't get that I'm not.

chapter 16

When I get to work on Monday, there's an envelope taped to the door. I pull it down, annoyed that someone wouldn't use the mail slot, but today I'm toting a new, heated chiropractic table for Brian, who's just gotten his lymphatic massage license. Naturally, the thought occurs to me that this is going to mean more space in my business hunt, but for all the good it will do it's worth more rent. Lymphatic is one of the best remedies for toxins in the system, and now my patients won't even have to leave my doors to get their systems flushed by a professional.

I schlep the table, which is in pieces, into the foyer, and drop my keys on the countertop. I wish I could ride my bike to work, but it just doesn't work out with the traffic and the dangerous route to get here, so I get up earlier and earlier to train as my race gets closer. Just a little more than a month, and I'm there, soaking up the Hawaiian sunshine, and eating goo in the race of a lifetime.

I tear open the envelope, and I feel my stomach plummet. It's an eviction notice. What the heck? I paid the rent. I have a lease. I— "Jeff!"

Without another glance at the pink paperwork, I exit my office door and head to Dr. 90210's staged foyer. Jeff's office is like something out of a model-home environment. There's a faux limestone fireplace crackling in the waiting room, with deep, rich taupe colors and Tuscan art lining the walls. A fake marble statue of the female form sits in the middle of the room on a marble pedestal, piano concertos play, these fabulous, natural candles fill the room with the most peaceful scent. I pick one of them up against my better judgment and smell its divine scent. I could use a little peace right now.

I'm telling you, this office makes *me* want plastic surgery. Man, it's like a cult of luxury in here, and all I can say is that when he pulls them in, they're like flies in a Venus's flytrap. No one's going anywhere until they're nipped, tucked, and well on their way to perfection.

"Where's Jeff?" I ask his plastic staff girl. Working here, some of the benefits are clearly obvious.

"He's in a consultation. Can I help you with something?"

"Can you ask him to come to my office when he's done? I have something to discuss with him." I try to put on my nice voice, but it's apparent from Plastic Girl's face I'm not succeeding. I take in a deep breath and exhale.

She looks down at her open calendar. "He's really swamped today. I'm not sure when he could find time to . . ." She looks up at me. "Do you know we carry mineral makeup? You would be a knockout with makeup. Just a touch to even out your skin tone. You are really stunning, Dr. Clayton."

"It will take five minutes of his time, all right? It's really important to the future of his business. Tell him that for me, won't you?"

"Anytime you want to come over for a free demonstration, I'd be happy—"

"I don't wear makeup. I don't wear anything I wouldn't ingest into my system," I snap.

Plastic Girl lets her mouth hang, "Why on earth not? You

know, pardon me for being so blunt, but you are, like— Well, if I was a guy, I would say you are totally hot and you have a figure to die for. So I guess I don't get the makeup thing." She shrugs, but her Valley speak continues. "I mean, you'd be, like, the kind of girl men were afraid to talk to. That's my dream. Scare them off before they even approach."

Yes, it would be. "I have to say as a makeup salesgirl, you are very persuasive." I tap the desk a couple times and turn to leave. I smile, thinking about the Tammy Faye look to her taut, flawless skin. There are some women who think of the face as a mere canvas, and where there's white they must slash it with color and glitter.

I'm about halfway to the door, next to the marble bust of perfect womanhood, when I realize it. I'm all about energy—if you give off good energy, it passes on, but bad energy kills people's emotions. And as I'm next to the marble figure beside me, I realize that's what I've just done. I've taken my eviction notice and passed it onto Plastic Girl. I mean, Dr. Jeff's assistant.

"I'll be sure and tell him," she calls out.

"What's your name?" I turn to ask her.

"Alicia."

"Well, Alicia, I have a big wedding coming up where I'm a bridesmaid. Maybe you could help me then."

"Sure," she says.

Of course, I have no intention of spending a fortune on plastic surgery makeup, but I can't stand the idea that I've tried to crush Alicia's day, either, just because I'm mad at her boss. I catch a glimpse of myself on the way out and see my eyes are red at the rims. Maybe I'm being a little hasty on the no-makeup thing.

Jeff opens a door to the back and appears before me. I'd like to say my first reaction is extreme disdain, because that would be the smart girl's reaction. Apparently, I'm not all that bright, because my first reaction is that I'm happy to see him in a friendly sort of way. And he's as handsome as ever. And even he makes more sense than Simon right now. At least to my well-addled brain.

"Poppy? I thought I heard your voice. Come on back."

"I thought you had a consultation."

He looks at Alicia and then to me. "Right, right. On the phone. I had a consultation. Very in-depth consultation. I'm done now."

I stifle my laughter and follow him to his office, where he shuts the door. "You're a terrible liar."

"I'm a Christian, so I take that as a compliment. I've been on the phone since seven this morning—"

"What is this?" I interrupt him and hold up the eviction notice.

He grabs it and peruses it with those deep blue eyes of his. "It looks like an eviction notice." Then he brings his gaze back to mine. "I got one too."

"You know, you don't even— What? What did you say?"

"The landlord is breaking all of our leases, Poppy. Yours, mine, the Greek café, the gym, everything. No one in government is at work yet, so what a time I've had getting as much information as I have."

"Did you know about this?"

"Of course I didn't know about this. I've been on the phone all morning with lawyers trying to figure out my next step."

"Why aren't you flustered? I thought you were planning to take over the entire building."

Jeff shrugs and gets up to put a book on the shelf. "Because legally he can't do that, and we can all file a class-action suit. He's planning to fill the building with a high-tech startup that has an extraordinary amount of cash. But I'm torn because maybe this is my sign to get my own building built." Jeff shrugs. "Either way, he's not kicking me out without a fight, and I can afford a better lawyer than him," he says with a laugh.

"Well, what good will a class-action suit do me if I'm going to be sent packing anyway?"

He lets out a long, haggard sigh. "Do you really think I'm going to kick you out if you don't have a new and better place for your practice, Poppy? Do you know me at all? You're the one who agreed to look elsewhere."

"Do you think I want to be next to a plastic surgeon?"

"You have this anger that simmers just at the surface, but you always manage to control it. You always manage to keep your emotions in check unless it's about some natural diuretic you've just discovered. Or me."

"This has nothing to do with us, or our differences. I just don't want to get involved in a lawsuit. I don't want to spend my life in strife. Maybe I want the peace that comes from above, and so I choose to focus on all that's good rather than what's bad."

"Maybe." He lifts an eyebrow as though he doesn't believe me.

"What does that mean?"

"You're angry, Poppy. You don't see it, but you are angry. And it plays out in little passive-aggressive garbage like taking my parking spot and coming over here and giving me an earful. You're not mad at me; you're mad at something deep." Jeff sits back in his chair and waits for me to react, which I'm not giving him the satisfaction of doing.

"What is this, your pop psychology? Do your patients get that for free?"

He crosses his arms. "Why do you run?"

"I like to run. As I don't plan any liposculpture in my future, that's probably a good thing."

"See? Passive-aggressive. You have never missed an opportunity to put down what I do, and I think if you're really comfortable with what you do, you shouldn't worry about me. So tell me." He leans in on the desk. "I think it's great you'll never need liposuction. I also think it's a blessing to women who've had children, watched men leave, and have lost all sense of self-worth. I think it's great for them. What do you advise—should I just avoid my calling because you think it's wrong?"

"Exercise helps endorphins, and a woman can lose weight."

"But she can't lose the skin. You're just not going to give in, are you?"

"Why should I? I'm right."

"So what?" Jeff asks. "What if life isn't about being right?"

His question stops me cold. *Life* is *about being right. Isn't it?*

I can feel the cortisone rising in my system as he continues to glare at me. My heart is racing, and I feel nothing but anxiety and the immediate desire to run it off. "I'm going running before my patients get in."

He stands up and blocks the door. "You can't do it without running it off, can you? We're getting evicted, the world is eating Big Macs, there are thousands of SUVs where there should be hybrids. What does that make you feel?"

I can't tell him that it makes my heart pound and my teeth clench, but if I'm honest, that's exactly what I'm thinking.

"Negative feelings are related to high blood pressure and heart disease," Jeff adds. "Toxic emotions, I believe you call them."

"I'll be in my office. Let me know what your lawyer says." I put my hand on the doorknob, but he doesn't move. "Are you trapping me in your office, Dr. Curran?"

He blinks slowly several times, and then he moves aside.

"Thank you," I tell him.

"You're welcome. I'll be in touch."

When I get out of his office, I'm like a gorilla let loose on the city. I'm just enraged that he has the nerve to say I'm angry. Who is he kidding? I'm not angry. Come and feel the positive vibe in my office, please.

I get into my office and rub my forehead, trying to shake the last ten minutes from my system. Emma is at her desk, nibbling on a whole-grain bar and downing green tea, her favorite snack. And it's only eight a.m.

"I see the new table came," Emma says.

"I have to run, Emma."

"No, no. You can't run. You're backed up this morning. You've got three people waiting already. Alan is in exam room one and Karen and Jason are in the adjustment room. Alan's first."

"Emma, I have to run."

"No, you have to *work*. Didn't you already swim?"

"I did," I sheepishly admit. "But I didn't get my full time in."

"I don't think Karen, Jason, or Alan really care. Oh, and your dad called. They're in Arizona and wanted to know if you found everything you wanted."

"All right, thanks."

I finish with my patients, taking special care with a sciatica case and a pregnant Karen, but I can't remember actually talking to any of them during the treatment. *God is in control*, I keep reminding myself. *How dare Jeff try to get me off kilter. It's my business day; what is he thinking?*

While I'm contemplating his incredibly bad manners, I trip over the new massage table and find myself splayed on the floor, looking at the ceiling.

This probably would have been a lot more feminine in my mother's skirt.

"Poppy?" Emma stands over me.

"I'm getting up," I say, laughing it off. "Just call me Grace." But as I go to stand on my left foot, I can't do it and crumple onto the floor again.

"Grace, let me go get Jeff."

"No!" I shout. "If I need a doctor, I'll find a good one." My patients are looking at me oddly. "Not that he isn't a great plastic surgeon, but I think I need an orthopedic guy."

I stand up again, and this time it's better. My left foot has been aching for a while, and I've just ignored it, but I'm at the point where I can't ignore it any longer. I go to my office to find my doctor's number while Emma moves the table from its precarious spot.

"Brian!" I call out. "I need help with the X-ray machine. I think I may have a problem," I yell. It dawns on me for a split second that Jeff is right about me being slightly angry. And maybe there's something to what Simon said about me avoiding him. But the thoughts quickly dissipate into the ridiculous notions they are. I'm a girl of thirty whose best friends are leaving me for the stability of marriage while I try to convince the world to give up hydrogenated oils and Teflon. So yeah, I have a few issues. Who doesn't?

chapter 17

"You twisted your ankle," Dr. Hopkins tells me in his monotone voice. Is it any wonder people don't like doctors? I mean, would it kill them to throw a little personality into their routine? It's not like he's diagnosing me with a terminal illness here. I was klutzy. I fell and sprained my ankle. It's the perfect segue to a joke. Doesn't he get that? The energy in here could kill a man.

"That's what I figured," I say, but I know there's more. Brian wasn't around to help me with the X rays and it was his stupid table I tripped over. My foot has a constant dull ache, with the stabbing pain every now and again, made worse when I run. Which is why the run on the beach was such a gift to my soul. Since Hopkins missed whatever's going on, I imagine I'm going to have to do it myself and wait for Brian's availability or get Emma to drop her crunch bar long enough to help out.

"And," Dr. Hopkins continues, "You have a hairline fracture in your metatarsals. Haven't you noticed it hurt?"

His words are a crushing blow. I knew it was something to that effect, but his saying so means I have to actually pay attention. "I have noticed, but I'm training for a triathlon."

"Not anymore you're not. You can swim, but there will be

no running for you for at least a month. No bike riding—too dangerous with a cast."

I just sort of laugh the idea of a cast off, wondering what type of shoes I can get where I wouldn't feel my toes. They have to be out there because I am not going to miss my run. "Thanks, Doctor."

"Don't write this off, Poppy. You'll do permanent damage to those bones if you don't give them a rest. As a chiropractor, there's no reason for me to be telling you such an obvious thing. You either stop running now, or you'll stop running forever. What's it going to be?"

His words sober me, mostly because I know they're true. I preach whole-body health on a daily basis, and yet I haven't listened to my own body for some time now. The irony is not lost on me. Nor is the fact that I don't feel the pain. I just stuff it somewhere deep and focus on the scent of the eucalyptus or the stars guiding me or even the crest of the waves. Anything but the pain. The pain eases, but if I miss my run, I feel it for a week.

"You've been on this fracture for some time now. I can tell." Dr. Hopkins says to me, and though I'd like to write him off as the typical quack I think all MDs are, I know this time he's for real, because I would never let a patient of my own run under these circumstances.

"Fine, no running for a while. When will it be fixed?"

"You need to be pain free for at least three weeks when you start up again, and even then, you take it slow."

"Three weeks from pain? My run is in little more than a month. On Oahu."

He ignores me and looks at my chart. "Take Tylenol for pain, and I'm going to give you a permanent cast. I could give you a removable sort, but I don't trust you as far as I can throw you."

"A cast? I'm in a wedding soon. The bride won't want me wearing a cast."

"Do you want a wood-soled shoe instead?"

"Doc, I can't do this right now."

"You've already done this right now. And Poppy, you have no one to blame but yourself. You, of all people, who worked in this office once upon a time, who has come in here and told me countless times of all the evil medicine represents—you, of all people, should have listened to your body. You'll get no sympathy from me." He rips off a prescription for a stronger pain reliever, which he knows I won't fill, and another order for a cast to be placed. "I'll have a wheelchair take you to casting."

I'm not missing my triathlon. I don't care what he says. With a little time off, I can be on this foot again in no time. I'm definitely not heading to casting. I'll just wrap it in the office. It will have the same effect, and I can be back quicker.

"By the way, when's the last time you replaced your running shoes?" Doctor Hopkins asked.

"I don't remember. They're expensive."

"Not as expensive as a stress fracture." He closes my file and leaves me in the office to dress. I'll admit, I mumble through the entire process. When I'm finished I look out the doorway and head to Sarah, the front desk girl I worked with for three years before I decided this was not my path in life.

"I'm leaving. Shh. What do I owe you?"

"You know he'd never charge you. It says here you're supposed to get a cast."

"I'm in a wedding. I'm just going to wrap it until after the nuptials. You know what it's like."

Sarah shakes her head. "You are so stubborn, Poppy. If you end up a cripple, don't call here. We don't need your malpractice suit." She slams my folder shut.

"Sarah, that's not funny." I laugh with her, except she's not joining me.

"It's not meant to be funny. You know, I put up with it when you worked here—how you would just ignore everything Jerry said—but he's been a doctor longer than you've been alive. He's learned a few things along the way and you can't even give him the respect he deserves. I mean it, Poppy. Don't come here anymore."

Now Sarah is like Dr. Jerry Hopkins' biggest cheerleader. She would take you down rather than see him hurt in any way. In some ways, she knows the old man better than his wife does. But that doesn't mean she's right here. Technically speaking, I need a cast, but realistically, I just don't see how it's going to work out. I've been training for months for the Tinman Triathlon with the hope that I'll eventually run the Ironman with a full marathon at the end. This is not just inconvenient. This is the end of a dream. I just close my eyes right there in the office. But when I step down on my left foot, reality shoots through my nervous system.

What on earth does God want from me?

"All right," I say when I open my eyes. "I'll wait for the cast."

"Go up the hall; they're waiting for you."

"You're not taking me in the wheelchair?"

"No, I'm not. Right now, I want to run you down with the wheelchair, so I think it's best that you just walk gently down there."

"Such a bedside manner, Sarah."

"You are beyond irritating, Poppy. Jerry loves you like a daughter, and you show him contempt every chance you get, as if to tell him his entire career doesn't measure up. You don't deserve him. Go get your cast. If you play your cards right Jerry will take it off before the wedding. Though if I got a vote, your leg wouldn't see the light of day until your wedding, and it's going to be a cold day down under—"

"Sarah!"

She rips off the code numbers for the cast and thrusts it into my hand. "Just try to make another appointment and see how far you get."

I should have known I couldn't solve the embarrassment factor for Morgan. Sure, Lilly's dressing me. Sure, I'm bringing a plastic surgeon, but I'm Poppy Clayton, and I will always find a way to humiliate my friends. This time in the form of an untimely cast.

I've been planning this for a year, and I'm in the shape of my life to do it, so I'm not letting a little toe get in my way. As I'm limping down the hallway to get my cast, I see the convertible, giggly blonde who's always trying to sell Jeff more than the medical wares in her bag. She's flirting outrageously with an older doctor who could be her father, and coyly speaking with her chin turned downward. It's the exact same pose she struck on Sunday with Jeff. She's like the Madonna *Vogue* video come to life.

She's wearing a crisp white suit, tailored so tightly it's nearly obscene. I wonder what Lilly would think of that—if it's in style or as pathetic as it looks to me. But I'm fascinated by the way this woman moves. She gives off the air that they'll be heading to the bedroom after the discussion, and while I don't think she's that type, I can't help but wonder why she would want to appear to be. If I had the personal expertise she seems to possess, I would most certainly use my power for good.

I'm trying to be subtle in my fascination with her, but she spots me and I hear her tell the doctor, "Excuse me, Hal."

As the doctor turns around, I see it's Hal Halperin, who always was the sort who seemed to have no interest in the medical profession other than how much he could spend on the golf course. He nods at me, and I wave. "Hi, Dr. Halperin." *You jerk*, I think to myself. Okay, that was definitely bad energy.

She appears at my side. "Hi, hi, do you remember me?"

"Yes, of course I remember you. Are you feeling better about life?"

"I am. My husband and I have decided to give it another try; isn't that great?"

Not if you plan to be flirting like that, it's not. "Yeah, really great. What God puts together, let no man put asunder." *I can't believe I just said that.*

Having her this close to me, I find her eyes are nearly turquoise. She is truly exquisite to look at, and it's no wonder men pay homage to her beauty. She's stunning. But her confidence is a thin veneer; her desperate nature is apparent to all who would care to look closely. Some women never stop fighting to be at society's popular table.

"Well," I say, backing up. "It was nice to see you again."

"No, wait," she grabs my arm. "There's a reason I stopped you. I wanted to ask you something."

"I have a doctor's appointment." I point towards the hall.

"It won't take a minute, and they always make you wait, anyway. Give them a taste of their own medicine. No pun intended." She laughs at her own joke. "Besides, I probably have their medicine in my bag."

I look down at the bag of pharmaceuticals she carries around, and let's just say, it's not exactly warming the cockles of my heart. "Sure, what can I do for you?"

"Well, I noticed when I'm at Jeff's office, you run a lot."

This statement makes my toes ache. "Yeah, I'm training for a half triathlon. The Tinman on Oahu."

"Yeah, I'm not interested in anything like that, but I wondered if you might be willing to run with me. I know I'd be slow at first, but I'm really competitive, and I'd catch up quickly. I'd pay you."

Her request catches me totally off guard. She doesn't exactly seem the girlfriend type, and the first time we met she sort of laughed at my offer of help. The second time, she flirted outrageously with Jeff right in front of me. And then she kissed Simon in my office and I don't care how much she was paid! Not that any of this matters of course, but still.

"Actually, I have a stress fracture and I can't run for some time." *Woo-hoo! Sometimes pain is convenient!* "I'm on my way to get a cast right now." Looking at her beautiful yet disappointed features, I really feel this tinge of empathy. Lilly would tell me that was my problem, but my greatest desire, besides bringing people to Christ, is to bring them to health, and I would love to do this for Blondie. She's obviously no couch potato, but if she's peddling pharmaceuticals for a living, there's a lot I could teach her.

"Look," she says. "I know you were angry the other day about Jeff—"

"Wait a minute, mad about Jeff?"

"That's just a part of the way I do business. I have no interest in Jeff Curran or any other doctor. Doctors bore me."

"Angry? I think you have the wrong person. Why would I be angry about you and Jeff?" Really, I just want to wring your neck for touching Simon, but only because any good woman would have done it for free.

"You slammed your office door pretty hard. I thought maybe you liked him."

"Oh that. Well, I was just waiting for him to go to church, and—"

"Here's my card." She takes out a business card and hands me her name.

Chloe Stanlis
Pharmaceutical Sales

I pull out one of my own, which lists all the specialty medicine I perform. Sort of the anti-drug card.

Poppy Clayton, DC
Chiropractic Care
Clinical Nutrition
Allergy Elimination
Holistic Healing

"Right." She puts it away in her obviously expensive brief-case pocket, clearly unwilling to ask what anything means. "So when will you be running again? My husband and I are getting remarried, to show our reconciliation, and I have to get into a dress."

Gosh, I'd be worrying about how to not scream at him publicly before I'd be worrying about the dress, but that's just me.

Granted, I want to ask her, "Do I look like a personal trainer?" But of course, if she said no, I'd be doubly offended. I'm just going to chalk this up to a God encounter and make the most of it.

"I'm not actually sure when I'll be running again. I'm hoping I can rig something up where I can run regardless of the cast. I'm not missing my trip to Hawaii. In the meantime, do you have a friend to run with?"

"Look at me." She runs her hands down her figure; all that's missing is the Vanna twirl to show me the dress. "No, I don't have friends. Women don't like me."

Did she just say that? "Well, I am a woman."

"But it's obvious you don't care about appearance."

I cough and sputter here looking for the right words. First, I hear about mineral makeup and now this. I can be friends with the pretty girl because I don't care. What does that make me, chopped tofu?

"Just how exactly do you sell things?"

"What?" she asks.

"Usually salespeople are good with the whole buttering-up scenario, schmoozing. What's with the homely-girl accusation."

"I never said you were homely. You've got that natural beauty. Dr. Jeff sure seems smitten and that's you without makeup. I just mean it's obvious you don't care or you'd wear makeup and make the most of yourself. Right now, you just look plain so no one notices. Like when they catch a Hollywood star without her makeup."

This is getting worse. "I have to go get my cast."

"No wait, Poppy. You said if I needed anything to call you. Didn't you mean that?"

I put her card in my tapestry bag. "Call me. I'll let you know how it goes with the cast."

I am seriously up a creek.

I can't imagine how I'll run the triathlon.

Morgan will have a casted bridesmaid—which will bug Lilly, too, since it's her design I'm wearing at the wedding.

Dr. Jeff thinks I have a crush on him. And so does Chloe.

Simon's trying to lure me to Hawaii by restoring my house in Santa Cruz.

In three months I won't have an office.

And I've been accused of being angry three times today.

Well, uh, yeah!

chapter 18

Miles run: 0
Laps swum: 0
Desperation scale: 8

I've had a long morning of prayer. The Bible says that plans fail for lack of counsel. I'm certainly not at a loss for counsel. My friends are more than willing to give me an earful, though it usually involves a discussion on a Poppy makeover first: "Can we talk after I put some makeup on you?" However, I do trust my counsel—and if Morgan and Lilly think I'm a little off, well, it's most likely true. The thing is I take pride in that. Anyone can play normal. It takes someone special to be her weird self. I think, from the flurry of phone calls today, my friends are hoping I can hold my weirdness in small doses for my date with running man. I do not have a good feeling about this. And maybe I'm sabotaging myself, but there's something about a blind date that someone picked up off the beach.

It doesn't remotely sound romantic as that tale you tell when you're relaying how you met. "Like a discarded clam shell, Max found him along Ocean Beach." Insert tinkling laughter. See? It just doesn't work. My friends will coach me on proper date etiquette, anyway.

"Act coy," they'll say.

"Wear makeup," Morgan will say.

"Wear the Nike running pants, not the sweats," Lilly will add.

All this in the hopes that I, Poppy Clayton, can play normal long enough to lure a man into my lair. The entire process cracks me up.

As far as strange goes, I do not have the corner on this market, and it's time my friends knew it. Driving up 280 toward San Francisco, my car just wants to stop and park near Crystal Springs Reservoir to take a run. But the cast reminds me that's impossible and that my friends are waiting for me. Soon, I'll be running along Oahu's shores in the Tinman. I don't know how, but I will be there. Soon, both this wedding and my run will be in my history, and I will have to look for the next goal. Maybe then, I'll think about it being male in nature.

I haven't told Lilly and Morgan about the cast, and I can only imagine their expressions when they notice it. Tonight's my final fitting for the wedding. I'm wearing my eggplant skirt and a buttery T-shirt Lilly made me. I tried to balance in the heels Morgan left me, but with the cast that proved impossible, so I'm back to my Clarks clogs—or clog. I look quite normal by their standards.

I arrive at Lilly's palatial Marina doorstep with a bottle of wine. Not because I'll drink it, and really, I don't think they will either, but it seems on the "normal" scale for a dinner invitation. At least that's what people always do for me and that's where this bottle came from in the first place. I'm not above regifting. Although maybe my wine-bearing friends just think I need to chill out, and booze will do the trick. One never knows. My Spa Girls know I don't drink (alcohol acts like a sugar and yeast imbalancer) so maybe they'll see my gift as a huge step for me and leave me alone on the dating/ nagging front.

"Hey, Poppy!" Lilly opens the door, grabs me up in a bear hug, and all my angst is quickly forgotten. "What's with the wine?" she asks, looking at the bottle. "Does it have some sort of natural digestive aid in it or something we're missing in our diet?"

"No, it's just something a friend brought me at Christmas and I thought I'd share."

"And the clothes?" She puts her hand on my forehead, "Are you feeling all right?"

"It's my attempt at normal," I say brightly. "People bring wine to dinner."

"Not people who don't drink it." She starts to nod her head in her bouncing fashion. "But a very good attempt, even if none of us drink. It's a start."

"Still, I stretched, you know?"

Here, she notices the cast. "What's that?"

"Stress fracture. I'll have it off by the wedding."

"Morgan won't care; if you need a matching sleeve to cover it, I'll just sew one."

"You don't think she'll care?"

Lilly shrugs. "Why would she?" Lilly grabs my hand and pulls me into the room, where sweeping views of the San Francisco Bay arrest my attention. It's a beautiful pink/purple dusk and the lights around the water are starting to stagger on and twinkle.

"Wow, Lilly, what a view."

She looks at her husband. "Isn't he, though?"

Max smiles at her and comes along beside me. "Hey, Poppy, how's the energy?" He gives me a hug and kisses my cheek.

I have to laugh at this. Max tries, I'll give him that. "Energy is a little slow with the fracture, but I'm working on it."

Max is the studious and cerebral type, the opposite of creative and slightly flaky Lilly in every way. He grins at her, and they share a moment that, quite frankly, makes me want to gag.

"Max was worth marrying for the house alone. Except for this cranky, old woman who lives downstairs." Lilly laughs at the mention of her Nana, who is not the sweet, baking-cookies sort.

She waddles her pregnant self into the step-up kitchen. She's still as thin as ever, and doesn't look pregnant from the back, but she's not used to any weight and has to maneuver herself around. She's clearly a bit off balance and grabs the counter to steady her gait.

"I brought my chiropractic table if you want me to do an adjustment tonight." I worry she's going to turn around and yell, but she softens her expression.

"I love our parties. We're such incredible nerds. That would be great, Poppy. Can you tell my back hurts? This kid is making himself right at home. I wonder if he'll ever move out. He's got it pretty good in there." Lilly pats her stomach.

I hadn't even thought about Lilly being pregnant and the wine. *Sigh.* I can't even be mainstreamed correctly. It takes all my willpower to not destroy the bottle right in front of her.

She opens her Wolf stove to allow the steam from her lasagna to flow through the room. Lilly's lasagna is 99.9 percent fat—there's usually a thin layer of grease-saturated spinach leaf to account for the other 0.1 percent. She uses a turkey baster to skim the oils off it when she's done, and I'll admit, the scent of its sausage makes me want to hurl. I just can't eat this richly. Pavarotti can't eat this richly.

"Don't worry," Lilly says, noting my horrified expression. "I made you a vegetarian version with low-fat cheese. It looks and smells disgusting, but you'll eat it, right?"

"I'll eat it, thanks, Lilly." Trust Lilly to think of my well-being.

The doorbell rings and Morgan arrives looking like one of those elegant mothers I see in the Silicon Valley. The kind who spend their days dressed in pressed slacks and full makeup, wondering how children can be such dirty creatures. Morgan doesn't think this way, naturally, and for all I know, maybe the mothers at home don't either. But she's carrying little Georgie, who's about five, and he's nuzzled into her neck like he should have been there all along. His almond-shaped eyes take in everyone in the room, and he gives an infectious smile.

George, Morgan's fiancé, is a top tax attorney in San Francisco. Morgan's father had him fired from his former firm, but he was quickly reinstated when Morgan's father went to prison. George is wearing the standard tax attorney uniform—a navy blue suit with a red power tie—and he watches over Morgan as if she's a tender butterfly taking off for the world. "Are you warm enough, Morgan? Do you need a sweater?"

She shakes her head and drops the Louis Vuitton bag full of videos and kid items on the travertine floor. "Georgie . . . Poppy's here," she whispers.

Georgie has a thing for me. I think he likes the red hair, but our energy is great together, and he reaches out his arms and transfers himself onto my hip with another wide grin. He's just pure love, this little one. I'd take him in a second. Morgan has been taking care of Georgie during the day while George works, and when she isn't on call for her part-time protocol position, which is really more about society than an actual political position. George and Poppy's marriage and living under one roof is going to make life a whole lot easier on her new son.

"Poppy." George kisses me on the cheek. "What happened to your leg; are you taking falling lessons from Max?"

Max fell out of a ceiling and broke his leg in three places before Lilly and he started dating. "Just trying to grab a little extra attention," I joke. "It's a stress fracture from running."

"From running too much," Lilly clarifies. "We have a surprise for you tonight."

"My dress, right?" I'm here for the final fitting of my bridesmaid gown, but something tells me, by the look in Lilly's eyes, it's not the only reason I'm here. I can take a lot in my lifetime, but Lilly's surprises are usually not on my top ten.

"A surprise for me?" I ask tentatively.

"You know how you were supposed to meet Jacob and run?" Lilly is giddy and I'm scared. While I'll admit I'm not exactly prone to dating long term, the idea that Lilly gets what's right for me is ridiculous. She doesn't even understand why I run or like to wear my mother's skirts. She just thinks I'm pseudo-crazy and so is this loon her husband found on the beach, so it's a match.

"Yeah?" I stretch out the word.

"Well—" At that, the doorbell rings, and I know exactly what it means. The only thing that surprises me is that no one has chained me down and thrown makeup and new clothes on me for the spontaneous "dating game" event.

"I'm going to hurt you," I growl through clenched teeth.

Morgan opens the door and outside stands someone I can only guess is Jacob Frawley. He's painfully tall, perhaps six-five, and his color is indeed good, but it's hidden behind a black cluster of facial hair and equally dark curls gelled to his head in a 1974 sort of direction—sort of a cross between Tom Selleck (remember him?) and the guy from Starsky and Hutch. When he smiles at me, I feel a shiver run up my back.

"Jacob." Max goes over and shakes hands and takes the balsamic vinegar Jacob is toting. *Why didn't I think of that?* "Come on in. Lilly's just taken the lasagna out and we're waiting for it to cool." Max looks over the vinegar and laughs. "Great vintage."

Jacob looks at me, and then Georgie, and his eyes linger a bit too long on my red hair. I can only imagine the Maureen O' Hara ideas he has in his head. I want to quickly extinguish them. In fact, if I had a fire extinguisher here, don't think I'd be past using it. His gaze is creeping me out, like he's thought long and hard about the red hair fetish, and I want to run screaming from the room.

"Lilly, can I help you in the kitchen?" I quickly hand Georgie back to Morgan and jump the step to the kitchen. Lilly peels back the foil on the lasagna.

"I don't know. I'm cooking with sausage here. *Can* you help me?"

I back away from the meat-infested noodles. "No, I don't think I can."

"Didn't think so. Why don't you toss the salad?" Lilly lifts a brow. "No tomatoes died in the making of that salad." She starts to giggle.

I'm not a vegetarian, but I don't eat a lot of meat, either, and I certainly don't eat sausage, which is the sum total of parts that shouldn't be considered edible. I mean, has she ever actually read Leviticus? But I look back down at Jacob, who seems to be licking his chops like I'm dinner. Jacob . . . or sausage. Well, no-brainer there. I quickly head for the sub-zero to get the salad. When I open the fridge door, Lilly appears next to me so that we're hidden from view by the door.

"Isn't he great?"

"He's really not, Lilly," I whisper back. "He's sorta creepy, if you want the truth."

She peeks around the door and looks at him again, "Really? How so?"

"Look at the way he's watching me," I say through a closed mouth, like a ventriloquist.

"That's called physical attraction, Poppy. Maybe it's been too long. He obviously thinks you're gorgeous."

"No, that's called the precursor to stalking. That's called 'How fast can you get a restraining order?' Physical attraction is what I feel for one of my patients and must fight to keep control over." My mind wanders to Simon, and I feel a smile emerge.

Lilly sets the salad on the granite and takes out her homemade dressing in an ancient Tupperware—one I can only assume is her Nana's. "What? You came down to earth with us peons and found yourself attracted to a patient? Wow, Poppy, I'm really impressed. First, physical attraction. Next stop, dressing better. Pretty soon, the earth is going to start rotating around the moon."

"Well, don't be too impressed. Simon's moving to Hawaii so my secret is safe for all eternity. But do you know what he did, Lilly?"

She leans against the counter and loses all interest in the food. "What did he do, Poppy? Did he get a colonic that you suggested?"

"Lilly, don't be disgusting." She shrugs and pulls out my wimpy little lasagna from the oven. "So listen, Simon is one of those guys who just knows someone. He has a friend who does this or that. He's just—he's basically Kramer with a brain. He just 'knows a guy.' You know what I'm saying?"

"Not really. Could we speed this up? What did he do?"

"He found out from Emma about my mom's house and he employed a contractor friend, who he claims needed work, and just started repairing the house. When I finally got there, expecting what the house had been for twenty years, it was gone. Stripped away and ready to be built again."

"Without your consent? Oh Poppy, I don't know if I'd like that. He sounds like he makes himself a little too at home."

I look at the lasagna, and I have to say even with the layer of grease on top, it smells utterly divine. Lilly puts a paper towel down to sop up the excess grease the baster didn't catch.

"I did like it," I admit.

"Poppy, are you actually interested in someone?" Lilly pulls her potholders off.

"Me? No, I'm not interested. I just said I was attracted. I'm not attracted enough to pack up my life and move to Hawaii. I just think if I ever did decide to find a man, it would be someone like Simon. He's not afraid to put himself out there, you know?"

"It's just I haven't really heard you mention anyone you thought was attractive, not in years. I know you dated that guy at church for a little while—that business dweeb. But then I heard nothing. I was beginning to wonder if you weren't beyond such a simple thing as a boyfriend."

"Listen, where do you want me to put this meatfest?" I grab the potholders.

"Just put it on the table. I'll get a warming plate." Lilly grabs my elbow. "We're not done talking."

"Talking about what? What am I missing?" Morgan comes alongside us, Georgie hiked up on her hip. She's brought him a bag of tricks, including a video. I've heard Morgan say how antivideo she is for children. But apparently, she's ready for a night out, because there in the pack are three Veggie Tales and she starts rifling through them with her free hand. "Don't talk without me. Unless you're talking about me?"

"It's nothing. Poppy was just saying how you look like you're gaining weight."

"Lilly!" I slap her shoulder.

"It's Morgan's fault; if she wasn't so paranoid she wouldn't be so much fun to tease. She's just 'candy from the baby,' you know?" Lilly opens the fridge again and gets out a pitcher of fresh-brewed iced tea. She removes the tea bags, adds more ice, and yells down to the men, "Let's eat."

I place the salad and the lasagna on the table and smell the sourdough bread Lilly's made by hand, and I have to say, this is not a good place for a diet. Especially a vegan's diet. It's a good thing I've never made that commitment. I think I'd have to banish Lilly and her grandmother from my life.

"Poppy's got a boyfriend," Lilly whispers, so Jacob won't hear.

"I don't," I explain to Morgan. "I just said I thought someone was attractive and Lilly took it the wrong way."

"Well, maybe that's because we've never heard you say that. Not in years. All we hear is that a guy's color is good or that he's such-and-such percentage body fat. But hot? No, we haven't heard that, I believe, since the last Johnny Depp movie."

"I didn't say he was hot. I said I found him attractive and told Lilly something nice he did for me. I don't even find him *that* attractive. It's just he went beyond the call of duty and I'm not used to that. He took me by surprise, which I thought was romantic." As I say it out loud, it just sounds stupid. "Maybe I made too much of it when I was telling Lilly." I think about what I've just said and admit it's not quite true. "Well, he is hot. But in an unrequited, patient sort of way, where I admire from afar."

"So maybe your hand could slip a little and you could send him that message," Lilly says.

"Lilly, do you have to take everything to the gutter?" Morgan asks.

"Yeah, I guess I do. It makes life more fun. Hey, this is about Poppy, not me."

"What about Poppy?" Jacob comes up to the table and smiles. He's got good teeth, I'll give him that. And they're his. Yet another point. "I'm looking forward to our run." Said with the same inflection as "I'll show you mine if you show me yours." *Eww.* He so grosses me out. Can my friends really not see this? One thing that's a dead giveaway is he's said nothing about my cast. He either hasn't noticed because he's too busy gawking at my red hair, or he must think it's a party trick.

"Lilly, may I speak to you in your bedroom a minute?" I grab her hand.

Lilly puts the rest of the meal on the table and tells the men to gather round. "Go ahead, start eating. Poppy and I have to discuss her gown; we'll be right back."

"Right now?" Max asks.

"Right now," Lilly confirms.

As we head to the bedroom, Morgan is on our heels with Georgie. The bedroom is done in rich, Tuscan fabrics, and a warm sienna, textured wall makes me feel as though I've stepped into an historic castle. But again, it's the magnificent view of the San Francisco Bay and the Golden Gate Bridge that dominates the room.

"Dang, Lilly."

"I know, isn't that awesome?"

"The food is getting cold," Morgan reminds us.

"So go eat, Morgan. Poppy said a guy was cute."

"I said he was attractive."

"Whatever. Is he cute enough where you'd wear something different around him?'

"He's been coming as a client for three years; he knows what I dress like."

Lilly groans. "Oh, so this is a one-sided thing."

"Lilly," Morgan chastises. "Maybe he loves Poppy for her beauty. Besides, engineers never notice clothes. Is he an engineer?"

"He's got his PhD in engineering. He invented some gadget and retired. Now he helps people get businesses started and golfs."

"So you're not really into Jacob then?" Lilly asks. "I have to admit, I sort of see what you were talking about. Maybe he is a tad creepy."

"He's positively *Ten Most Wanted* creepy, Lilly," Morgan says. "And I supported you."

"Yeah, he does creep me out a little, but so do you sometimes, Poppy."

"Lilly!"

"Well, she does. Why would anyone work so hard for that body and then put it in a garbage sack?"

"Speaking of which, can I have my skirt back now?"

"Not until after the wedding. They say if you do something for three weeks that it becomes habit, so maybe you'll decide the skirt isn't all that, you know?"

"You wish."

"So what did you want to talk to me about before the dinner gets cold?"

"That guy is a creep." I point to the door. "I don't want to run with him. Ever. Unless I'm running *from* him. I do not like him on the beach, I do not like him within reach. I do not like creepy man Jake. I do not like him, not even for your sake."

Morgan starts to laugh, but Lilly has no idea what I'm talking about. She will, in about four months.

"So what do you want me to do about it? I made a mistake in judgment."

"I want you to break up with him for me. You've got a

built-in excuse. I obviously can't run with a cast, anyway. You got me into this, you get me out."

"He didn't seem to notice your cast."

"Which is not a good thing, Lilly. Will you do it? Or should I ask his cholesterol numbers and maybe about his intestinal tract? That should make for good dinner conversation."

Lilly crosses her arms. "Fine, I'll do it." She shakes her head. "I just really didn't see it until you pointed it out tonight. The hormones must have me off my game."

"Nice excuse."

"Come on, now, I worked all day on that lasagna, and you're not ruining my dinner party."

And with that, one slightly creepy date down. The couples' shower, rehearsal dinner, and wedding with Dr. 90210 to go.

chapter 19

Miles run: 0

Laps swum: 19 with self-made plastic wrap over cast.
Duct tape really is a miracle in itself.
Update: Learned cast is waterproof. Duct tape unnecessary.

Desperation scale: 4

It's been nearly a week since I last ran. I've replaced running with organic chocolate. The feeling/high is the same, but I imagine the long-term results won't be. I can feel my body-fat percentage slipping as I chew, but is it stopping me? Heck no. I'm one of those challenges on *The Biggest Loser*, and I'm losing. But oh, I'm losing gracefully. *It tastes so good.* And just when I think I'm ready to stop? I feel my fingers unwrapping another small bite.

I Tivoed an entire week of reality television, and I'm sitting on my sofa with Safflower the cat on my lap, nervous-eating and downing ginseng tea with cinnamon in it to keep my sugar and insulin from spiking. It tastes disgusting, but a girl's gotta do what a girl's gotta do. There are little foil wrappers strewn about the sofa, and as I yell at the television and a catty bachelorette, I realize it's over for me. This is my life. I'm sneaking chocolate, wallowing in my lack of exertion, yelling at women I don't know from Adam, and petting a cat who allows me to live here. I went to college for this? This has eating disorder written all over it.

I pick up my cell phone and punch in a number, but then I realize I'm overreacting. It's the lack of exercise endorphins in my system, and I hang up before it rings. I forward through a set of commercials and my phone trills. Pausing the DVR, I see it's Simon on the line. I take in a deep breath.

"Hi, Simon."

"Did you just call me?"

"Yeah, but it was nothing. It hadn't rung yet, so I just hung up. Sorry I bothered you. Are you golfing?"

"On a Saturday? Are you kidding? That's when all the weekenders golf."

I laugh. "You're such a snob."

"Seriously, everything okay? Are you going to the house today?"

"I am. I'm driving up to the city this afternoon and thought I'd take Highway 1 to get ready for Morgan's couples' shower tonight."

"What's a couples' shower?"

"It's this vindictive thing that women do to force the men in their lives to be as bored as we are with inane party games and the opening of gifts. We're sharing the wealth."

"Ah. So who are you being vindictive to?"

"Dr. Jeff next door."

"The plastic surgeon?" He starts laughing.

"We made a deal."

"Well, he got the better end of it. Why didn't you ask me?"

"Because I didn't want you getting the idea I was going to run away with you to Hawaii."

"Poppy, I'm an intelligent man, am I not?"

"You are," I admit.

"I've stated my position, you've stated yours. Am I right?"

"You are."

"You can't blame a guy for trying, Poppy. Now what did you call for? Really."

"I was sitting here, eating chocolate and feeling sorry for myself, and I thought about my quest for normalcy."

"Your what?"

"Don't ask. Anyway, I thought what Morgan and Lilly would most like to see is me as them. Normal and mainstream. So I thought I'd go to the shower dressed to the nines."

"All right. And how can I help you?"

"Well, I started to think I'm not all that familiar with mainstream or normal, and I can't ask the Spa Girls, or it won't be a surprise."

"You're not going to ask me for fashion advice?" Simon asks.

"Of course not. But you're the guy who knows someone in every business. I thought maybe you know a girl, you know?"

"Well, my sister's a hairdresser, and she's a makeup artist. When can I pick you up?"

"Simon, really? It's Saturday. Won't she be busy?"

"Yeah, she's probably busy, but I'm her brother, Poppy. Besides, I would pay money to see this. Not because you need makeup, but because the idea makes me laugh. It's the antithesis of you."

"Well, join the makeover club. I have the feeling Lilly and Morgan will welcome me back into their fold, and they'll see that really I'm no different with makeup than without."

"I'll pick you up in an hour. I'm just mowing the lawn."

"You mow your own lawn?"

"Why wouldn't I mow my own lawn?"

"I just thought you had a staff or something."

"All the more reason you need to get to know me better, Poppy."

"So are you upset I'm going to the shower with Jeff?" I probe, looking for a little harmless jealously on his part.

"I figure the sooner you get that ridiculous notion out of your system, the better off we'll be."

I bite down my smile. Looking down at the wrappings surrounding me and feeling my hair, which is not brushed and full of split ends, I realize I'm not exactly the picture of health at the moment. *What if his sister thinks I'm human vermin?*

"I'll be ready in an hour." I hang up, knocking the cat off my lap, picking up the foils and throwing them in the recycling. I, Poppy Clayton, am getting a makeover. The concept makes me laugh out loud. Safflower, a huge orange-and-white tabby, meows at me to show her disinterest, which only makes me laugh all the louder.

I found Safflower outside an auto-parts shop. She was drenched in motor oil and it took a half a bottle of Dawn to clean her up. That's right, no organic soap would touch her. From that day forward, I vowed she'd never know anything but natural oil, and so her name, Safflower, came to be. Her full name is Expeller-Pressed Safflower Oil. Safflower for short. She's about as slippery as oil, without a cuddly gene in her.

"Will you even recognize me this afternoon, Safflower?"

She meows, moves into a patch of sunlight on the hardwood, and collapses into a long, lazy Saturday stretch.

I'm heading to the shower when my phone trills again. It's a number I don't recognize, and I pick up. "Dr. Poppy."

"Poppy, it's Dad."

"Dad, where are you? After that weird reunion, I haven't heard boo from you."

"Listen, I'm sorry about the way we left the house. Sharon was finished living there, and we just had to get out of town before our temporary housing was gone. Packing up an entire life is more trouble than it's worth. So far, anyway."

"Why were you living in temporary housing?" I mean, I know he wasn't in the house, but I never thought to question why he wasn't in Arizona yet.

"Didn't you see the leak in the roof?"

"No, Dad. A friend took care of it for me."

"Well, it ruined Sharon's coffee table. She was thinking of filing an insurance claim."

"What about an insurance claim for the leaking roof?" I ask, trying to keep the *duh* from my question. While I love my father, his idea of maintenance is to allow something to fall apart and find someone to pay for the new one.

"That's homeowner's insurance," he tells me. "You would have had to file the claim." My father can't hide his bitterness. Admittedly, what my mother did to him—emasculating any claim he had to their house—was not the wisest thing as a wife, but the fact is there wouldn't be a house if she hadn't. She loved him despite his downfall, and I suppose I must too—and at the same time be understanding of his position.

"Daddy, I would have to have known there was a leaky roof to do that."

"Poppy, don't get angry. We've kept that house up for two decades. It's just in need of major repairs now. The ocean air is hard on any structure, darling."

My father is a jolly man who's never given a second thought to money. In his mind, it flies down from the sky and rescues him at the last moment. Somehow he's managed to escape bankruptcy, and most bills when they come due, for an entire lifetime. He sells Amway, Avon, and a litany of health supplements, and he has always managed to get by. I don't know how he does it, but he drives a Lexus the size of an oil freighter. Sharon drips in diamonds that Morgan tells me are all D in color, and nearly flawless, and Lilly tells me Sharon's shoes are worth a mint. Like I say, I don't know how they do it, because I've never really seen my father work, but they always manage to come out smelling like roses.

"I'm not angry, Dad." The truth is I can never get mad at my father. He's irresponsible. I dress like I'm in 1970. It's just who we are by nature. "Where are you?"

"I'm in Arizona now. Sharon and I got into our condo just this morning, and already we've been told we're not allowed to move in on a Saturday. Have you ever heard of such a thing?"

"They must have a homeowner's association. They like moving to be done quietly so the rest of the neighbors aren't affected. My condo made me do that too. It's ridiculous, but that's when people are home, and in big complexes, they argue that would ruin nearly every weekend for homeowners."

"Sharon's been yelling at the manager all morning. We bought most of the furniture new, so we just had to wait on the delivery trucks. That could have been anyone here who bought a new couch. Some people don't have enough time on their hands. We found out you can't drape a towel over the balcony either. What kind of place did we—"

"Tom!" I hear Sharon screech.

"I'm on the phone!" he yells back.

"The coffee table is here. He says it's COD!" Sharon yells.

"I have to run, Poppy. Listen, the foster program is going to call you about us. Turns out we can't just take Sharon's sister's kids without some paperwork. Just tell them we'd make great parents, and I'll talk to you soon. Let me know if I can help you on the house at all. Love you, honey!" He hangs up on me. Very unlike my father, but I know he'll find a way to charm me back into his good graces soon enough.

"Is it any wonder I'm weird?" I ask my mirror. I hope Simon's contractor knows about the roof. *This is going to cost me a fortune.* My mother didn't leave that house to my father for a reason. She signed a prenup long before they were fashionable because she loved a man who loved money. I love my father intensely, but somehow I can't help but hope that COD coffee table doesn't arrive on my doorstep with a note of how to ship it back to him. My dad would give you the shirt off his back, but you probably paid for it.

I enter my bathroom and turn on the tabletop waterfall that makes it sound like the spa. Then I start the bath, pour eucalyptus bath gel into the water, and let the mentholated steam fill the room. I'm curious if Simon will notice I used something different. I light a few candles, grab a *Natural Health* magazine, and step into the bathtub (one footed—yes, the cast is waterproof, but it takes forever to dry out). I ate chocolate. I didn't run. I'm getting a makeover. Today, I enter normality. Even if it's a brief tour to show my friends I can play nicely.

I close my eyes and let the scalding water embrace me. I think about the chlorine warnings that other natural health doctors give their patients about the hot water—an excess of the chemical chlorine can enter your skin through osmosis. This is a rule I never had any trouble avoiding. There is nothing better than relaxing in a bathtub and water-logging a magazine, lulling yourself into a pure and blissful state. Sometimes, people can go overboard.

After reading through the magazine, I toss it over the edge of the tub and allow myself to enter into a state of total leisure, and not for the first time I think this feels really good. This is how the other half lives. But naturally, I can't stay here. A control freak is in a constant state of motion and this moment comes but ever so briefly.

The doorbell rings.

Sometimes even more briefly than one hopes for. I look at the handmade rock clock on the wall and realize it's been over an hour. Simon is here, and I am definitely not ready for my close-up.

chapter 20

Miles run: 0

Organic chocolates consumed: Never mind

Desperation scale: 0

I get out of the tub quickly, which proves to be detrimental to my current state of cleanliness. My cast isn't nearly as agile as I would hope, and in an instant I am splayed out on the ceramic tile, buck naked, listening to the doorbell.

"Just a minute," I wail.

In all my makeover images, this was never a part of it. I grab the side of the tub, and pull myself upright. I have cat hair stuck to my legs now. So attractive. My cell phone rings, and I look at it wondering if I should answer. Naturally, it's Simon. "Hello!" I try to sound calm.

"Poppy, are you all right in there?"

"I'm having a little trouble with my cast. I'll be with you shortly."

"What cast?"

"I have a stress fracture. It's a long story." Right then, I realize how long it's been since I've seen Simon, and that just isn't like him. "Can you give me another ten minutes?" Why couldn't they just give me one of those buckling casts? Oh, wait. Because I ticked off the doctor, and he was determined to make my life as miserable as possible.

"Take your time. I'll go out and listen to the game in the car. My sister is expecting us, though, so hurry a little, will you?"

Simon's going to think I'm high maintenance. And I could not be less high maintenance if I were a brand-new Toyota. "I'll be out as soon as I can, Simon. Sorry about this."

I punch the button and dip myself back into the tub on my good leg, washing off the scattered cat hair. I just washed this floor yesterday! That cat must roll around on the cold tile as part of her hourly ritual.

I pull on a skirt. Yes, it's one of my mother's. I have many more of them. Lilly just took my favorite one, and with this cast, it's by far the easiest thing to handle. I brush out my hair, throw on a T-shirt, and slide into my Clarks clog. I'm ready.

Opening the door, I can see it's a typical spring day in California, and the sun blinds me as I look for Simon's car on the street. I spot him in a red Prius. I would have never figured him for a hybrid man. I would have thought Hummer or two-seated sports car. It's strange that I never noticed, but he usually comes at the height of my workday, and I guess I never cared enough to look.

"Sorry," I say as I get into his car.

"What happened?"

"I had a little bathtub incident."

He raises his eyebrows. "Well, sorry I missed that."

"You really aren't. It wasn't pretty."

Simon starts up his car, and we pull into traffic. "My sister's in Belmont. I hope you don't mind the drive, but I thought it would give us a chance to get caught up on the house."

"I haven't seen it since we were there. It's just been a busy week, and—"

"And what?"

"I'm not really all that anxious to go. My dad called me today and said the roof leaked."

"Poppy, I had everything inspected. It's all on a list, and the contractor is taking care of it."

"Why would you do that?" I ask him. "We've never had any kind of relationship that would warrant that kind of help. I don't understand."

He grins. "No, you wouldn't."

I decide it's best just not to have this conversation.

"How are you going to get your hair done? Are you going to rely on my sister's advice?"

I shrug. "Well, it's my best friend's wedding in two weeks. I don't want anything too drastic."

"Just tell her that, and you'll be fine. Listen, I'm glad you called today because there's something I need to tell you in the interest of full disclosure."

I certainly don't like the sound of this. I shut my eyes instinctively, waiting for the shoe to fall. He's married—eight times over. He's got a fiancée waiting for him in Hawaii. He used to be a girl. (Okay, nix that one. He's far too big to have ever been a girl and his fingers are the right length. He has the most manly hands I've laid eyes on.) He'd like to me to pay back the housing costs in 'favors.' My mind runs amuck.

"My mother's in Hawaii. She's sinking into dementia, and I have to get there sooner rather than later so I'm heading out on Monday and meeting with a realtor. I need to find a place to house her with a nurse, have room for my sister to visit, and for me to have my own life."

"Your mother?" I let out the breath I've been holding. "You're not going to Hawaii to play golf?"

"I hope to play golf, of course, but my mother is there, and she's barely remembering my sister and me as it is. I thought I should tell you I'm leaving before my sister did."

"I don't understand—why is that a secret?"

"My father—" He stops. "Well, my father's been looking for her for a long time. Let's just say he wasn't very nice to her in our youth, and she left here after the divorce. He doesn't know where she is, and we've sort of allowed him to believe she's gone on to greener pastures. Which of course, she has. They're just tropical in nature, rather than heavenly."

"Oh my goodness, I don't believe it. You actually have a weirder family life than I do."

Simon laughs. "I'm sure my dad knows the truth, but he's married again, and we just figure it's best to keep things the way they are. Don't ask, don't tell. Mom's remembering the past like it was yesterday, and since he still lives in the same house—"

"You're worried she'll call him."

"I'm worried she'll call him and think she's still in that marriage. She doesn't have access to a phone right now, and she has great care, but it's something my sister and I want to take care of ourselves. She was the kind of mother who protected us against all odds. I think we owe her the same dignity."

Suddenly, Simon's taking care of me doesn't seem all that far-fetched. I can't find words that will offer any kind of peace, so I grab his hand off the steering wheel and clutch it tightly over the parking-brake handle. I'd like to say this is purely to comfort him, but upon reaching for his hand, I'm not so sure.

"My sister wouldn't have told you about my mother, but she would have told you that I'm leaving Monday."

"This Monday!"

"Relax. I'll be back, and I'll make sure I'm watching the contractor. Though he's a buddy of mine, and I can't imagine he'd do anything less than the best."

Simon leaving? As I look at his profile, I realize I haven't been truthful with myself about my feelings in a very, long time.

How did I not know?

I want to say something, but every time I open my mouth to speak, I just hear a sputtering sound.

After a long, silent drive, Simon pulls up in front of his sister's salon. He stops the car, grabs my hand tighter, and looks into my eyes with such force I have to close my eyes. "It's been an absolute pleasure knowing you and offering you a serious commitment." He smiles with a twinkle in his eye. "You be sure and invite me to your and the doc's wedding."

"That's not funny."

"It wasn't meant to be. It was meant to say you have my blessing. I just want you happy in life." He shrugs his shoulders. "That's all I ever wanted."

"People always say that. It's not true, Simon. I don't believe it's true for a minute. Not if you really cared about me. You said earlier you could wait while I lost interest in Jeff."

He gets out of the car, comes around, and opens my door, offering me his hand. I grab it a bit too gustily and stand face to face, willing him to kiss me. I move in closer and shut my eyes. I do everything but pucker, but I hear him slam the door. "Spare me the pity kiss, Poppy. Unlike Chloe, I'm worth more than fifty dollars. My sister's the blonde inside. I'll pick you up in a few hours."

Simon gets back into the car, and before I know it, he's backing out and his Prius is tearing off into traffic. Someone honks at me to get out of the parking space, and I startle and stumble to the sidewalk.

I wish I'd brought a set of crutches. I'm suddenly feeling very woozy and wondering what in the world I set myself up for. The man redid my house; is that not enough for me? No, I have to call him and ask for a makeover, then make a complete idiot out of myself and throw myself at him. Unconvincingly. Leave it to me to finally make a pass at a guy, and not only does he reject me like yesterday's salad, but he doesn't even believe me. I'm that wilted.

I wobble into the salon, and everyone turns to look at me. *Yes, I suppose I do need a makeover. So what of it?*

A blonde woman approaches me. She's big like Simon, but the absence of shoulders on her makes for an extremely obvious bust line. It's almost like her A frame makes an arrow pointing to the area.

"Are you Poppy?"

I nod. "Alma?"

"Come on in. We'll get your hair washed." She walks around me. "When's the last time you cut it?"

"It's been awhile." I shrug.

"Have you *ever* cut it?"

"Yeah, it's just been awhile."

She rolls her eyes. "I guess. And I guess you're not into plucking either?"

"Plucking?"

"Shaping your eyebrows so they don't look like two orange caterpillars on your face. It's a shame to hide those blue eyes."

I instinctively reach for my eyebrows. *Orange caterpillars?* Is it just me, or is that kind of rude?

"I'm open to most anything, except I don't want to dye my hair."

Alma laughs at this. "Honey, do you know how much of my business is trying to get this color? You can't get a perfect red like this from the bottle. Trust me, we're leaving that alone."

"Okay, great."

I sit in a chair, and she flops me back with a lever. I feel every bone in my foot when she does it and muffle the cry. I look around while she warms the water up, and I note the salon is average at best. Everyone has their own mismatched station, all of them covered with personal items describing the particular stylist that goes with the station. Alma's is black lacquer, faux painted with gray stripes and spackling to look as though it's marble. But it doesn't even register as good plastic.

Alma pushes the lever again and moves my neck into the shampoo bowl. "Ouch," I say aloud this time.

"Sorry, you all right?"

"Fine," I say.

"So what do you want to do today?"

"I want to look stylish, like I live in this decade. My best friend's getting married and tonight's the couples' shower so I want to surprise them."

"My brother says you like to dress like that. What's changed?"

"Well, nothing's changed. I do like to dress like this. I just think it will be nice for the wedding pictures if I look a little more mainstream."

"You don't look like my brother's type. That's what surprised me. I wouldn't have recognized you if it weren't for the cast. He told me when you were running late that you had a—what was it?"

"A stress fracture."

"Right."

"Wh-what is your brother's type?" I ask while she sprays my forehead with a jet of hot water. "If you don't mind my asking. I only see him at work. He's my patient, you know?"

"He likes them dark and ethnic looking. Hispanics, Indians, Italians—those kind of women with the piercing brown eyes, you know? I think his perfect woman is J. Lo."

"Uh huh." It's all I can think to say. Ethnic? Somehow, red hair, pale skin, and blue eyes hardly seem ethnic. Unless Irish is ethnic. And J. Lo? With 14-percent body fat, I'll tell you one thing I don't have that J. Lo has. I have the flattest derriere in the world.

The whole conversation fills me with dread, and suddenly I understand why he rejected me at the car door. His offer, his protesting his emotions on the beach, it's all to get what he wants in Hawaii. Golf and good chiropractic care. Simon has not learned that his money can't buy him everything. Clearly.

"But he seems to like you. Maybe his tastes are changing." She rubs my hair just a little too hard, and I clamp my eyes shut against the pain. I thought this was supposed to be relaxing? This is like the pedicure I must endure every time we go to the spa. I hate having my feet touched, and I'm afraid my head is no different.

"I think he just likes good chiropractic care. He has a special back."

"It's inherited. We all have it. When my son came out with shoulders, you could have heard me scream throughout the hospital! I did not have Quasimodo for a son." She laughs at this.

"Quasimodo? You and your brother hardly look—"

"Listen, we survived grade school. I just didn't want that for my kid."

"How old is your son? Simon's never talked about a nephew."

"He's twelve. I had him out of wedlock, and Simon's been like a dad to him, but I think he still gets embarrassed to tell my story."

She rinses out my head and flops me up with that lever again like I'm a piece of toast. I swore I'd be ready for it, but nope. She wraps my head in a towel, and suddenly I'm anxious about this woman with scissors. "You know, maybe I don't need to have my hair cut after all. Maybe we can just do the eyebrows and makeup."

"You have split ends like wishbones. Do you do a lot of swimming?"

"I do," I admit.

"It's drying out your hair something fierce. You should really wear a cap."

I suck in a deep breath. "All right. Let's get it done." We move to her station. There are several pictures of her son on beaches, and a few with Simon in the picture. He's smiling and has her son, in younger years, hoisted on his shoulders, posed in a strongman pose. The image makes me giggle because I can just hear him boasting about how fabulous he is and teaching his nephew to do the same. When it comes to "trash talking," Simon is probably the best in the business.

"Don't take too much off, okay? Go easy on me," I say.

"Poppy, every woman in here is wishing for your hair right now. I'm not going to do anything but clean it up and make your style look slightly more today. All right?"

Alma is the tough-talking, practical sort. But it's clear by the memorabilia on her shelf that she knows how to cut loose and have fun. There's a picture of her in a bikini with her son, and let's just say she's not exactly a small woman. But there she is, enjoying the beach and her son and it's like none of that matters. She's not homely by any sense of the word, but she hasn't given up on life. Though one could obviously say it's dealt her a rough blow. I don't know what happened with her father, but her mother is being hidden away, her father is out of the picture, and her son's father long gone. Yet here she is, all smiles and into her career.

She starts to cut, and I can't bear to watch. My hair hangs down to the middle of my back, and she's been quite clear that this is not stylish for a woman my age, and I can feel her snipping off sections of hair. Watching the three-inch long strands fall to the floor, I cringe with each cut.

"Poppy, you're going to look great. Relax." She drops her scissors for a moment onto the table and starts to massage my shoulders. "You're going to have a heart attack in the chair if you don't chill."

"Why would your brother help me with my house in Santa Cruz? Do you know?"

Alma laughs and picks up her scissors again. "I don't know why my brother does anything. What's your house in Santa Cruz got to do with it?"

"He had it fixed up. It was severely damaged, and I guess I want to know what I could do to pay him back."

She stops cutting again, which brings my breathing back to a normal, steady rhythm. "My brother has too much money and too much heart. It's as simple as that." Then Alma's eyes thin. "Don't read too much into it. Do you plan to pay him back?"

"I do, of course."

She's got those scissors perched precariously over my head, and the threat is a little frightening to me. "I see why he likes you."

"Likes me?" I know this is way too high school, but I can't stop myself. "Has he said that about me?"

Alma shrugs. "You're not his type. I think it will pass once he gets to Hawaii. He'll find a cute little Hawaiian girl who will cook for him and give him babies. Simon learned one thing from my dad. He learned how to care for a family because our father didn't." She drops the scissors. "You're done. Now, I'm going to shape your eyebrows before I dry the hair."

Before I can react, she slops hot goop all over my eyelids and then presses a strip of muslin on my face. With one fell swoop, she rips off the strip of cotton and I scream. "Dang! What was that?"

The other women in the salon look over and start laughing. "You don't want to give her a bikini wax!" one of them shouts.

A bikini wax? I don't even want to know. There is something worse than having just had your first eyebrow waxed unwittingly. It's realizing the second one needs to match and seeing that little wand o' wax coming towards you. My right eyebrow is still stinging and yet I feel my searing flesh on the other side as the wax reaches it. *Riiippp!* Oh my gosh, *au naturel* is the way to go, ladies. Why on earth would anyone do this to themselves willingly? Have they employed this in the war on terror?

So now, instead of two red caterpillars on my face, I have two Charlie Chaplin scarlet eyebrow marks. And because I run, the space where the eyebrows used to be is paler than my normal pallor, which is white at best. Alabaster. That was a word created by a pale woman who couldn't tan, to make herself think she was pretty.

In a world where Eva Longoria, J. Lo, and Beyoncé are the ideal, I am like a ghost straight out of the last century haunting an Irish castle.

Alma dabs cream on my eyebrows and convinces me to calm down. "I'm going to give you a little facial just to clean out those pores."

I am already bored stiff. I look around and all the women are chatting, reading fashion magazines, and seeming to enjoy this entire process. I want to hurt someone. I cannot sit still like this. I could be vacuuming the cat hair off my floor, power walking with my cane, or even updating patient charts. But I'm sitting here with charred eyebrows and short hair, waiting for more pain, more beauty treatments that would make Queen Esther cringe.

I breathe in deeply as Alma uses a paintbrush to paint on

yet another potion and leaves it while she dries my hair. After what seems an eternity, she pulls the now-rubbery mask off my face, applies a spray and then a cream and deems me ready for makeup.

She takes a sponge and pounds (I repeat, pounds) foundation onto my skin (the makeup artist is busy, lucky me) until I can't see one remaining flaw in my face. I am like a tan mime. She even paints the eyelids so you can't see the bright white stripes she's left from waxing. She applies blush, three lipsticks to make me shimmer, and finally, mascara.

"You're ready," she says as she spins me towards the mirror.

"Oh my goodness!" It feels as though I have that rubbery mask still bound to my skin. I am covered in color. I think this might be a little too extreme. What if Lilly and Morgan think I'm going to a street-walking festival rather than coming into this decade? I should have stuck with the clothes makeover and listened to Lilly.

"Do you like it?"

"Uh, yeah. I'm just really shocked, that's all." I vow right then and there to scrape it all off as soon as I get home. My hair is enough of a change for one day. That is, until Simon walks in and all the women zoom in on him with laser-like intensity. Simon looks at me. I see his expression warm at the sight, and I'll admit inside, just for a moment, I wonder if I'm enough to keep him in California. *Can't his mother come here?*

Simon looks at me thoroughly. In fact, I'm not sure I've ever seen him take the extreme notice he takes right now. Truthfully, I don't know if it's his sister's handiwork he appreciates or my changed appearance. Whatever it is, if he's expecting J. Lo, he's still sadly disappointed. There are some miracles a beautician just can't perform.

"I told you she was a miracle worker." Simon grins at me and leads me from her station. I hear the buzz of the women discussing our exit, and I almost wish I could give them something scandalous to discuss. But yeah, this is me we're talking about.

"Keep some ice on those brows if they continue to hurt. You're a wax vir—"

"Never mind." Simon kisses his sister. "Thanks for fitting her in."

Our ride home is silent and strained. Whatever emotions Simon expressed on the beach that night under the stars, the spell has more than worn off and I feel he's more chaste than he was with his own sister. He doesn't look at me like he once did, like he was lucky to be in my presence. Now, I feel like little more than an annoyance.

In the car, I keep thinking of a casual way to discuss my virtual pass at him in the street, and his subsequent avoidance. But what point would it serve? I had my chance, and I suppose he figures I shanked his shot.

chapter 21

Desperation scale: 9

Tonight is Morgan and George's couples' shower. I'm not a couple, but I play one tonight. I decided after an extended period in the beauty chair, seeing the house makeover was the last thing I needed in my life. Simon dropped me off after an uncomfortable drive home. I didn't know what to say to him, and will he even call me before he leaves for his new Aloha life? That remains to be seen.

I dress in the new peasant skirt and flowing shirt that Lilly created for what she terms "Poppy's unfortunate style" and wear a red sandal to downplay my cast. I'm not home for more than an hour when the doorbell rings. It's no wonder Safflower the cat thinks she's the mistress of our home; she spends far more time here.

"Hi," I say, opening the door to Jeff. He's carrying flowers and dressed in a casual pair of khakis with a short-sleeved Tommy Bahama shirt (which I only know because it says so, right there on his collar; I guess that way there's no mistaking he spent money on his clothes). "You look great. You didn't have to dress up."

"Ah, but I did. You were willing to give up your office

space. I'm going to play the knight in shining armor with gusto. It's the least I can do."

"Well, I hope you get the space after all this. I don't know where you're going to find the time to fight a lawsuit."

"I just have to find the money. My lawyer will fight the lawsuit. What are your plans? Have you found anything nearby? Because really, that offer stands. I have a great commercial real estate agent who could find you something in a heartbeat."

"I'm thinking about my options. I might go back home."

"Home to Santa Cruz? And start your practice over again?"

"Most likely not. I'd just drive over the hill. I'm just thinking out loud. Are you ready?"

"No wait. First—" He puts the flowers on an entry table. "First—" He takes both my hands in his. "I want to look at you. What did you do, Poppy?"

I bring my hand to my hair. "I had a makeover. Too much? Do I look like a streetwalker?"

He laughs. "Poppy, the makeup is very natural. You look more gorgeous than ever. But Alicia will be mad. She wanted to get her hands on you with the makeup. Not that you need it, but now you're like a lethal weapon."

"Spoken like a true plastic surgeon. I'm telling you, you really should sell cars on the side. I think you might even get me to buy a Hummer." I smile at Jeff, and for once in our tempestuous relationship, I am truly glad for his friendship. I suppose he does deserve most of the credit.

"You can't take a compliment to save your life."

"I'm sorry. Thank you for the compliment."

Jeff walks around me, taking in all the sights. "The eyebrows were a nice touch. They really opened up your eyes. Now they're unmistakable. Nicole Kidman, look out. You've got competition."

"I don't think she does, but I appreciate your playing the knight-in-shining-armor role. I need it at the moment."

"Why is it so tough for women to watch their friends get married?" He sits on the sofa and puts his feet on my coffee table. A little forward, perhaps, but it's not like I have date options, so I keep quiet.

"It's not nearly as tough as it is to watch the *last* friend get married because that leaves you on a playing field all by yourself. You have to get more, new single friends, or you have to hang out being the third wheel all the time with them setting you up with a series of losers they call perfect for you. It's hard to make new friends at thirty, you know?"

"Poppy, I want to show you something." Jeff walks with me to the mirror and stands behind me, with his head propped on my shoulder, his gaze steady with those amazing blue eyes. "Do you see what I see?" He says this exactly like my father would tell me when the boy I wanted to ask to the Sadie Hawkins Dance went with someone else.

"Hmm," I say. "I see a girl with too much makeup."

"What else?"

"I see a girl with too many options and not enough certainties."

"You sound beaten, Poppy, if you want to know the truth of the matter. I thought you sounded that way when you left me in the parking lot before church the other night. Why don't you go ahead and call me a jerk? That always makes you feel better."

I turn around and face him, and his striking eyes meet mine. For all Jeff may be, strikingly handsome is always the first thing that comes to my mind. And I don't even care about such things. I look down at my red sandal. "I don't want to call you a jerk, Jeff. You're just a man who knows what he wants. Something in me, I suppose, respects that."

I watch Jeff's chest rise and fall with his deep breathing and I try to remember all the reasons I fight with him on a daily basis. I clasp my eyes shut, repeating the mantra *Jeff is a jerk. Jeff is a jerk. Jeff the jerk. Jeff . . . jerk. Jerk. Jeff.*

But when I open my eyes, he's closer than ever, and the distance between him and me diminishes. I bite on my lip, looking for the excuse to move. I can put the flowers away. I can tell him we're going to be late. I can offer him a glass of water. I can call him a jerk.

But I don't need an excuse. Jeff backs away on his own, and I run to the kitchen to get a vase. I can't tell if he's really making a pass at me, but the thought leaves me cold, and with thoughts only of Simon. "How's the sushi chef?" I ask.

"He's back to work. He only got the very tip. It wasn't that big of an injury. Fingers just bleed."

I nod. "Right. Lot of blood supply in the hands. It's no wonder. Just like the head wounds, you get one of those and you're going to have a lot of blood. Lot of blood," I repeat.

I slide the flowers into the vase. "They're beautiful, Jeff. But really, you didn't have to do that. I know what this night is about, and I appreciate you doing it." (What I'm really saying is, *Do you know what this night is about?*) "It's just going to make things a lot easier on me. Remember we're not allowed to talk about things like bloody fingers or slicing people open or anything that has to do with health, especially the digestive tract. All right?"

"I know I'm going to regret this." Jeff moves the flowers aside on the table and grasps my cheeks in his hands. "Why do you pretend this doesn't exist?" he asks about our attraction. Attraction is a funny thing. Linebackers and quarterbacks are brought together by the football, but the collision is never pretty and this won't be either.

"Because this—" I step away and motion between us.

"This is nothing more than an illusion. People who are completely wrong for each other are attracted to each other all the time. It's just the way God made life. You have this certain amount of energy, and when you're around certain people that energy feels really good. And remember God's first building block was energy, or light, as the Bible translates. And who knows why certain people—"

"Shut up, Poppy." Jeff's lips land on mine, and they're soft and firm at the same time. I finally pull away and frantically push my hair behind my ears "Well, it's a good thing that's out of our system, right? Now we can just go on our date, and we don't have to worry about a goodnight kiss. We already took care of that. Monday morning will already be extremely awkward and uncomfortable, and it will force me to get to work on finding a new office space. So yeah. Yeah, that was really good."

"See? I knew what I was doing. Grab a sweater. It will be cold in the city."

I open the hall closet and wonder how on earth I'm going to explain to Jeff that there really is nothing between us. Do I think he's hot? Absolutely. Do I want to take this anywhere? Not on your life. I grab my old grubby sweater, but put it back realizing it ruins the effect of all I went through today. Instead I get a white cashmere cardigan that Sharon bought me for my birthday. It's interesting how my new lifestyle is conducive to all the gifts Sharon purchased.

Jeff puts his arm in the center of my back, and I look back at the flowers he brought and grab the gift for the shower. I feel my face flush at the sight of the bouquet. "Jeff—"

"Just never mind," he says, apparently understanding my meaning and a shared belief in not overanalyzing it.

Sometimes being cherished, even if it's a facade, is not all that bad of a feeling. I'm glad I kissed him. It shows I'm not completely without adventure. I tried. But when all you get is an image of another man? That's just a sign. Sure, Simon dissed me on a Belmont street, but he also used the word *wife* in a sentence in Santa Cruz. And most important, he's the only man I want to kiss me.

I talk when I'm nervous. And apparently I'm very agitated, because I don't think I gave Jeff's ears a break for the entire ninety-minute traffic-ridden drive to San Francisco. When he stops the car in front of Lilly's house, he looks at me and laughs. "Are you sure you have any words left to go in there?"

I cover my mouth with my fingers. "I'm nervous."

He gives me a close-mouthed grin and laughs. "But you're beautiful. Let's go be Barbie and Ken."

"That's Morgan and George. We're more like Skipper and Allan."

"Skipper and Allan?"

"Barbie's less attractive sister and Ken's friend."

"All right, Skipper and Allan it is, though I think you'd give Barbie a run for her money any day."

Jeff helps me out of the car, which is no easy feat because of how low that Lexus is to the ground. He practically has to get a corkscrew to make it work, but eventually, I'm up and in his arms. He steadies me and takes my hand, leading me to the door.

"This house is something. What does your friend's husband do?"

"He's a TV critic. And he dabbles in San Francisco real estate. Oh," I add as though I've forgotten. "And he's an heir to a hotel fortune."

"I guess." Jeff whistles at the sight of the elaborate house in San Francisco's posh Marina District. He knocks on the door, and Lilly opens it as though she hasn't seen me in a year versus a week.

"Poppy!" She squeals. "What did you do? Dang, girl." She takes my hands. "You look hot! And you're dressed in my skirt. See? See how simple it is to make a statement! Max, come look at Poppy!"

"Lilly, this is my date, Jeff."

"Hi, Jeff. Doesn't she look hot? Oh my gosh, what is up with this?"

Max comes to the door. "Lilly, let them in. What are you doing? Whoa! Poppy?" He lowers his eyebrows, trying to decipher if it's me.

"It's me." I point to Jeff. "And this is my date, Jeff."

Max thrusts a hand towards Jeff "Nice to meet you. Come on in, make yourself at home. Lilly's been working all day on this shower. Morgan's not going to know what hit her."

"I really wish you'd let me do more," I say to Lilly. But I know exactly why she didn't. She was worried I'd serve tofu and grape leaves with hummus. Which are some of my very favorite foods. But Morgan's from the San Francisco socialite set, and even Lilly, who can cook like a fiend, hired a catering company for the shower.

Two by two, Lilly's house fills up with people I've never seen in my life. They are all sophisticated and well dressed, and Jeff and I retreat to our corner. Since we're not allowed to discuss what we do, and I'm not dripping in diamonds, and Jeff isn't wearing Armani, we're both at a loss for conversation. Apparently, Cupertino chic is not San Francisco chic, and I think even Jeff feels out of place.

After an hour of idle chitchat and finger food, we sit down for the first game. "All right, couples. We're going to play our version of *The Newlywed Game*. Whoever knows each other best wins a night at Max's dad's hotel complete with a nine-course meal in the Starlight Room."

"Whooo!" A collective gasp goes up around the room of

trendy couples, who all look as though they've stepped out of the Neiman Marcus catalog. Why *free* would mean anything to them is beyond me. They look like they relish paying a lot for things.

Morgan has tried to bring Jeff and me into the fold, but it's apparent neither one of us is in the mood for more pretending. Morgan is wearing a crisp, white pantsuit that Lilly designed, with a touch of lace at the top. It screams *I am the bride* and she looks happier than I've ever seen her. Not because she's the bride. Morgan has always been the center of San Francisco attention and written up for social events since before she was in puberty. But this is about family. She finally has one, and all of this fanfare is mere trifle to her, who looks at George like she wishes the rest of the room would disappear.

"You each have a pencil and several cards with your names on them. Write your answers down and number them, and we'll check them." Lilly's in her element here. She loves to be in charge. "First question: what's your idea of the most romantic date?"

That's easy, I think. *The beach*. I write it down, and Jeff scribbles his own. Then we all hold up our answers.

"The first question goes to . . ." Lilly pauses, reading the cards. "Poppy and Jeff."

I look at Jeff and we laugh. "Beginner's luck, I suppose."

"Next question: what would your mate say is their favorite food?"

Easy again: *organic chocolate*.

Jeff guesses my answer. And he continues to guess. Until we get to: if your mate could go anywhere on vacation, where would it be?

"She'd go to Hawaii and run," Jeff says directly to me.

"That's right. I would. I love the tropical weather, and I

love to run on the beach more than anything else. I know the beaches aren't huge there, but I'd run back and forth, back and forth and take in every single wave and memorize them."

"Who's the best onscreen couple?"

I say Bogey and Bacall, while Jeff names John Wayne and Maureen O'Hara. At least we both see the romance in the classics, but there's something about the wise-cracking, aloof Bogey that gets me every time.

"It looks like our winners, with nine out of ten questions right, are Jeff and Poppy." Lilly says our names slowly as though she doesn't understand and places the envelope in my hand. "Of course, they won't be needing a night in a hotel room, so the winner is Paul and Winnie!" She pulls the envelope from my hands.

The other couple shout and hug one another, and Lilly shakes her head at me. I glare back. Did I ask to win such a stupid contest? I didn't even want to play! I look at Jeff with tears in my eyes. Not because I wanted a hotel room, but . . . How could Lilly do that to me? Make my singleness so public? Did she have to make sure that all her friends knew *this* couple at the couples' shower is a sham and that Jeff and I are only pretending? I blink away the tears and Jeff sits closer to me on the couch and kisses my cheek ever so gently. Nuzzling against my neck as though we're a longtime couple. I smile in gratitude.

"Well, great night, Lilly. You throw a wonderful party. Poppy and I have to get up early tomorrow for church, so we're going to head home. If I know Poppy, her foot is starting to throb and she's said nothing." Jeff stands up and pulls me up from the sofa. "I've got your Vicodin in the car, sweetie."

Lilly walks us to the door. "You okay, Poppy?"

I nod, just wanting to get out of the house as soon as possible and into the crisp night where I can breathe "single" air. Jeff helps me on with my sweater and we head out the door, thankful when it shuts behind us.

"Thank you, Jeff."

"It's nothing."

"No, really. You went beyond the call of duty tonight and you've earned your extra office space. Now do you see what I mean about being single in a married world?"

"Oh, please. I'm a single doctor, Poppy. Every time I show up anywhere, the mothers come out in droves trying to set me up with their Drusilla."

This makes me giggle. "Well, my big foot thanks you." I hold out my cast. "You did me a huge favor."

"Did I? You seem to think everyone's doing you a favor, Poppy. Perhaps my motives aren't purely selfless. Did you ever think of that?"

I laugh uncomfortably. This is not going well and I try to remind him of our deal. "Well, considering you're here because you want my office space, I did have a clue to that." I wrap my sweater around me a little tighter as the brisk spring evening in San Francisco is moist and frigid.

He wraps his arms around me, and we look down at the darkened Bay, whose outline is ringed with lights. The Golden Gate Bridge is lit like a magnificent, red sculpture and our eyes both go to the landmark. "Sometimes I don't think you do have a clue, Poppy."

"Join the club." I say, wondering how I tell him I just don't think about him that way. I think I am going to be dateless at the wedding after all. See, I said I couldn't make it two months. Heck, I can't even make it two weeks without an arrangement blowing up in my face.

"So you're really not interested in me in *that* way?" Jeff asks, bringing his arms tightly around me.

His question captures me by surprise. For some reason, I

thought a doctor would be far more eloquent than to ask a high school-note kind of question. But more important, I can't believe he'd care. And I just don't want to hurt him or his ego.

"It's obvious we have chemistry—" I say by way of a gentle entry.

"But I want to know what you really think about *me*. And I don't mean that line where you think I'm a selfish jerk who mutilates women for a living. I mean the part of you who knows I love my patients as much as you love yours and that I want them healthy, just like you want yours healthy. I mean, let's get over that we are flat-out, stone-cold attracted to one another and we always have been."

I look up at him, and I do give into the temptation I've felt for two years and snuggle into his jacket for warmth. It must be the sea air. I wonder if that intoxicates me from childhood. I pull back and stare into his eyes, feeling the stubble on his cheeks from the long day.

God, I am so confused. I thought I loved Simon, but what on earth am I doing here if that's the case? What do You want from me?

"Let's get some coffee," Jeff says, pulling away. "You do drink coffee? Or you can get some soy concoction there, all right?"

"Soy mochas. One of my favorite things in life."

"Good, because there's not a cold shower nearby, and we're in front of your best friend's house, and I want to make out like a couple of teenagers. It's beneath us."

"Jeff." I stop in my tracks. "I can't do this to you."

"Do what, Poppy?"

"I just can't trust my feelings today. This is convenient, you and me."

"How so? You hate what I do for a living."

"You know what I mean, Jeff. I'm convenient for you. You don't even have to step out of your office, and I'm there. I'm as good as the next girl at church."

"Is that what you think?" He pulls away.

"I just told you, I don't know what I think. But I think a patient has my heart."

And how would Jeff know what I think? I did kiss him earlier, and I played *The Newlywed Game* with him like we'd known each other for a decade. But I can't get Simon out of my mind, and I don't know what to think.

Jeff opens his car door and helps me in. I'll say one thing. When it comes to playing my knight in shining armor, Dr. Jeff is an overachiever. Leave it to me to finally figure out what I want out of life. And for Simon to promptly tell me where to stick it. I really have to work on that timing issue.

chapter 22

Miles run: 0
Laps swum: 0
Motivation: 0
Desperation scale: 9

I take it back. I am desperate. I can't run, I can't bike, and I don't want to swim. Jeff is avoiding me by not returning my phone calls to his cell, and my hopes for a "normal" wedding date have diminished, and he's taking my office space with him. Leave it to me to be the only person to lose on a California real estate deal. I suppose it serves me right for trying to pretend "normal."

I sigh aloud. Maybe I was always desperate, and I just never bothered to name it. It's Sunday morning and the May weather is perfect. Seventy degrees at eight a.m. Usually, it's my favorite day of the week because I run a full eight miles with a Starbucks CD, and it makes me feel like I'm relaxing with the Sunday paper in the coffee shop like the "normal" people. That's what I want to be doing, if only I could sit still long enough. But for me, I just need the endorphins that running (and chocolate) brings. I look down at my cast. I hate sitting still and my foot is throbbing.

As I get to church and take a seat in the back row, I find my eyes keep searching for Jeff, but I don't see him, and my guilt envelops me. Maybe I did give him the wrong perception. I tried to give Simon that same perception, and he left me standing in the middle of the street. Clearly, I'm doing something wrong.

I listen to the worship music, and the hymn "It Is Well With My Soul" is sung. Is there a better song to remind you no matter how big your problems are, they are not what this man went through as he penned this great hymn—the loss of his entire family at sea? It really puts things into perspective. It is, indeed, well with my soul. Well, mostly. Don't get me wrong. I'm grateful. But I am desperate.

After service, I call Simon to say good-bye, and his cell number has been disconnected. I try dialing it again, hoping there's a forwarding number, but there's nothing. I try one more time, just because the third time is the charm, and again, just a loud, busy signal. (Something I thought went the way of the rotary phone since call waiting.) When Simon doesn't answer, I wonder if there's the possibility that he could be in the house in Santa Cruz. He wasn't leaving until tomorrow, so he's got to be somewhere.

I stop at Starbucks after church, and there's an entire contingent from church, and the line is nearly to the door. I look around and see all the people reading the Sunday paper, couples sipping mugs of coffee, and my heart beats a little faster. I don't think I've ever really felt alone like this. Perhaps I have always lived sort of a solitary life, but it was full. I had my running groups on Saturdays, and my swim meets during the summer, and even a biking group. And then, of course, there's the Spa Girls. And Wednesday night singles' group, which I occasionally attended. Lots of things to allow me to gloss over the true loneliness I felt.

I suspect none of those are really intimate relationships (other than the Spa Girls). It was all event related. Which I guess I'm just more comfortable in. But now that life's events have ceased with my stress fracture, I notice there's more in my life that's broken than my foot.

"Aren't you the chiropractor?" A woman in front of me asks this of me, and I turn around in line and face her.

"Yes, Poppy Clayton," I say.

"Yeah," she nods. "You told me once that hydrogenated fats would ruin my life." She turns back towards the cashier. "I'll have a vente mocha Frappuccino. Extra whip on that." She turns around and clucks her tongue at me. "You're a chiropractor, not a doctor." She rolls her eyes and walks over to wait for her fat fest.

The human in me wants to tell her it *has* ruined her backside, but I refrain because it is well with my soul. "Iced tall soy latte." I scratch my head. "No, make that a mocha."

"Whipped cream?"

"No, thanks," I say, getting in line behind the woman clogging her arteries.

"You know," I say to her. "I told you that because in Bible study, you said you'd been unable to lose the last ten pounds and you said that you didn't like to exercise. The body doesn't digest trans fats. It's like putting plastic in your system. I was trying to be helpful. Sorry if I offended you."

This disarms her and she softens her expression for a moment before a call for her Frappuccino reminds her where we are. "Are you a Christian? Or a tree hugger?"

"I suppose I'm both, depending on your definition."

"You can't serve two masters." She says, walking out with her supersized cup o' calories.

Of course, I could tell her the same thing. She can serve God and the temple he gave her, or her craven desires for drinking her calories. But what's the use? I leave the coffee shop more depressed than ever. As I'm walking out, Jeff walks in with the blonde from the convertible. This girl is like a bad penny; she shows up everywhere.

"Jeff, hi. Chloe, what a surprise to see you both." *Together. So soon after you kissed me.* Granted, I'm pining for another man, and I kissed him back. But still. A little loyalty should last at least twenty-four hours. Is that too much to ask?

"Hi, Poppy." Jeff purposely takes his hand and places it on Chloe's back. "Guess who's coming to church?"

I want to ask where the reconciled husband is, but I've learned enough to keep my mouth shut for the moment. If people want advice, they'll ask for it.

I lift up my drink. "Off to Santa Cruz. See you soon."

"You're going to call me." Chloe makes that annoying phone fingers next to her ear like she's starring on *American Idol*. "To run, when you're up to it, right?"

I lift up my cast conveniently. "If I'm still in town, most certainly." I reach for the door and Jeff opens it for me and follows me out to the sun-kissed patio.

"You know, if I were you, Jeff, I wouldn't get involved with that. First she's with her husband, then she's having coffee with a single man on a Sunday morning. Don't you ever see the Lifetime channel?"

He laughs. "No, what does that mean?"

"The boyfriend is always the one to die."

"Boyfriend? No, no. You've got it all wrong."

"The husband always has it wrong too. And then . . ." I shape my finger like a gun. "Bam! The boyfriend's family is fighting for justice in the court scene."

Jeff lifts his brows. "So where's this elusive man of yours? The one who has your heart." He looks around the parking lot as though I've made the entire thing up. "If you wanted to be rid of me, you know, you didn't have to lie. I'm a strong guy."

"I didn't say I had *his* heart." *Maybe I did once, but I sure blew that.*

He gives me that lopsided grin and the blue of his eyes just sparkles under the sunlight. "So have dinner with me Wednesday and we'll talk about it. I think—" He puts his hand to his chest. "I think if you really analyze the situation, you might not be as head-over-heels as you think. I mean, who needs rejection like that?"

Certainly not me. "I'll think about it. I've got to get over the hill before all the beachgoers clog the road."

"You want to trade cars?"

"You'd let me drive Katie on one of the most dangerous roads in the Valley?"

He drops the keys in my hand. "Now, give me the keys to Granola," he says about my Subaru.

"I don't think so." I hand him back the keys and he grasps my hand.

"I'll see you for the rehearsal dinner."

I nod. "Thanks." I climb into my car, amazed that even after I've damaged his ego, he's committed to our deal.

The traffic to Santa Cruz is a nightmare. Bumper to bumper all the way over, with kids screaming their music from their convertibles and beaters. Surfboards sticking out the tops of vehicles. And it brings back memories of cruising Friday night, honking at the popular boys and giggling wildly if they honked back. Those were the days when you only had to worry if you were worthy of a honk.

"Oh my goodness!" I say aloud as I approach the house. In the daylight, it's like something out of a movie and I've just gone back in time thirty years. It's perfect. The white clapboard siding has been replaced with new, vinyl siding, and the roof is a bright composite gray. I smile at the front door, which has been painted red, and I know that had to come from Simon. I'm sure he's listened to my explanation of color more than a few times.

I clamber out of the car as fast as I'm able with my awkward gait and race to the porch. The door is ajar and inside, the drywall is up and a painter—at least I assume he's a painter; he's in whites with paint splatter all over him—is standing there. He looks over the plans and, finally, at me.

"Did you want imperfect smooth or elephant hide?"

"Pardon me?"

"The wall texture."

"What's better?"

"Imperfect smooth is more popular now. It's that old-world look."

"Yeah," I nod. "I think that's good. Have you seen Simon?"

"Nah. Been here all morning getting everything prepped." The painter shakes his head. "He hasn't been here."

I walk out to the back porch and look to the spot where I had Simon in my grip last time, and I ponder the previous day in his sister's salon. I'm probably just anxious over this because he's leaving, and he doesn't believe that I'm truthful. This is probably just pre-wedding jitters I feel for Morgan. I'm just worried I'll be alone. The truth is I've been alone a long time emotionally. This is nothing new and Simon's leaving will change nothing.

I walk down to the beach and watch the waves roll in and the kids chasing them and running back in. I can't recount the hours I spent doing just that before my mother's death. I smile at the memory.

"One of these times, the waves are going to get tired of being taunted, and they'll catch you by surprise," my mother warned me.

I retaliated by sticking my tongue out at the wave and running even closer to the cresting water. Then, just as my mother prophesied, the wave encapsulated me and took me down into its undertow. I remember water everywhere, like being in an agitation cycle, and not knowing which way was up and which was down, just tumbling violently while bits of sand hit me in the process like tiny darts. I thought I'd never see the sky again, or breathe the air, as I fumbled and flailed, unable to do anything against the power of the water. I was nothing more than a piece of seaweed against the force.

Until my mother pulled me upright and stood me up. I was still in the water to my knees and wanted to run. "No," she said. "Wait until the wave goes back out. You'll just get stuck in it again. You can't fight the undertow."

I looked up at her, so fearful of the water, but knowing I couldn't let go of her hand or I might go under again. I clung to her leg with my free hand.

"Just wait," she said reassuringly. "It will be gone soon."

As the wave dissipated, I pulled my feet from the wet sand, which had buried them above the ankles, and my mother calmly walked us to our blanket and surrounded me with a towel. "Let's eat a sandwich. I'll bet you're starving. I made your favorite."

I nodded, trying so desperately not to cry, but angrily staring at the waves as though they had betrayed me.

"You're crying. Poppy. That's what the waves do. They come in, and they have such force you can't play with them and not be ready. Don't be mad at the waves or scared of them. Just know that's what waves do, and I'm here to protect you because that's what mommies do."

She fed me an almond butter sandwich and made me go right back out into the waves. She stayed with me, and held my hand, but she wouldn't let me go home. Not until I'd faced the Pacific again and prevailed.

As I gaze out into the depths of the ocean now, I have tears again, remembering those words. *That's what mommies do.* I use the back of my hand to wipe away the tears and I listen to the laughter from the children below. It's not what all mommies do. Not when mommies have more pain of their own than they can handle. Not when a tidal wave of full force captures them and won't let go. She didn't cling to His hand, though she told me not to let go.

Why did you let go?

"You promised me!" I rage at the sky, though I know how ridiculous my words are now. Decades late, and more useless than driftwood on the beach. I sink to the ground, cross my legs, and watch the surf go in and out again. The children playing chicken with the waves, and their mothers hovering closely nearby.

I never told my mother I loved her before she died. I was so angry—livid, actually—that she'd allowed herself to get sick. *Disgusted* might be the proper word. "I loved you more than life itself," I whisper. "I loved you and Aura more than anything. We never talked about her death, but I loved her, too, Mom! I was her mommy too!"

I wipe away the tears, remember when life in our home ceased to be alive, when the prevailing emotion was sadness and grief. Life changed when my sister Aura died from SIDS. Suddenly, my mother went from being a good mommy to being a failure—in her mind anyway.

Like a fresh wave, the truth finally hits me.

It was the guilt!

I stand up again, watching a pelican race along the crest of a wave. "I blamed you, Mom. I blamed you for not taking care of yourself, but it was because you couldn't take care of

Aura!" I feel the tears come again. "I never knew," I say to the sky. "But you were a good mommy."

That's why she told me I was strong when she was sick. She thought Aura needed her more than I did.

"Poppy, are you looking for me?" I shield my eyes from the sun and turn to see Simon like the angel of light he is right now.

"Oh, Simon." I fall into his barrel chest and breathe in his familiar scent. He doesn't know what to do with his arms, but I don't care. I wrap my own around him and hug him with the passion I feel. "Simon."

He doesn't hug back, but I don't care because I am finally free. I understand with amazing clarity. I've put into health all that my mother put into destroying her body from guilt. I had my own guilt that I couldn't save her and this has been about proving to her I could do it.

"Simon." I look up into his eyes, which soften, even though I can tell he's working hard to keep his expression from changing. "I let life go by without telling people what I really felt for them, how I hurt for them. I was so angry at my mother when she died that I never told her how much I loved her. I never told her that I loved her more than life itself or that she was a good mother."

"Poppy? What are you talking about?"

"Granted, maybe I was too young to know all those things. We never talked about my sister's death. I never told her I loved my sister, and I knew it wasn't her fault, but I never told her, Simon."

"Poppy, what sister?"

"My sister, Aura." I try to talk over the sobs. "She was a cranky little baby, who I tried to mother when her screams drove my mother crazy. But she died, Simon. SIDS, they called it, but she was never healthy, I don't think. Her death broke my mother, and I think I always blamed her for not taking care of herself after that, and for letting the diabetes get her. But now I know, Simon. I know that she couldn't help it."

Simon's arms finally come around me, and again I breathe in deeply and relish his familiar and warm scent.

"She once told me that mommies take care of their babies. I never thought of what that meant to her. It meant *guilt*, Simon. It meant that she didn't care for Aura like she should have. Which of course was a lie." I wipe my face again. "It didn't mean that she'd given up on me. Only that she couldn't deal with the guilt." I look up at the sky. "All these years, I've been so angry. Why didn't I know?"

Simon's arms come around me tighter, and I bask in his warmth, allowing the decades of tears to fall. "She knew, Poppy. I promise you, she knew."

I pull away from him and meet his deep brown eyes. When he looks away, I lift his chin and force his gaze to mine. "So you see, you might have to go to Hawaii alone and do what you need to do to be a good son. But I can't let you go now without telling you that I love you. I've joked with you and kept you at arm's length because I wasn't able to face what I really felt. I think I must have loved you years ago."

"Poppy." He shakes his head. "Don't say this now. You're not in the right place to say this now and I'm not in the right place to hear it."

I nod, and sniffle. "I am, Simon. I am."

Simon takes a golf handkerchief from his pocket and wipes my tears away, softly patting my cheeks. "Let's get you home."

"No." I stop him by grabbing his arm. "I don't want to go home, Simon. I want to have this out right here and now at the beach. It only seems appropriate. I want to know what changed between the other night on that very same beach down there and right now." I point to the dusty ground. "If you don't love me, why did you spend a fortune to fix up my house without even asking me? Why did you stand up to my father that day in the office?"

Simon sucks in a jagged breath, but he doesn't answer me. He twirls me around in his arms so I'm facing the children on the beach. I want to turn around and beat his chest until I get an answer, but I'm so comfortable in his arms as I think about what really happened to my mother, I can't bear to hear what he might say. For now, his being here is just enough.

chapter 23

Miles run: 0
Blocks walked with Simon: 2
Desperation scale: 0

We walk back to the house after staring at the ocean for an hour. Simon's back is hunched over, and I can tell he's hurting. I almost feel it myself, as I can see exactly where his spine is curved strangely. Instinctively, I put my hand there. "I have my table in the car. We'll adjust you when we get back to the house."

Simon nods as though he really hasn't heard what I've said.

"Simon." I stop walking and face him. "What is going on with you?"

"I've just got a lot on my mind, Poppy. I've got to finish packing, and I shouldn't have come over here. I have a million things to do to close up my own house. Hearing what you're struggling with, and that I can't help you right now—it bothers me, all right?"

"Simon, today was a good thing. I understand a lot more than I did yesterday."

He grabs his back. "It doesn't mean you have all the

answers, Poppy. This is all fresh and you're still going to fight the obsessions. You know that."

As we approach the house, my father's Lexus is in the driveway. My father, who's supposed to be in Arizona.

"Isn't that your father's car?" Simon asks.

At that point, my father comes down the front stairs and waves at us. He's wearing the same Tommy Bahama shirt Jeff wore on our date, and I can't help but laugh at the sight. I run the last few steps towards him and hug him frantically. "Daddy, I'm so glad you're here. What are you doing here?"

My dad keeps his arm around me and reaches out and shakes Simon's hand. "Good to see you, young man. You've done a good job on the house." His nod is his form of masculine thank you, and I watch adoringly as my two men meet each other in respect.

"Thank my friend, Jim. He's the contractor." Simon stretches out his hand again. "Well, it was good to see you, Mr. Clayton. If you'll excuse me, I've got to get home and get the final things packed for Hawaii."

"Going on vacation?"

"Something like that." Simon starts for the car. "Poppy, if you need anything just ask Jim. He'll take care of it."

"Simon." I go chasing after him. "You're just leaving me?" I can't keep up on my cast. "Simon, wait."

He turns around, and his brown eyes warm at the sight of me. I know what he feels; I can see it. I just don't understand what's changed, and I know if he leaves, that will be it.

"Why is your cell phone not working?" I ask him.

"I'll get a new one in Hawaii. I'll call you when I get there, Poppy."

"Do you promise?"

He smiles. It's the warm grin I'll always remember. The

one that would light up a room. "I promise." He tips my chin towards him. "Stay out of trouble."

"Are you going to kiss me good-bye?" I ask.

He chastely kisses my forehead. "Stay out of trouble and stay off that foot. No running, do you understand?"

"I didn't mean aren't you going to kiss me on the forehead. If I want that kind of kiss, my father's behind me."

Simon laughs. "You're asking me for a kiss? This is rich, Poppy. A man just has to redo your house for the privilege?"

"Jim redid my house, and I'm not asking him for a kiss, am I?"

"I'll be sure and tell him."

"Make no mistake, Simon. I am asking you for a real kiss, and you're avoiding the subject quite adeptly. I'm starting to feel . . . Well, I'm starting to feel a little dissed, quite frankly."

He steps closer to me. "I can't have my best chiropractor feeling dissed." He bends down and kisses me tenderly, but briefly on the lips.

"That's it? That's the best you got?"

"In case you haven't noticed, your father is right there, and I'm not sure he thinks much of me."

I turn around and look at my dad, who is indeed staring at us. "He'll get over it." I pull Simon down toward me, and I give him a real kiss. Whatever Simon's saying to me, I can feel the truth on his lips. I pull away with a sly smile on my face. I don't think Simon knows exactly how goal oriented I am, but I consider myself in training for not just a triathlon, but wrangling a slippery young entrepreneur.

"What are you up to?" he asks me.

"Just saying good-bye to a friend." I shrug.

"That was *not* a good-bye. Everything in that kiss was a 'hello, baby.'"

This makes me giggle. "I'll be in Hawaii for the run in a month."

"How are you going to run on a stress fracture?"

"You let me worry about that."

He bends down and kisses me again, and I feel it to the tips of my toes. I feel like I could leave with Simon right now. I could walk away from everything, and we could set our goals together. But of course, that equates with stalking, and I have enough self-control to know better.

"You're worth the wait."

"What?" he asks.

I clamp my mouth closed. "I'll see you in Hawaii."

"Good-bye, Poppy." Simon slips into his Prius and waves.

I walk back towards my father after watching Simon drive off and I just have all the confidence in the world that I'll see him again soon. Though, in hindsight, he didn't leave a phone number or a forwarding address. A lesser woman might think that was a bad sign.

"What's that about? Poppy, are you interested in that boy?"

"Do you remember that time Mom pulled me out of the undertow?"

He grins. "I do. You were scared to death, but then you relayed how you got right back in, and that the water would never get you again." He laughs again. "It did—the Pacific is faster than a six-year-old—but you were never afraid after that. You kept your cool."

"That's exactly what I plan to do with Simon, Daddy. In his own way, he plucked me out of the ocean again, and I'm going right back in."

"Do you always kiss your patients? It's not very professional."

"Dad!" I start to laugh. "What do you think?"

"I just don't know what you see in that guy. He's all money and bravado. What's attractive about that?"

"Dad, look at this house! What's not to see in Simon? He takes care of everything. I like that in a guy. I know that I can rely on him."

"Reliable is something you want in a mechanic, not a husband."

"Actually, I think I want *both* a reliable mechanic and a husband. I'm particular that way."

"What about passion? Does he move your senses at all?"

"Dad!" *I'm so not having this conversation.*

"Sharon and I knew from the first moment. She looked at me, and I knew everything would be okay."

That might be because you'd just lost your wife.

"What about Mom? How did you know with her?"

"Your mom was a good woman, Poppy, but she was too practical for real passion in many ways."

It breaks my heart to hear this, because I don't think for one moment that it's true. My mother bore and bred passion. I think about her giggles at the beach, and her spinning me around in the house, and our sewing together, and her passion for art. Everything she did was done with zeal: the garden, her dancing, her baking. I think about my dad's statement and I realize he doesn't really remember my mom before Aura died. He just couldn't and think she wasn't passionate.

At the same time, I imagine my father forced the practical in her. Though my daddy may be passionate about a lot of things, work was never one of them. Don't get me wrong—I love my father deeply, but I know his weaknesses well. He never grew up. When my mother finally died in her coma, Sharon helped serve food at the funeral.

I'll never forget seeing her in the kitchen, wearing my mother's apron, as though the interloper had made herself at home no shortage of time. Later she told me, "Men need to be married, Poppy, and I wasn't about to let another woman get her hands on a good man like your father. In those cases, one must move quickly. Let mourning protocol be saved for kings and queens. You needed a mother."

Yeah, I was her top concern. But of course, Sharon was a good mother to me; she just wasn't my mother. And it's time I remembered the good in that.

"What are you doing here, Dad?" These memories temporarily wipe the empathy from my voice.

"I drove all night. I just felt there was unfinished business here. Something drew me back, and Sharon tried to talk me out of it. She's worried about nesting for the kids before they get there. But I don't know, Poppy, I just had to come." He looks at the house. "It looks good, doesn't it? Hard to believe we lived in it the way we did all those years."

I nod.

"We have to get your mother's things out of storage. It's time. I'll be back in a month for the wedding, but I didn't think this could wait."

Yes, it was time twenty years ago, but facing things head on is not something either me or my father is good at—unless we're talking someone's health issues. I can take all the conflict in the world for a bad kidney.

"Sharon didn't come with you?"

He shakes his head. "She feels we should have done this ten years ago. She offered to."

"Maybe we should have let her."

"Come on, I'll drive you to the storage locker. Simon said the key was in the left-hand kitchen drawer."

I watch my father go into the house and schmooze with the plaster guy. He really could charm a snake from its hole, and this makes me smile. My daddy was the man every girl wanted in school, and I feel lucky to have him. Though money disappears in his presence, he's worth every penny to those he delights.

He jangles the key in his hand. "Let's go."

Let's go. My thoughts exactly, but somehow I'm picturing white sandy beaches and a burly hero at the end of my travels. Simon's picture invades my thoughts, but it's a good thing because somehow going through my mother's things doesn't feel nearly as unpalatable as I might have thought.

My cell phone trills, and I pick it up hopefully. It's Morgan.

"The bride is calling me? What did I do to be so special?"

"Lilly and I are worried about you, Poppy."

Oh my goodness, how sweet is that?

"Worried about me? What's to be worried about?"

"You're dating a plastic surgeon who looks like he's straight off Dr. 90210, you're in a cast from over-exercising, you're telling us you might lose your office lease, and you have the nerve to ask that question?"

"I'll have the cast off for your wedding, and Jeff and I are just friends. The office will work out. My clients will follow me."

"It didn't look like friendship on the sidewalk," Morgan says, referring to my brief lack of judgment.

"Were you spying on us?"

"Of course we were; what kind of friends do you think we are?"

I walk away from my dad so he can't hear my conversation. "Well, I explained to Jeff all about Simon. Jeff felt sorry for me after the shower."

"Simon? The guy you told Lilly about? The patient?"

"Not anymore. He's moving to Hawaii. He was a patient for three years though."

"And you're telling me I shouldn't worry. You finally have a crush on someone and he's going to Hawaii and it took you three years to realize you had a crush?"

"Yes," I answer. "But Hawaii's just a plane ride away, and I have my ticket already for the race, so I can track him down easily enough when I get the new office settled."

"What on earth? Poppy, you're not thinking clearly. What supplements are you on now?"

"I'm on nothing, just a little kefir in the mornings. Listen, I have a plan, Morgan."

"Oh no, Poppy. A plan? It doesn't include some magic potion you've concocted in your office, does it?"

"Ahem."

"You're not going to think this is romantic to have an unrequited love scene, are you? You didn't watch *Wuthering Heights* lately, did you?"

"Simon!" I shout with all the passion of Heathcliff on the moors. But Morgan doesn't laugh.

"That is not funny."

"Come on, it was sort of funny."

"Let me see if I have this straight," Morgan says. "Jeff is your date for the wedding. The guy you were snuggling with on Lilly's sidewalk, and the guy who you got a nearly perfect score on *The Newlywed Game* with, right?"

"Right."

"But he's not the guy you want."

"That makes me sound flaky, Morgan. It's not like that. Jeff needs a place to expand his business, and our landlord is going to kick us all out, so Jeff hired a lawyer, but I'm not into that lawyer/lawsuit thing. Oh, no offense to George. But anyway, I made Jeff a deal—"

"Poppy?"

"Yeah?"

"How does this have anything to do with the guy you supposedly want?"

"I'm getting to that. Okay, Simon, the man I want, comes into my office all the time, and we've been flirting for years, but really never did anything about it because I was his doctor, he was my patient, that kind of thing. Then, Simon was in my office when my dad was there—"

"Oh, your dad likes him."

"No, not really. So Simon overheard my dad say that I had this house in Santa Cruz that needed a lot of work."

"Poppy, you're making my head spin. If you want Simon, but he's moved to Hawaii, explain to me how you think this is going to play out."

"Okay, well, I don't exactly know that yet. I just know that Simon is the man I want to marry. I'm going to pray about it, and you know, God says he can move a mountain, so Simon shouldn't be all that difficult."

Morgan sighs again. She seems to be doing a lot of that lately.

"So will Simon come to the wedding now as your date?"

"No, he's going to be in Hawaii, aren't you listening? Besides, he says he's not serious about me, but I know he's lying about it because when he kissed me— Oh well, just never you mind. But wow! This is it, Morgan. This is it."

"I'm glad I called. Lilly reserved the spa for the weekend because she was worried about you, and I told her she was full of it, but now I think I must have been blind. Lilly thought we hadn't spent enough time with you and wanted to get together just the three of us before the wedding."

"Don't you have a million things to do?"

"Poppy, you forget. I used to plan these parties weekly. George will be home for the weekend with Georgie, and this is our last chance to play free and clear."

"That would be great." I hold up a finger to my dad, who is tapping his foot outside his Lexus and ready to get this errand over. "I'll explain about Simon then."

We hang up, and I have a big smile on my face. Today, I

remembered who my mother really was, and I learned how a broken heart damages everything. If Simon thinks he's any match for my zeal, he's got a lot to learn. I did not figure this all out for nothing.

I get into my dad's Lexus and he dashes us to a nearby storage unit that looks like a good place for a murder. The metal cubicles are all locked, and of course I can't help but wonder what's inside each of them. Maybe I've watched too many movies of the week, but I keep hoping one won't smell and there isn't a body inside.

"Poppy, what are you doing lollygagging?"

"I was just thinking about something. Do you think anyone's ever been murdered here?" I hop quickly to catch up to him, and he looks at me strangely and gets to the number Simon has marked. He opens the door, and whew, talk about smells! "Oh, Dad! What died in here?"

"I think it's the sofa. It was out in the rain." He shrugs. "I should have taken it to the dump, but I guess Simon didn't know to throw it out."

The good news is Simon values used items. The bad news is he may be a pack rat like my father.

Dad starts to pull out the items. My mom's old sewing box. "Oh, Dad, I want that."

He nods. "Everything in here is yours. There's only one thing I came back for. I used to keep it hidden from Sharon. It made her feel bad."

"You kept something hidden from Sharon?" This intrigues me.

He pulls out a wooden frame with the family picture in it. My eyes well up seeing the photograph of me at nine beside my father, and baby Aura in my mom's arms. "Sharon thinks it's morbid to have this around since half our family is gone, but it makes me happy to remember what we were."

He holds up the frame. "Do you remember when we took this?"

"I fought over the green dress. You wanted me to get the pink one."

He laughs. "That's right. Your mother wanted to sew matching dresses for you and Aura, but you said you were too old to dress like a baby."

"Where are you going to hide it now in Arizona?"

"I'm not going to hide it anymore, Poppy. This is my first family. Yeah, we're not the same and we've added Sharon to our mix, but it doesn't make your mother or Aura obsolete." He dusts off the photo. "You know why I'm here?"

"I haven't a clue." But I feel my tears at the sight of all my mother's things. There's not a day goes by that I don't think of her. You never forget. You just never forget what it feels like when your heart has been broken.

"We're going to do foster care for Sharon's nieces and nephews. I told you that, right?"

"You did."

"God really nudged me the other night that I hadn't finished my first job as a father. I left you with this house and all it entails, and even though that man Simon helped you, it wasn't his place to do so." My dad looks down at the photo in his hands. "That Simon's a good man, Poppy. I still think he's not for you, but what father ever thinks a man is good enough for his daughter?"

"Daddy, I love you, but I want you to know, I'm strong enough to do this alone. I want to take my time and go through everything methodically."

"I know you are, Poppy. You always were. But sometimes it's about not having to be strong enough. Sometimes, it's about knowing that you can be weak and someone else will pick up the slack. That's been you far more than it's been me."

"Dad, you're a good father. We just got dealt a raw deal, and we didn't handle it all that well."

"I wanted to be the best father. I think I was better before Aura came along. I suppose that's a cop-out, but somehow everything fell apart after that. Once your mom lost her, nothing was ever the same. She ate her pain, and the rest of us suffered right along with her."

"You've got a new life now, Dad. Someone else will benefit from the lessons learned." I hug him and realize how grateful I am for all he is—and, really, all Sharon is too. She really walked into no bargain, and I've forgotten that. All this time I acted like my father and I were the prize, the reward for a life well lived. *Hello?* No wonder Sharon thought I was nuts.

No, my father's never been the kind of dad who made sure my shoes didn't have holes in them. But more important, he was the kind who supported me in whatever I wanted. Even when that meant dropping out of medical school. "Yeah, Dad. God broke the mold with you. You're the perfect daddy."

"And you're the perfect daughter."

We continue to sort through the many things in the storage unit, and there are quite a few more gauze skirts. I'll have fun with those this weekend. Lilly will completely lose it, and just the thought of it makes me laugh out loud.

One thing about death: the memories go on forever, and it's a choice to remember the good ones.

chapter 24

Miles walked: 3
Weights lifted: 60 minutes
Desperation scale: 4

Spa Del Mar has been such an important part of my history. Our history as friends. The Spa Girls started coming here during college—to get away, to study and have the quiet necessary to escape our stressful collegiate lives. Morgan tried to escape an overbearing father who choreographed her every move and saw her future as an investment. Lilly tried to escape her finance major and the life she architected for her Nana's approval. Back then, I thought I was escaping nothing more than my routine, that I was just along for the ride to help my friends.

I was escaping more than either of them. I just had buried it so deep that I didn't know it. As I come back to Spa Del Mar for this final soiree, I've emerged a new person from my carefully constructed cocoon, so light I feel like I could fly.

We get into the room with its familiar faded green walls—which get more and more faded with each trip—and it dawns on me that we've outgrown this place. *It's a dump.* I suppose it always was, but it held so much comfort for each of us no one wanted to be the one to say out loud what we all thought. I toss my tapestry bag on the floor, and I open a brand-new Samsonite suitcase with the fancy, twirling wheels.

"Poppy, you bought something new?" Morgan asks.

I nod. "It's for my trip to Hawaii."

"About that trip." Morgan and Lilly look at one another. "We think you should postpone it. Hawaii is always having triathlons. You're not going to be able to run this one now, and we're worried you're going to push it. And about this Simon character—"

I shake my head. "I'm not going for the run. I haven't run since I put this cast on. I've been doing weights at the gym at work. Simon will work out fine."

"Really?" Lilly says.

"We're not concerned about the exercise. Even if it is extreme, you've always been extreme, so it's not like the obsessive-compulsive thing worries us. Poppy, we're worried about this guy Simon. You can have any guy you want. Why do you want to chase someone?" Morgan extends her French-manicured hands to her suitcase filled with expensive couture relaxation outfits and unpacks as gracefully as possible in a plastic dresser.

"I don't really *want* to chase Simon," I say. "But if training has taught me anything, it's that I can outrun him. Probably even in the cast. Which is coming off next Thursday for a removable one. That should make you happy, Morgan."

"Men like to be the pursuers," Morgan says like the star of the fairy tale she is.

"Do you remember that song *More than Words* by Extreme?" I ask.

Again, they look at each other, wondering what I'm really asking and not quite sure how to proceed.

"It's not a trick question. I'm going to assume you remember it. Well, with Simon there's more than words. I can't explain it. When I'm near him, I just feel alive. He's like this great energy source, almost like I'm plugged in! He's the water to my houseplant."

"Honey," Lilly says. "That's lust."

"No," I shake my head. "Dr. Jeff was lust. He's hot and I can't deny I thought he was completely attractive and I almost lost my head to lust. But no, Simon is different. I even learned to appreciate Jeff's zeal for plastic surgery. But that's different from what I feel for Simon."

The two of them back away from the bed, as if to show me it's again mine. They obviously feel my life is the most pathetic at the moment. Which I understand. After all, Lilly is married to a multi-millionaire living on an expensive knoll in San Francisco's Marina District. Morgan is marrying a top tax attorney in San Francisco and becoming an instant mother to his child, Georgie, who sees in her genteel nature the mother he always needed. Likewise, Morgan sees the ready-made family she always craved. So it's not like there's any real competition for pathetic, but I'm glad they recognize it just the same.

I'm fixing up a decrepit house, trying to find a new office building, paying an escort for his services to the wedding (with my pledge of office space, but still), and I'm chasing a man who left me for the Aloha Spirit and golf. So I can see why they think my life is bad energy personified. But they're wrong. Simon loves me. We just have a few kinks to work out.

"Poppy, we just want you to be happy," Morgan says.

"And bring a decent date to your wedding. I've taken care of that. Simon is a little boisterous for your tastes, I'm sure, but Jeff will be fine."

Morgan shakes her head. "If you want Simon to come to the wedding, I'll pay his way, Poppy. Lilly and I are sorry. We gave you the wrong impression—that we wanted you to act a certain way—and the fact is we love you for all your foibles and spirit. You're like Pollyanna. You see everything from the good, and maybe we were just jealous."

"True," Lilly says. "But at the same time, we still don't want you discussing leaky-gut syndrome at the table."

They both start to laugh, and in a sudden awakening of the rational, I do see their point. "I'm still going to Hawaii after the wedding."

"Then let us help you," Lilly says.

By this, I can only assume she means "Let us dress you. Let us swathe you with makeup."

I hold up a finger. "I'm already going to do that—let you help me." I open the brand-new Samsonite hard suitcase that's fresh out of a catalog. I'm sure it's not recyclable, and I did have trouble with that, but in an act of faith, I purchased it anyway, knowing that it was time to invest in new baggage—and not of the mental type. I lift the lid, and there's about six of my mother's skirts. They smell from being in the storage unit, and I see Lilly reach for her Lysol. Which I thought she'd given up with pregnancy. But there she is, in *Charlie's Angels* pose, pointing a spray can at me.

"What are you doing with those?" Lilly asks after she's sprayed the collection.

"I'm giving them to you, Lilly. If you want to burn them, you're free to do so."

Lilly's expression is that of a fiendish cartoon character when she realizes what I'm saying.

"Really?" Lilly drops the Lysol and reaches for the skirts. She wrinkles her nose as she does so. "This Simon must be something special if you're able to get rid of this garbage. I'm going to find a match to light these." She gathers the skirts up in her arms. "I don't want you to change your mind."

"It's not Simon, the reason I'm burning those." I point to my temple. "It's that my memories are right here. I don't need to wear them anymore."

Morgan comes to the bed and sits beside me. "We let you down, Poppy. You've supported us through everything, and we haven't returned the favor. You're sure this is *him*?"

I nod.

"So what about the doctor at the wedding? I'm sort of excited if you're leading someone on."

"I'm finding new work digs. Don't worry, he's getting what he wants out of it."

"You know, I don't think I'm like a normal bride. I just want my wedding day over with. I want to be married. I want to stay with my family all night. I'm sick of acting like a high school girl going home to my empty apartment. Shouldn't I be more excited about being the princess?"

"You've spent your life being a princess," Lilly says. "It's no wonder. Besides, you're ready to sleep with your man. How surprising is that? You're a normal, healthy woman."

"Lilly, do you have to take everything to the gutter?" I ask.

"Sleeping with your husband is not going to the gutter, Poppy. Or don't they teach you about those endorphins in chiropractic school?"

"Lilly, would you leave her alone?" Morgan says.

"Fine. I'm going to burn these before my facial." Lilly exits the room and leaves Morgan and her tender concern alone with me.

"I'm sorry about that. You know how Lilly can be. The pregnancy hormones aren't helping her any."

"She's Max's problem now," I laugh.

"So listen, about the wedding—"

"Jeff's all set to come. You liked him, right?"

"He's a great guy, Poppy. Smart, bright, good-looking. You're sure there's nothing between you?" Morgan asks hopefully.

I shake my head. "Jeff's a great friend, but that's it. I'm sorry to disappoint you." *And him.*

"I know you said you and your dad had a great time together last weekend, and you worked out a lot of the issues surrounding your mother and baby sister. But Poppy, we don't know about this Simon deal. You're just all of a sudden up and in love with someone? And you're going to fly to another state to track him down? Poppy, you have never even talked about a man with a serious commitment in mind. We just think you might be confusing your childhood issues with this."

Morgan is all tact. Translation for us common folk: "Poppy, we think you've actually lost it this time. Go for the doctor!"

I stand up and walk towards the sliding door and out onto the patio. I can smell the eucalyptus trees in the distance and feel the cool prick of ocean air. "I love California."

"So why would you be thinking of Hawaii?"

I'll admit, her question stops me. I never thought about that. I never thought about being away from the eucalyptus and the redwoods. Sure, there's plenty of Pacific Ocean in Hawaii, and there's Simon. But is that enough? "Simon said it would be a good place to offer a health spa where I could help people get better in a vacation environment. But I don't know that this is my future. I just know I have to try, Morgan. I don't want to live anymore in my cocoon."

"Is that what you want to do? A spa of your own?"

I look at her in her silky, pressed slacks, while she smoothes her sleek blonde hair. "I don't think so."

"It sounds like you don't have all the answers you think you do, Poppy."

I kick my shoes off and look at my wheat-colored toenails from our pedicures. Lilly always tells me that's not actually a color, but I like it. It's as natural as you can get with painting toxins on your toenails. "So what's with you, Morgan? Why do you all of a sudden trust me to come to the wedding and not tell everyone how to have better organ function?"

She laughs. "I don't trust you to do that, Poppy. When my father was being hauled off to jail, you thought he might need some liver support." Morgan shakes her head. "Do you think the warden cares about his liver?"

"I just thought if he thought clearer maybe he wouldn't be so greedy, and he'd realize what he had in you and his family."

"It was sweet of you, if not a little naïve. He threw a brass paper weight at my head, Poppy. His illness goes deeper than a supplement can handle."

"You're probably right."

"So the rehearsal dinner is next week. Are you up for this? Coming with a man who is just a friend? A man who just wants your office space?"

I nod. "At least that's all he wants now." I slide out of my mother's last skirt and get into my loose-fitting sweats. "I'm going for a walk."

"Poppy, I didn't mean to depress you."

"You're not depressing me. You're just making me take a new look at reality."

I so much prefer fantasy. It has better energy.

chapter 25

Miles walked: 3
Times I tried Simon's old number: 3
Desperation scale: 7

Did you see the paper?" Jeff comes into my office with a copy of the *San Francisco Chronicle*. It's not a paper I get down here in the South Bay, so I wonder where he got a copy.

"What are you doing with that?"

"Just look at the headline."

It reads, "Malliard Wedding Off."

"Jeff, what on earth?" I grab the paper and scan the article as quickly as possible.

"His ex is suing for custody of Georgie."

"Of Georgie?" My head starts to throb.

"You haven't heard from Morgan?"

I shake my head. "It has to be Georgie's mom. George has offered her money several times. Thanks, Jeff."

"I have to get back to the office. Let me know how it goes. I'll say a prayer."

I call Morgan, and she's not answering, so I call Lilly instead.

"Lilly, what's happening?"

"The wedding's off for now."

"What?" My heart is in my stomach.

"Don't get upset, Poppy. Morgan is fine with it. I think she's almost relieved."

"What are you talking about? They've put a fortune into this wedding."

"But not their hearts, Poppy. Haven't you noticed that? Morgan says they can't take the chance of having a high-profile wedding if it means publicity about Georgie being away from his mother. George would love to give Karen more time with Georgie, but not this way. He's not going to drag Morgan through another public battle in the media."

"Oh my gosh, Morgan has to be devastated. Where is she?"

"She's at work at the protocol office, and she's not answering her phone for fear the press will catch her. She's going to call you as soon as she finishes answering questions from the caterer. George is going on the offense and trying to get Karen to talk to him about this with a mediator."

"The wedding is next Saturday, Lilly!"

My heart grieves for Morgan. All she ever wanted was a family. This is her family, and that other woman never wanted Georgie. She abandoned him when he was born with Downs. How could she come back now? Right now, a week before Morgan's big day.

"They'll get married, Poppy." Lilly says with all the calmness of a yoga teacher. "Don't fret over this. They're just not going to make it so public, and George is going to make sure all his ducks are in a row, so that Georgie doesn't get pulled into the middle of this. Morgan is really calm."

I feel myself break down at the thought of Morgan not marrying the man of her dreams. Granted, I know the wedding is just an event, and it means little in light of Morgan's history. But Georgie and George? They mean everything to her, and they've just drifted farther from her than I could have imagined. Her own father couldn't have inflicted this kind of pain.

"You can't fix this, Poppy. Morgan is fine. She'll be fine. This storm she endures with George and God. She's fine, I swear to you."

"Is there anything I can do?"

"I don't think there's anything any of us can do. We just have to wait it out. The wheels of justice turn slowly. Listen, I have to run and let the hotel know we may not have a wedding. Don't worry, Poppy. You can't fix this, so don't try."

I hang up the phone and start to go through all the scenarios of how I might fix this, and of course, I come up with nothing. But here's the thing: for once in my life, I realize there really is nothing I can do. I can't obsess. I can't run and change anybody's mind, and I can't get Morgan out of trouble. I can only pray.

I look at the newspaper again and open it up, and in the local news section is a mug shot of Jacob Frawley. The runner they set me up with has been detained for lewd behavior on Ocean Beach. *I knew it!* But now is hardly the time to do my "I was so right" dance. I know Jeff told me life wasn't about being right, but sometimes it feels good to be vindicated. I just wish I could spend my morning gloating to Lilly, but I quickly decide that's probably not in anyone's best interest.

My office door jangles again, and Jeff's assistant, Alicia, opens the door. "Hi Poppy."

"Hi, Alicia. Did Jeff let you out of your cage?" I smile at her. "He sure likes to work."

"Like you're any better," Emma pipes up.

I hand Emma a file folder. "Here, do something with yourself. Act busy. Alicia, what can I do for you?"

"Well, we got a bunch of mineral makeup samples, and I'm bringing you some. Not because I think you need them. I was just trying to make peace."

"That is so sweet! I had a makeover. Did Jeff tell you?"

"He did. Listen, can I talk to you a minute?" Alicia gets that serious look that I hate on someone I barely know.

"Sure," I say. "Let's go to my office."

She follows me back, and I shut the door wondering if my mineral makeup isn't the Trojan horse of a new era. Alicia hands me an envelope.

"What's this?"

"It's the injunction against the landlord. No one's moving anywhere."

I look over the legal document in my hand and feel a smile come to my face. "Jeff did it."

"Well, his lawyers. But yes."

I finger the paperwork with a hint of sadness, looking around the office. I can't believe I agreed to move out of here. Sometimes I really don't think things through.

"This is great, Alicia, thanks."

"Jeff wanted me to tell you the Greek café is leaving. We're taking over their shop for space."

"I beg your pardon?"

"There's no reason for you to move, Dr. Clayton. Jeff has more space across the way for our expansion until we build."

"I don't understand. Jeff was just here. Why didn't he tell me?"

"He thought you might think it was a favor he was doing you. I'm here to assure you it's not and that we can all be one natural-healing, liposucking, neighborly office again." She pushes the makeup boxes towards me and smiles. "Jeff thinks the world of you, Poppy. Can't you throw him a bone and let him know you respect him, as well?"

I nod. "It's the least I can do, Alicia. Thank you."

We come out of the office together, and Jeff is in the foyer with Emma as she munches on a flax-seed health bar. He looks at us oddly, as though we're meeting for a clandestine plan to oust him from the building.

"What are you two up to?"

"Alicia was just filling me in on your real estate dealings. Maybe the Supreme Court needs a new nominee with your expertise, Dr. Curran."

He smiles at me. "I came to check on Morgan."

"As of this minute, the wedding is postponed, but there's no telling what Morgan can pull together in a split second so don't go ditching me on Friday night for the rehearsal dinner." It's at this point I realize he owes me nothing now. My office is mine. But being a gentleman, Jeff says none of that.

"Keep me posted. Alicia, are you coming back?"

"It smells good over here. How come we don't have a waterfall?"

"We have a fireplace," he says to her.

"It's eighty degrees out," Alicia complains.

"Jeff, before you go, can I tell you something?"

He shrugs. "Yeah. Alicia, I'll be right there." Jeff follows me into my office and I just feel an overwhelming gratitude towards him. He smiles at me and takes a seat, pulling the chair closer so our conversation can be more intimate, I guess. "So, I have a message for you."

"A message?"

"From Chloe."

"Oh right. How did your coffee date go?"

"It wasn't a date," he clarifies. "The message is to tell you she doesn't want to run anymore. She's seeing a colleague of mine to do the work for her."

This makes me laugh out loud. "So you're not going to be a Lifetime channel statistic, is that what you're telling me?"

"Listen, I know we're friends, and I appreciate that we're friends, and I just wanted to apologize for maybe coming on too strong. I think that your playing hard to get all these years confused me. So . . ." He thrusts a hand towards me. "Friends?"

I reach out and take his hand. "You've really taught me that life isn't about being right all the time, Jeff. And something else: I was wrong about you. From the very start. You're a good man, and you do a good work. Accept my apology?"

He grabs his heart. "Oh man, I don't know if I'm strong enough for this. Do you have a blood pressure cuff?"

"Very funny. Jeff Curran, here's to our workaholic ways. May we leave them in the past and find a future for us both."

"Amen."

I hear the bell ring to announce more clients, and I watch Jeff leave my office. He's charming, and when he really finds the time to date for real, I have a feeling it's going to be harder on me than I think. Not because there's anything between us. But because I have defined lonely, and Jeff and I have been extremely lonely in our constant chaos. Here's to finding romance for both of us that doesn't fit into a schedule, but works because it's ordained.

My phone trills, and I see with relief that it's Morgan.

"Oh my gosh, Morgan, are you okay?"

"Poppy, I'm fine. George and I are still getting married. We could go ahead with the big wedding if we wanted, but you know what I've been through. I don't want my wedding to be a zoo over more printed gossip. We're going to hold off a month and do it quietly."

"You're so calm. How can you be so calm?"

"I'm calm because I already have what I want. Karen just wants her son sometimes, and I'm thankful for that. But I refuse to let the world invade my day again. This marriage is not about a wedding. This is for us, and I'm not allowing the San Francisco society to steal it."

"I'm so proud of you, Morgan."

"You saw that couples' shower. I don't know any of those people anymore, and were they there for me when my dad went to jail? They weren't."

"So when's the wedding, then?"

"George is going to finish negotiations with Karen, and we'll get back to it. In the meantime, he surprised me this morning. Well, after he showed me the newspaper," she giggles.

"I can't believe you're laughing."

"I have everything, Poppy. Everything! I have George's heart, I have a son who loves me, and this is just one of the complications that comes up in life and makes you stronger. Am I going to deny Karen the right to her son? How could I blame anyone for loving him as much as I do?"

I want to point out the woman abandoned her child, but if Morgan's okay with the situation, who am I? "So what's the surprise?"

"It's for all of us."

"All of us?"

"Lilly, you, and me."

"What is it?"

"Lilly still has a month where she can travel by plane, and your race is coming up, right?"

"Well, but I don't know that I'm going to be able to run."

"But you've got a ticket to Hawaii."

"Right."

"We're going with you. George's father has a friend who has a hotel on Oahu with a great spa. We're going to Hawaii, Poppy!"

"Together?"

"The Spa Girls are moving up in the world! Good riddance, Spa Del Mar! If you're going to get Simon, we're going with you."

I'm smiling from ear to ear. I spend the rest of the afternoon listening to complaints about TMJ (jaw-locking pain), peanut allergies, and *plantar fasciitis* (heel pain), and none of it invades my thoughts. I'm going to Hawaii. With the Spa Girls. Aloha!

chapter 26

Oahu with the Spa Girls.
Miles run: 0
Laps swum: 0
Pineapples eaten: 2
Desperation scale: 0

The spa in Hawaii takes on an entirely new dimension. The air here is always moist and misted with the sweet floral fragrance of the tropical plants and soft rains. The turquoise of the ocean exudes peace, and as we make our way to our hotel room, the open-air lobby beckons for us to come back outdoors as soon as possible. There's a lanai outside our room, with plush upholstered chaises for each of us. The hotel has left a giant basket of fruit, and there are flavored waters over ice for our convenience.

"If this isn't a step up," Lilly says.

I look out the French doors, and open them to the soft sounds of the Hawaiian music and childish sounds from the pool below. *Somewhere out there*, I think, *is Simon*.

Morgan, who I thought I'd find in a desperate and depressed state, is rabid like a Labrador puppy. She has already unpacked and is ready to get to town to shop. We flew in today purposely. It's actually the day of the triathlon, and they didn't want me tempted, so we're here after the fact. I still can't wait to get into town and see who would have been my fellow racers.

"Morgan, how are you going to go to your massage?"

"I knew she'd regret making that appointment," Lilly says.

"I cancelled it," Morgan says. "Are you kidding? I'm going to the beach. All that money my dad had and we never left the city. What good did it do us? Come on, Poppy, your race is finishing. Let's go see how bad you would have looked."

I look down at my cast, which is removable but still won't allow me—because of the stress fracture—to run. I've adjusted pretty well. I've learned to walk and go to the eucalyptus trees without running there. Besides, I can hardly feel sorry for myself in paradise with my best friends.

We each throw on the skirts and tie-tops we bought at the outdoor market. Lilly's is bright pink flowers on white, and sticking out with the baby's shape below. Morgan's is yellow and clings to her figure, matching her golden hair. And mine is turquoise like the color of the bay we're staying on and just slightly tacky.

We're giddy and giggly as we make our way to the race's finish line. Seeing all the paper numbers discarded and the runners coming in at the finish is hard for me to digest. I mean, it should be me. I trained for a year to do this, and I'm standing here looking like a turquoise popsicle with all the other tourists—who are digging in on shaved ice and screaming for the triathletes as nothing more than a tourist site. My leg jiggles with anticipation. I want to be out there, and I want to run across that finish line with everyone else. But my friends take my hand and smile at me. Even Lilly, who's not the warm type.

"There's next year, Poppy," she nods.

I bite back a sob.

"Maybe next year you'll do the full triathlon, not the Tinman," Morgan says.

As I watch a large group of women come across the finish line, I feel a tinge of regret, but it's short lived. Life is too fleeting for that. I'm free. I'm calm, cool, and adjusted. Looking to the sky, I lift up my fist to show solidarity to my mother and little sister. They're together and they're in real paradise. Seeing my Spa Girls, I know that the Lord has replaced what the locusts have eaten. I'm not allowing them to eat anymore. From here on out, it's organic pesticide, baby. I'm not living for tomorrow. Well, within reason.

"I'm going to see if any of my running group came." I walk closer to the finish line, and I look back to see them both looking worried about me. "You girls go shop; you don't have to stick around for me."

Lilly lifts her brows. "I wish I was having a girl. I saw this little bikini that was darling! Want to shop, Morgan?"

"I'll be fine," I say to them both. "I promise."

They nod and take off for the row of stores behind the race's finish line. The ground is covered with race numbers, and I pick one up and lament for just a moment that it's not mine. I kick some of the paper cups as I get closer.

"You're still in a soft cast?"

I turn around and see him, and I feel my entire face light up. "Simon!" Leaping to him, I bring my arms around his neck and kiss his cheek. "Simon." I snuggle into his neck, nuzzling as close as I can get. I can't believe how I missed him.

"I knew I'd find you here," he says quietly, while clinging to me fiercely. It feels like I've never left his side.

"Right, well, no running this year. You're not going to believe this, but I'm here with the Spa Girls. We decided to come when Morgan's wedding got postponed. Well, and besides that, it's the last month that Lilly can travel because of the baby. So George—that's Morgan's fiancé—he called his travel agent at home at five a.m. and they got us these great seats in first class, because George travels a lot and gets all these upgrades, so he got the upgrades—" I notice that Simon's eyes have begun to glaze over and I grab him tighter. "Oh my goodness, I missed you. Shut me up."

"Not as much as I missed you. Do you know how quiet it is without you in my life? No one to nag me about golf. It's not nearly as fun that way."

"I imagine it's far too quiet. How's your mother?"

"She's doing really well, Poppy. I was hoping to introduce you."

"Now?"

"Well, I thought you'd have to check with the Spa Girls."

"They'll understand." I nod quickly. I don't want to let him out of my sight for fear he'll disappear again.

Simon grins. "Don't you want to call them?" He hands me his cell phone.

"Why did you disconnect your cell phone?" I ask him with a hand perched on my hip. "I mean, a lesser woman would have been offended."

"A lesser woman wouldn't have come to Hawaii for me." He winks.

"Who says I did? And why did you just abandon California?"

"Sometimes a man has to find out the truth, even if it might hurt."

Simon weaves his arm through mine and we step over all the discarded water cups and running numbers until we get to a scooter.

"Simon, you are not driving this?"

"Only down here. I figured it would be a madhouse due to the race, and I was right. All you tourists. Besides, the scooter's good for the environment. I thought you'd be proud of me."

After a weaving drive through the lush greenery and floral scents, Simon drives up to a magnificent house perched on a hill, with a wall of windows overlooking the Pacific. "Simon, this place—"

"It's where my sister is going to live. Isn't it gorgeous?"

"Your sister?"

Simon nods. "She's moving here to take care of Mom and run her hairdressing business. Her son was getting involved with a bad crowd, so she was looking for a change and we decided she was better suited to this lifestyle."

"So you're not living here?"

"I'm bored here. This island is—well, it's an island. There's nothing to do but golf. I was golfed out in a week, and without a good chiropractor, I just want to sit on shaved ice all day anyway."

"So where are you living? When you come home, I mean. To California."

"I was hoping to move in with my wife. She's got this great little cottage right on the ocean close enough to a place called Pebble Beach."

I bite on my lip, praying that Simon isn't trifling with my emotions. "Your wife?"

"The offer still stands. I'm a man of my word, you know."

I crumple into his arms, and the strength of his embrace comes about me full force. "Shouldn't we date?"

"Is there something you have to say that you haven't shared with me in three years?"

I look up at him and shake my head. "I don't think so."

"Nor do I. Come in the house." Simon leads me up a walkway of small pebbles all the way to the front door. The house is nice, but simple in both design and size. It looks like Simon. Ever practical and yet elegant. He opens the front door, and I see the house is furnished with typical man furniture. Big, bulky, and reclining. I have to laugh at all the blues and greens and ocean hues. While I'm sure he bought it all new, there's something that gives off a garage-sale feel to everything he's put together.

"I know, it needs a woman's touch. My sister will get here soon enough."

I'm looking around for his mother and gingerly walking through the house, but there's no sign anyone's home.

"She's not here. Neither is her caregiver."

I feel my heart begin to pound at the idea of being alone with Simon. This is chemistry. This is the energy I wanted to feel. "Simon," I turn around to see Simon on one knee with a jewelry box open and the most perfect diamond the size of a . . .

"Simon, is that a golf ball?"

"No, Poppy, it's a diamond. I have a friend in the business. You might know her."

"Morgan. Morgan knew about this?"

"Dr. Poppy Clayton, will you do me the honor of becoming my wife?"

I feel the tears rolling down my cheeks, and I fall on top of Simon's shoulders, knocking the ring from his hand, so he's lying in a heap on the floor. He groans. "Does anyone know a good chiropractor?"

"I do, and for once in her life she's calm, cool, and adjusted. Now I just have to help others with that." I go scampering to get the ring, which has rolled across the painted cement floors, and allow Simon to place it on my left hand. "Yes, Simon, I will marry you. Now let's get a table. I can hardly have my husband walking hunched like that."

I let the diamond sparkle at the window, sending off a myriad of rainbow colors in a brilliant display of nature and wealth all compacted into one incredibly gorgeous package. I'll tell you, this thing ought to put out enough energy for the lot of us. Maybe I was desperate all along, but not for reasons I might have thought. Being single was never the source of my desperation, but being alone was. It went a lot deeper than a boyfriend, and it took a bigger Man that even Simon to root it out.

"So are you marrying me for my chiropractic care or my great beachside real estate?" I quip.

"Hmm. I think it was your girlfriend in the diamond business. You were definitely the best deal. I don't think Morgan would have given me a deal on a ring for Chloe."

I swat him, and he wraps me tightly into his arms. "I can't believe you don't know the answer to this question. I'm marrying you for the perfect energy between us. God's first building block."

I smile up at him. Energy indeed.

Don't miss the second book in the Spa Girls series!

Sometimes the end
is really the beginning . . .

CPSIA information can be obtained
at www.ICGtesting.com
Printed in the USA
LVOW08s2301210717
541937LV00009B/156/P